MINDHOPPER

JAMES B. JOHNSON

DAW BOOKS, INC.
DONALD A. WOLLHEIM, PUBLISHER

1633 Broadway, New York, NY 10019

Cover art by Les Edwards.

DAW Book Collectors No. 738.

First Printing, March 1988

1 2 3 4 5 6 7 8 9

Printed in the U.S.A.

For my son Blair
whose traits and growing pains
contributed to Manny's character.

1: The Hub

I felt like an experiment gone wrong.

Then, a little later, came the shock.

Limping, I was being escorted across this giant concourse. People in government blue were scurrying in different directions—typical government, all walking every which way, none going the same. Ceilings four or five stories high. Airy. Lots of glass, plastic, steel.

These two big jerks were kind of leading me along. They were, I knew, "Special Security" men. Big and tough. Jailers.

Why was I limping? I didn't know. Then it occurred to me that I didn't know why I was here.

"Why am I here?" I asked, but it only came out a mumble. And exactly where the hell was here? I wanted to ask these questions, not yet caring enough to want to know where we were going; but a lethargy enveloped me. I limped on.

Something was bad wrong.

Men and women glanced at us and then away. Why? The SpecSec escort?

I held onto my questions. This curiosity was lifting me above my normal state. It was becoming the fence post on the lonely prairie of my life, something on which to anchor myself. Jeez, I oughta be a poet.

An escalator took us up another level. The jerks and their beefy hands handled me like I was a goddamn child, hustling me on and off like I was dangerous and gonna escape.

Jerk number one unobtrusively elbowed a military man out of the way. "Sorry, sir," he said like he wasn't sorry. The GI, a colonel, started to call them on their manners, but swiftly closed his mouth and walked on. Special Security guys do that to you. SpecSec and doctors was all I knew about this place. Number one grinned at number two. "Gives me pleasure, I was a corporal." He smiled again showing even teeth. He was a clean-shaven man with widely-separated eyes and a fresh haircut. No hair for prisoners or foe to grab, I thought.

"I never did like colonels, either," said number two, a tall, lanky fellow with quick, darting eyes. "I am glad there aren't many military left—especially officers." He grinned like he'd personally stomped a roach dead.

Well, I could agree with that. Don't think I ever met a colonel I liked, either. Though I couldn't rightly remember any.

On that level, we took a speedwalk, and the belt carried us, I swear, a mile. There were metric position markers along the way, but I don't speak much metric. Which was an interesting fact in itself on accounta it suddenly occurred to me that I didn't know a hell of a lot about myself. Like, for instance, who I was.

Trying to concentrate on this last thought, I stumbled getting off the speedwalk.

"Easy, pops," said number one.

Number two mumbled something about old geezers.

My right leg throbbed in a haunting echo of the past. My nose was taped and it ached. I had back trouble, too: I couldn't remember back.

We entered a skybubble, one of them new, almost freefloating, elevator-like things. Sometimes called bubblevators. Number one punched a code: they didn't think I was paying attention. The skybubble went up, through a channel in the ceiling, shuttled sideways out into the sun, then lifted on a track and I felt the G-force.

The side of the building stretched well above us a couple of hundred stories. I looked out and the giant complex spread out before me. I had the feeling that I was seeing only a portion of the place. But it was enough to give me information. Only one place we could be.

The Hub.

At about fifty floors past one hundred, I could see the two great roadways feeding from the haze into their intersection like an askew giant T with great loops at the crossing point; one, I-10, running east-west; the other, I-75, north-south.

The Hub. The Fedcenter in Lake City, Florida— though, I realized, the state name, Florida, was no longer an operative concept, what with the Fedcenters and all. I recalled that, on reorganization, Lake City had been selected as the site for this republic's Fedcenter because there was so much open land hereabouts; additionally, it was right in the middle of the transportation lanes established by I-10 and I-75. Though I called 'em Interstates, they were now simply called 10 and 75, there no longer being any states to interstate on. They were supposed to be called Fedhighways, but that hadn't caught on yet. Anyway, seemed to me this Fedcenter was here instead of Atlanta or somewhere more centrally located. The Hub was the administrative center for Cuba, too. Not to mention the fact that Atlanta, like most big and/or important cities, certainly had a few buried A-bombs remaining under it; Lake City most likely did not.

Remembering the Hub put the thought of the American Federation and the Soviet Federation into my mind. The date now would have to be sometime after the turn of the century. This thought cheered me somewhat because in the fear-recess of my mind I'd been avoiding the possibility that I was a clone; and while I still could be, I didn't think the cloning process was perfected yet. At least I hoped not. But the facts were beginning to point against me being a clone. Besides, who'd want to clone me? Whoever I was.

Onliest thing this remembering stuff was doing to me was confusing me. Maybe I was dead and somebody forgot to tell God.

Bing went a binger just like in a department store, and the skybubble came to a comfortable stop. Number one stepped out and number two urged me out.

Immediately I knew I was in the Halls of Power. I might not know who the hell I was, but I could recognize a Hall of Power when I saw one. It smelled crisper—though what crisp smells like, I ain't sure. Parquet floors in this day of more people and less lumber, whenever this day was. Long hall with executive doors leading off at irregular intervals. Secretaries coming and going observing strict pecking orders. Occasional men and women dressed formally, less hustle and bustle than in the caverns below, more smiles and personality expression on faces. Glimpses through open doorways not revealing the proliferation of those goddamn ubiquitous terminals.

Curious glances at me. They'd called me an "old geezer." Which made me wonder what year it was again. How old I was. And why. Everything was ending in why. Of course, none of the offices had "Ace's Automotive Supplies Calendar" hanging from the wall.

Another fact: automotive. That felt comfortable and I tried to wrap myself in it, but anything concrete eluded me, and I felt an unaccountable longing for something well past.

We trucked to the end of the corridor and stepped through an open door into a well-appointed reception area. Real wood. Cypress and other hard-to-come-bys.

Number two moved me aside and we waited while number one went to a long desk behind which a man in a formal blue tunic waited. They talked and I couldn't hear what was said. They glanced at us occasionally and the secretary hit an invisible key and spoke softly.

With nothing to occupy myself, I let my eyes wander. This being passive was beginning to irritate me. Perhaps triggering my curiosity had freed some other emotions. The room had light blue ceilings and walls, soft, ever-wear carpeting, and plush seats and couches. Behind one set of couches, several photographs were inset in the wall. Not hanging on the wall, but inset, and covered with several panes of glass, all of which gave the photographs a three dimensional appearance.

For some reason I wasn't aware of, I didn't want to show shock. Though I don't think my face would register it anyway. If you don't want somebody to know something, don't show or tell 'em that thing.

The photos were obviously of the mifwicks of this Fedcenter. (I realized I must of been a GI once, what with my feelings about colonels and all, and my use of the acronym MFWIC for mother fucker what's in charge.)

The chief mifwick in the first and largest photograph I recognized. The Administrator. While I didn't discount the fact that her face must be plastered throughout all the media, print and electronic, and in various chain-of-command photos like these spread everywhere here in the Hub, there was an even more compelling reason to recognize her. But I couldn't recall that reason. It was a slippery thing worming through my mind like a small eel going in and out of a Budweiser can in the sea. That is, over and above her position as Administrator of the Republic of Dixie, she had some other special meaning to me.

Amber Lee-Smith. From Singapore. Hired to run the charter government of the Republic of Dixie, all of which was required by the U.S.-U.S.S.R. settlement.

And why they didn't call her position Administrix or something genderwise correct, I'll never know.

She was Chinese-Oriental with an obvious trace of Caucasian. Recessed lighting accented the dark, intelligent eyes.

What shocked me was my own reflection in the glass

overlaying Amber Lee-Smith's photo. Her nose fit right over my bandage as if it were my own. My hair was ash blond with a few shards of auburn and incipient gray. While my face wouldn't grace Mount Rushmore, there was a similarity, charitably speaking. It was interesting because somehow I knew I hadn't seen a mirror in a while. The beard stubble reminded me of times irrevocably past.

So I knew who Amber Lee-Smith was, but I didn't know who I was. Real neat.

I'd been going through more periods of rationality recently and seemed to be more a part of the world than I'd recalled having been lately. Old geezer? Could it be senility? If so, why the interest in me? Why was I atop the Hub in the Administrator's office? Another thing I'd been dodging the possibility of was mindblocking, mindwiping, memorytampering; i.e., somebody screwing with my brain, say electronically or chemically. (Don't even *think* biologically.)

Whatever it was, I was becoming increasingly more uncomfortable the more I thought about it.

It was then that I began to feel a strong presence. A familiar feeling, but one I still couldn't identify.

Then things began to happen.

The Administrator stepped through a door and I felt unaccountably tired. I hadn't been this alert for this long since I didn't know when.

She walked straight toward me. Yep, maybe an inch or two shorter'n me at the most—maybe five nine or ten. All other observations right on the money, especially the penetrating gaze bit. But younger than me, much, I could tell.

One man had come out of the same doorway behind her, and flanked the Administrator to the right with his eyes locked onto my face. He had Doctor written all over him. From occasional periods of lucidity, I recognized him from checking me, doing doctor stuff. He was smiling, and it wasn't an institutional smile.

I'm not certain whether my condition would have

allowed me to physically react, something which they all were obviously watching for. But having seen the photo in the wall and figgered something amiss, I was prepared.

Their intense concentration on me made me uneasy. What the hell did they want? Then the strong presence intruded on me again: it wasn't the Administrator. It seemed unfocused, reaching out, curious, but not understanding. I *knew* that presence, but I couldn't think of who it was. This strain was beginning to drive me back into myself, away from this current rational awareness.

"Nothing," said the doctor, hands lifting from the pockets of his regulation blue smock.

"Nothing?" repeated the Administrator in a low voice.

"No, ma'am," said the doctor. "Some rapid eye movements we've associated with stress—it's in his profile. Perhaps all this activity has tired him . . ." He looked at SpecSec number one who shook his head. "Nor any sign of alertness when brought through the activity of the Hub."

"Enough," said Amber Lee-Smith. She stepped forward and stared into my eyes from two feet away. "Do you know me?"

If I coulda answered, I might have. What I would have said I don't know.

"His mind's clean," said the doctor, who seemed to smile a lot.

The Administrator continued to stare into my eyes. Maybe more like a glare. With a little hate thrown in. "You wouldn't admit it, if you did recognize me." Her voice had acid in it.

La Tee Goddamn Da, I wanted to say, but didn't even try.

The Administrator turned and walked to the doctor and they talked between themselves for a moment. "All right, do it," I heard the Administrator say, and the secretary spoke quietly into the desk unit.

You could feel the air of expectancy rise in the room. Strong Presence was coming out next. What the hell kind of tricks were they playing? But I began to anticipate, too.

Another door opened and a goddamn kid appeared in it. He was five years old with a thin face and eyes that made the Administrator's penetrating gaze seem like the minor leagues. This kid had light brown hair, pert nose, and quick eyes which riveted on me. His tan skin did not bely his Hispanic heritage.

His Dodger blue eyes locked onto mine and a surge from his mind hit me like a goddamn tsunami.

"Uncle Wyndy," he shouted and ran to me like a thirsty cowboy after free beer.

My heart wrenched my face, I just knew it. I knew I shouldn't react. Goddamn sonofabitches fucking with me and the kid, me and the kid, me and the kid . . .

The kid had me around the waist and was crying. If they'd mistreated him, I'd burn this Hub down around every manjack and woman in it.

I forced these thoughts from my mind as another surge from the kid hit my mind. It searched, groped, snaked, felt, got *inside* my mind. I sensed worry, concern, helplessness, curiosity, and a nonunderstanding of events which a child endures—only more so this time. He yearned for family and familiar surroundings.

My arms had gone around his shoulders and I squeezed him to me, my mind cautioning my adrenaline-spurred muscles.

Amber Lee-Smith stood alone in the middle of the room, her eyes squished shut to thin lines, her shoulders and neck reflecting great concentration. A few strands of black hair hung loosely from her carefully groomed bun. Her legs seemed to tremble in the baggy trousers she wore—though that could have been a breeze from the air conditioner. Her hands were clenched into fists.

I sensed another, but this time inimical, presence

through the kid's connection with my mind. Somehow I knew it wasn't the Administrator.

Over wet cheeks, I saw another man, tall and bald, step through yet one more door. "Got him. My people confirm the mental activity."

The kid's mind reacted furtively and withdrew immediately. Yet his comforting presence was etched into my brain. Right then I knew not only my name, but that I could receive something from the kid's mind. And I was certain that I could not transmit like he had been. It was all the kid; he had the ability, I did not.

"We'd better terminate this now, Madam," said the doctor. "It might have an adverse effect on the old man's mind."

Effect, hell. Did Krakatoa have an effect on the surrounding sea? Did Madison affect the Constitution? Did Daytona ever affect auto racing?

The lady from Singapore opened her eyes and squinted and was back, fully aware, shaking her head. "Nothing," she whispered.

The smiling doctor came over and tried to pry the kid's arms from around my waist. The baldheaded guy started for us, too. I knew I didn't like that sonofabitch a lot, too.

"No!" the kid shouted. I could tell he was near tears.

I held him tighter.

Number two jerk stepped quickly to us and reached for us. I picked up the kid, whirled, and made for the door. Number two caught me from behind and I lashed out with a booted foot, missing his groin and connecting with his lower stomach. Out of practice many long years. He "ooofed" and kept coming. I made it out the door before they could react fully.

In the corridor outside, the kid was squeezing me around my neck, and I was breathing hard. I swiveled too quickly on my bad leg and almost went down. Number one jerk was alongside of us, leg swinging to kick mine from under me. I got a feeble four fingers into his throat before I went down and rolled on my shoulder to protect the kid.

I came up, bad leg hurting worse, almost not functioning, and saw several aghast faces in the hall watching us. Number one jerk punched me right in the already-injured nose with a good old American haymaker and I went down again, this time spraying blood all over the kid.

The doctor knelt beside us and I felt a stinging on the side of my neck. As I struggled to rise again, a lethargy overwhelmed me. No part of my body seemed to work. Somebody peeled my arms off the kid and pried his loose from my neck.

"Who'd have believed it?" asked jerk number one.

"Amazing," said the doctor. "Absolutely amazing."

I didn't share their wonder.

"Bastards," I managed to say and felt right proud of myself. "Why?" I wanted to demand, but bastards would have to suffice.

"Wyndy," cried the kid and I was gone.

2: Bar Codes, that's why

Awakening from the drug, I knew. They hadn't raped my mind again—because I remembered. Some, at least.

The kid. Me and the kid.

We'd been together from the beginning . . .

They'd reorganized the world and left me out. A relic. That's why I worked at a horse farm, and, no, I don't know why they call it a farm. I'm in favor of internal combustion engines myself, you don't got to shovel up after 'em. 'Course there ain't many of them old engines left any more, either.

Not that I really cared then. In the thirty-five years since the turn of the century, the U.S. of A. done blasted by me like a moon shuttle accelerating. Then U.S.A. was gone. Now the country was split up and labeled the American Federation; and over there was the Soviet Federation. See what arms control can do to you? The worst part was bye-bye Constitution. TJ, you guys gave it your best shot and it worked for a long time. But technology overwhelmed the process.

Early that morning, when this all began, I limped to the stables—that bein' my job and all. Shovel and hose the place down before the handlers and trainers and vets and bosses all arrive later. I wondered if the shepherds had gotten in from night shift yet. That was always a confrontation. I was supposed to clean up

after horses, not sheepaloe. The three shepherds were
wise guys, just on accounta they had fancy Ph.D.s and
all. Hell, I got a GED.

I looked into the predawn skies right over the top
of Ocala, ex-Florida. Well, not exactly. A few miles to
the west of Ocala and 75 toward Williston in the
rolling green hills. Right above us was a supernova.
Just where the scientists had predicted it would be.
Ever since they got telescopes into orbit they been
able to do amazing things. And there it was nice and
bright, a friendly companion for me alone in the night.
Like a match flaring to light God's cigarette.

Not that I really gave a damn about anything any
more.

To save effort later, I hitched up the three-quarter
inch hose to the water faucet. We'd dug the well
ourselves, thankful that the water table in this part of
ex-Florida was still high. I'd sluice down all the cement floors after shoveling and carting drums and
wheelbarrows full of the night's leavings. I checked
the bottom of my favorite wheelbarrow to see if they
hadn't put a bar code on it yet. Republic bureaucrats,
get 'em started and you can never stop 'em.

When I rose, I realized my age-aches weren't bothering me this morn. Which told me it wasn't gonna
rain today and reminded me to eat breakfast.

The building was long and high. Rafters and cross
beams. Twenty stalls down the right side mirrored by
twenty stalls along the left. Occupied now by fourteen
horses and three or four sheepaloe scattered here and
there. Maybe forty million dollars worth of animal
flesh. When I thought about all that money, I wondered if we should ought to lock up the stables. But
them sheepaloe herders, they were in and out most of
the night, getting stuff out of the storeroom in the
back, checking on some of their sheepaloe which were
in two or three of the stalls either sick or giving birth
or whatever them weird animals do.

In the storeroom, I ate my morning yogurt and shot of Jack Blue, no longer an eye-opener, but tradition.

Today I decided to start at the back. The horse in there, Ralston Peerina, who no longer raced, just played the stud (not a bad life even if you're not a horse), was used to me and stood aside while I shoveled. Sometimes I gotta move the horse to an empty stall. Anyway, old Arpee, he watched me but seemed agitated this morning. With my pitchfork I fluffed his straw and hay. Maybe if they let him out, I'd douche out his stall with that special antiseptic stuff. I swatted old Arpee on the ass and closed only the bottom door to his stall. Let him hang his head out and check out the action.

My hands were getting used to the wheelbarrow handles by now, callused actually, and I pushed it on down the row.

Sometimes during the day they move horses or sheepaloe in and out, so I had to check every stall every morning. I checked the one next to Arpee, one which hadn't been used in a while.

"Jesus Christ," I said and Arpee snorted a response.

What I saw was old Fargield, our virgin-white Abyssinian cat who lived there to keep the field mice down to manageable, sitting on his ass watching this kid—well, young man (they're all kids to me)—kneeling between this girl's legs. But it wasn't what it looked like.

Her face was contorted in pain. Sorta. Then a rush of happiness hit her face. Some people just exude attractiveness, and she was one. She had clear brown eyes and wore pigtails. And she saw me see them.

"Oh, sweet Jesus," I said again, pushing my straw hat back on my head and remembered times when I was young.

The young man peered at me through dark and long lashes, eyebrows overhanging. "Hello," he said pleasantly. "We had to stop here."

"Yeah, I noticed," I said as I noticed the girl was about a hundred and ten percent pregnant. And, when

I peeked over his shoulder, I saw how much. "Dilated, can't really see, but I'd bet my Uzi she's nine or ten centimeters." Almost the only metric I knew.

"You know about childbirth?" he asked and I could feel the suppressed panic eeking its way into his voice.

The girl was sweating now. Or maybe I'd missed it before. "Jest a minute," I told them and ran to the storeroom. Ten cm dilation means "right now" comes the kid.

They were a nice looking couple. Hispanic, I'd guess from their looks and his accent. He was wearing jeans and blue work shirt, she a baggy sack-looking thing.

In the storeroom I got the hidden bottle of Jack Daniels Blue Label, a blanket and some clean towels—they use 'em for sheepaloe birthing—and one of them sonic sheepaloe shears. Neat little thing, sonic waves cut the fur or hair or wool or whatever those strange beasties wear over their skin. I'd adapted it to shave with, every couple days, and I just knew that somebody would figger that out and market it as a new electronic-sonic shaver. They'd probly call it something like Tronicsonic.

I trotted back to the stall. Arpee watched me with interest. I had to nudge Fargield out of the way to assist the boy in the delivery.

"Damn," I muttered. "Maybe I should go for help."

"No time," the woman/girl gasped. Her voice, while stressed, was controlled and clear.

"We got a vet lives here on the property," I said, "he might could help."

She forced her legs up and apart and the boy looked at me questioningly.

"Get behind her, son." While it was true I hadn't been interested in life in years, sorta hung it up, I could still make a decision. I ushered him behind her, moved some straw around, and got her heavy body more or less upright against him. "Put your arms around her, right under her breasts," I directed.

"You *are* experienced," the boy said.

"Betcher ass, jack. Pembroke Wyndham at your service. Most folks call me Wyndy, save for the time I went by the name of Sandy Creek for eight, nine years." And several other names I wasn't gonna mention. I stood aside and poured Jack Blue over my hands. Fargield the cat scampered to lick up the drippings. Either way, a shame to waste good sour mash.

The boy colored each time I'd cussed, so maybe I oughtn't to do that thing—but I always cuss when I get excited, when the action begins, and my blood begins to flow.

"This is . . . my wife, Maria. I am José."

"Sound more like a New York Yankee to me than you look like you should." I paused. "Oops. That wasn't a ethnic anything, just a comment." Some folks these days are so touchy you never know.

"Kew Gardens in the city. My family settled there long ago." His voice challenged.

"Long damn way," I said. "You're probably like me, a no-tech in a hi-tech society." I tested the sonic cutter hoping it would work for what I was gonna use it for.

"Yes and no," he said. "I had a good job, union. Worked construction. Carpentering. Installed cabinets in nonprefab houses being built. Sanded edges, planed doors and stuff in prefabs. Like that." He sounded more midwestern than Hispanic and NYC. "But the taxes, I just couldn't stand them. Had to leave for my sanity. New York City income and sales. Ex-state of New York which were never removed when they deleted the state, income and sales. Republic of New York, income, consumption and now that new value-added tax." He looked guiltily at Maria.

This couple couldn't be all bad. Us Americanos are screwed up: We actually pay assholes to steal our money as taxes and then spend more than they steal. Ought to be a natural, physical law against it.

"His favorite subject," Maria said, then gasped. "He will lecture all day," pause, pant, "against taxes."

Her voice held more of a noncity nasal twang. She tensed. José pulled her sack the rest of the way off. Nice body. I always thought pregnant women were special. But I do prefer my women a little more substantial than Maria would be ordinarily. A cross hung from a chain around her neck.

"Push only when you have a contraction," I cautioned. "Helps you rest between contractions, and the two forces together help expel the baby better than individually." I was quoting from a manual I'd once had to read. I soaked a towel with Jack Blue and sponged off the inside of her upper thighs and lower pelvic area. "How long you-all been hitched?"

"That is cold!" said Maria.

"You know about childbirthing well, then?" José prompted, avoiding my rude question.

"Goddamn right. Had to." I swabbed some more. "And stop gushing. It don't become you."

"Where?" He ignored my accusation.

Good thing he didn't ask when. "Tak Rahaeng. Old Thailand, before the Division." Dusty plain, I remembered, in the dry season. Hot.

"I recall a famous battle or two occurred there."

I grinned wolfishly. "Yep. The battle to end all battles. Burmese and Thais, right there in west central Thailand. Against the Vietnamese. I was a mercenary. Last good job I ever had."

"But that was forty years ago!"

"Yeah, and them sumbitches keep upping the Social Security age. I'll get there yet."

"How *old* are you?"

"Today? About twenty years younger than I feel." I used to quote Bernard Baruch about old age being fifteen years older than I am. But not lately.

"What?" he asked. But his eyes told me he understood.

"Not much more than ninety," I said. "And to answer the obligatory question, yogurt and a shot of good sour mash every morning. Read a lot. Old stuff written before the Reorganization." They always ask.

These two were strangers, but they'd asked the question. Soon people who lived here would start asking; they always have. It occurred to me that it was time to think about leaving this place. I've always had very low blood pressure and a slow pulse rate. But when the action starts, I always feel younger. Maybe there's something to it. Backwards aging. More articulately, what happens to me is more akin to age *wearing* off like a snake's skin. And I never been anywhere long enough for anybody to notice or think twice about it. I had been kinda layin' low hereabouts for too long.

"Kid's coming, I can tell." I didn't say how. The baby moving down the birth canal presses on the rectum making the mother-to-be think she has to do a BM. And sometimes thinking is doing. I cleaned that up quickly. "As familiar as I am with you, Maria, I don't know anything about you."

"Ahhh," said Maria. "I like," pause, pant, "fried dill pickles," pause, pant, "on a stick." A contraction hit her. "And I know," pause, pant, "that Mickey Mantle won the Triple Crown in 1956," pause, pant, "and Richard Petty," grit teeth, breathe, "won more than two hundred NASCAR races." She smiled. I could really get to like her. Fondly, I remembered stock car racing. And ole Mick would be ashamed of gloves, balls, and bats with electronic trackers and proximity beepers. Times don't seem to be changing for the better.

"When she contracts like that, you help her by pulling under her breasts—yeah, that's it." My instructions to him weren't all that clear, but he seemed to follow what I was saying.

"Forty years ago mercenaries needed to deliver babies?" he asked. Tenacious bastard. At least he wasn't gushing any longer. Maybe it was my smooth manner.

"Yeah. Them fuckin' feminine fascists. Half the mercs were women. Some of whom wouldn't take the pill or or implants or inoculate against pregnancy, and most of us guys didn't worry about birth control either.

Interesting thing, giving birth during battle. I didn't used to be a wrinkled ole geezer with a bum right leg. Here comes his head, push with the contraction now."

"You are doing well, Maria," said José. He touched her cheek. How touching. There was a bond of some sort between these two you don't usually see these days.

I heard a squawk and knew it was old Oscar the Owl. He lived in the building to get the mice old Fargield the Abyss was too lazy to chase. Between them, we didn't have too many mice. I wondered why, thirty-five years into the twenty-first century, there was no better mousetrap. Oscar was perched on a cross beam watching. Arpee, next stall over, had his nose jammed against the chicken wire separating the upper part of the two stalls. A regular sideshow.

Most of the kid's head was showing. "Most of his head is showing," I said.

Suddenly it occurred to me that this was a simple birth. Maria wasn't screaming in pain. José wasn't really panicked—in fact we were having a relatively intelligent conversation. "This isn't your first child," I accused.

They looked at each other and I couldn't read anything about it.

"This is my first," Maria gasped.

The head was coming out, sort of poking in and out, turning a degree or two, not much. I put my fingers down there to help ease his way out. "You from New York, too, Maria?"

She shook her head. "I was," pause, pant, "in the hills and mountains of ex-West Virginia." Accounted for her accent. It was obvious they didn't want to tell me anything, but equally they didn't want to lie to me, either. WVA was now administered by the Cincinnati Republic. NY had one of its own, it was so fucked up.

"I always said the prettiest girls came from Westby-GodVirginia." That sexist comment earned me a fleeting smile. But when I thought about it, she wasn't a bad combination: she eats weird like me, had to have old values because baseball and philosophy go together, she liked stock car racing, and she was from ex-WVA. What else could you ask for?

The two of them were in perfect synch now, she breathing and pushing properly, he pulling and encouraging. Just like old pros.

"Just like old pros," I said. "Minds me of a time we were in the hills, way outside of Chiang Mai, sorta where they used to call it the Golden Triangle. Old Lulu, she was giving birth. I was alone with her. I'd fire an occasional shot and help her with the birthing. Helluva situation. It all happened in a hollow on a mountainside where we were hiding."

The kid almost squirted out in my hands. I was the first to hold him. I dug around in his mouth with my pointy finger and plucked out most of that gooey stuff. His chest was beginning to heave, needing air.

"Had my old Uzi, one of the originals made by the Israelis, not one of them electronic fuckin' things they got today, just a simple self-contained unit, you know? Kill people and get it over with, don't need electronics to kill people. Shit, don't need electronics to do nothin'." They don't call me Wyndy for nothin'. I don't know if José and Maria noticed, but I did: in the midst of a peaceful birth, here I was talking death. Real smart, Wyndy. Maybe that's one of the things wrong with you.

The kid started breathing like he'd been doing it for years.

"We really need a doctor," I said. "There's stuff you put in their eyes, viral agents to check for. 'Course they'd probably stick a bar code on his ass." I'd heard they were experimenting with that, God help us all. I touched the kid's ass and got a good reaction. A nurse in a maternity ward woulda stuck a pin in it or whatever they do, I ain't never been present at a normal birth. "Without bothering to check further, I'd say this kid has a ten-ten Apgar score, at least."

"What's that?" Maria gasped, needing to be distracted and grabbing for her kid already. Bonding.

"Not sure. Just something doctors use to rate babies when first born and then a few minutes later. Has to do with reflexes and maybe intelligence—I dunno. Scale of one to ten, ten highest." I set the baby boy down on his mother's tummy. "Now that's a boy," I said emphatically. I felt some of that bonding, too. The first time and certainly not the last.

I poured some Jack Blue over the handle of the sonic wool-cutter, having forgotten to do so earlier. Got two two-dollar bills outa my wallet. Checked the stretch on them: good. Poured some more 100 proof on them. "Hate to waste all that good likker," I said. Bills were dated 2010, making them a quarter century old. When they said they made 'em to last, they were right. Can't even tear a corner off them any more.

"Anyway, like I was saying," I said while fumbling with all my stuff. "That old Uzi—had my special sixteen point one inch barrel. Muzzle velocity up to fifteen hundred feet per second." I tied the umbilical with one of the two-dollar bills, near the kid's navel. A doctor could fancy it up later. "Good range, too. Twenty-two hundred yards, sometimes." I tied the other two-dollar bill about six inches up the umbilical (which was still attached to the inside of her). "And I was loaded down with dozens of twenty-five round clips of that nine millimeter ammo they used."

I snatched the sonic cutter away from Fargield who was fixin' to lick the booze off it. "I'll tell you one goddamn thing, that weapon beat the shit outa anything them sons of Kalishnikov ever came up with." I could hardly ever pronounce the name of that Russkie colonel what invented their basic gun a long time ago. Fuckers always been incompetent.

"Maybe there will be no more wars?" José said hopefully.

"Yeah. Big fuckin' deal." Rather have wars than Fedcenters. It took the threat of nuclear destruction of the Earth to finally kill the Constitution. I preferred the former and *keep* the Constitution.

Maria jerked back like I was gonna gut her when I flicked the switch and sliced neatly through the umbilical—coming awfully close to the kid's penis. "Take it easy, Maria," I said to comfort her, "I wasn't gonna cut his pecker off." They both looked blankly at me. They were beginning to get my dander up. They were inperturbable—or something like that.

"What happened to Lulu?" Maria asked.

"Lulu?"

"In Thailand, the woman who . . ."

"Oh. Yeah. Damn if I ain't forgot. Think our kid— yeah, it was mine—was big and dumb and healthy as a goat in a hog pen. Until a launched fragmentation grenade from a remotely piloted vehicle—an RPV, that's a flying drone to you civilians—bounced into our little hollow." We'd been lucky, if that's the way you want to look at it, flak jackets and luck. The kid hadn't been lucky. We buried him right there and went out and avenged him. Lulu leaked blood all over the mountainside. I bled inside and stained the hills with commie crimson.

I pushed on the kid a little. "Pull him up 'tween your breasts or something. Cute little fucker, ain't he?" He wasn't all that cute. All babies got this gunk all over 'em and their faces are scrunched up like they was gettin' a enema for the first time. But there was something about some babies, something peaceful, something nonstressful. Hell, my verbal diarrhea was proof that I wasn't a bundle of nerves. I remembered Lulu. My fourth wife. "Lulu was good with explosives. Give her a plastic cup from McDonald's and she'd have a fistful of plastique explosive in ten minutes. She went back to California and I never seen her again." Another mail-order divorce.

"I did my stint in the UNESCO Peace Cadre," José said. "We don't like wars and fighting."

Eyeing him carefully, I said, "Wars should not be

fought by young men; they should be fought by old men like me who enjoy them. And you can quote me on that." Jeez. I ain't been philosophic in years. At least I'd kept my voice flat, dodging the dramatics.

Maria was still having contractions. "This here is called the third stage of labor," I said like I knew what the fuck I was talking about.

"There's more?" José asked.

Maria was resting almost comfortably.

"I don't think it's twins, if that's what you mean. Placenta. Afterbirth."

I tugged on the umbilical cord stretched into her, not hard, but easy. "Shouldn't take ten, fifteen minutes," I said. I put my hand on her abdomen and pushed down to speed up the process. *Babbling is for politicians and priests.* I remembered the quote from Trevanian.

"Forty years ago was your last good job?" José asked. He stroked Maria's brow with a clean cloth from my stack.

"Yeah." How'd he know that? Maybe I told him. "Jerks quit having wars, I wasn't qualified to do nothin' else. Except be a mechanic. Worked on cars for a few years."

"Uh oh," he said. "Another vocation which died." He examined a tiny hand.

"Them fuckin' bar codes done it," I said, pushing down on her tummy with a contraction. "Whatcha gonna name the kid?"

"I will call him Manuel," Maria said.

José nodded. "It's already decided."

I eyed the kid who appeared to be gurgling happily. "Manny. That's all right."

"I don't understand the bar codes. Please?"

People in New York haven't driven anything for years. "That started The Change. Some gummint asshole decided to regulate all automobiles while they drove. So they put bar codes on the bottom of them. Just like at Safeway. Run your car over a laserlike trigger on 75 and a computer knows who you are and where you are. If you ain't paid a traffic ticket or your taxes, they got you." I think the placenta was beginning to come. "Them sunofabitches."

"Why?" asked José, still shrugging off my profanity.

"I was making a fortune—had to on accounta my seventh wife—by painting over the bar codes with this special lead paint I made up in my garage."

"But there aren't any more bar codes on vehicles," he said.

"Yeah. My idea spread like worms on hot concrete so they took the next step, they put them little transponders on your car. Welded 'em onto the frame, your car stopped working if you tried to take 'em off or apart. Big fuckin' brother. Tied 'em in with the computer unit in your car; governed speed, gas mileage, emissions. All that. And their computers could override and control your computer. You weren't the master of your car anymore. You couldn't speed or even get a parking ticket. But they could stop you if you ain't paid your taxes or libary fines." The placenta was oozing out, just like another kid. Maria was breathing properly and all.

"What with all the improvements and stuff, next thing I knew you hadda be an electronics technician to work on a damn car. Even the old antiques. More mechanics than you'd ever need for them. I'm out."

"Why, Mister Wyndy," Maria said, "you seem a person," pause, pant, "who is quite resourceful. Surely," pause, pant, "you could make out better than . . ."

"Shoveling shit? Ah. Hell with it." I wrapped the mess in a towel and set it aside and began cleaning her up. "Sometimes the world has gone by, you know? And you don't care. You done what you think is your part. You can't fight an alien society. And you don't wanna. Shoveling shit is my way of commenting on life."

They looked questioningly at me. Well, hell, I didn't really understand all that myself. "Look," I said. "I

read some. I work some. I drink some." The idea
struck me and I sucked at the neck of Jack Blue. "I
wait. I write in my journal. I try to understand. See,
they reorganized the world and I don't fit anymore. I
exist." Jesus, I couldn't believe the bullshit I was
feeding them. I wasn't all that articulate anyway.

"No excessive bleeding," I said. "No retained placenta. We're doing good." I had her pretty well cleaned
up. Soon, I could call for a doctor—though it would
take away the first responsibility I'd had in years.

"*What* are those?" José demanded and pointed.

I glanced up. A pair of baby sheepaloe (they haven't
decided whether to call 'em calves, kids, lambs or, for
that matter, whether they travel in herds, gaggles or
schools) had nosed into the stall with us. They were
bigger than regular sheep already: they grow quick
which is one of the advantages they were engineered
for.

"They're new. Genetic engineering. Part sheep, part
buffalo, part longhorn steer. The Bossman here is very
future minded." Their broad faces, stout, low-slung
bodies, long wool which needed cutting often, and
long tails were eye-catching. "Call 'em sheepaloe. Eat
damn near anything, tough as a longhorn, their grass-
fed meat is as good as grain-fed beef and more nutri-
tious. Their wool is as good as synthetics." I pointed
to the incipient horns. "For self-protection. Bossman's
gonna be ready for the first colonization off Earth,
you know?" Maybe I should bide my time and make
the trip. "Lots of advanced husbandry terms they speak
here. Them sheepaloe herders, they're all licensed
animal-engineers." The jerks. "They should be here
soon, seein' as how their advance guard has beat 'em
in."

Besides gettin' a jump on the future, Bossman ran
an intelligent operation. We had solar panels and wind-
mills everywhere. We had several microhydroelectric
units at all the streams harvesting all that free power.
We burned our own garbage "clean" for more power.

My horse and sheepaloe manure was perhaps the best source of power we had. We had more power than we could use, so we sold it to Florida Power, mostly for Miami and Tampa and the Hub, where they needed all they could get.

I covered Maria with a couple of towels and then one of them horse blankets. She was resting comfortably now. "Tell me again how come you're here?"

José said, "We couldn't get a room at the Holiday Inn." He was dabbing his towel at the baby Manuel, trying to clean him up. "We do have a little money and wanted to get a room. We sort of expected the baby might come and were planning to be near where we could go to a hospital or find a doctor if we needed to."

"Keep the kid wrapped up, son," I cautioned. "He ain't used to providin' his own warmth."

"Sorry. Anyway, we took a wrong turn and it was easier to hitchhike that way to get back to town when we figured out our mistake."

"And here you are."

"Boy, you can say that again," came the nasal voice of Bully Base, the sheepaloe herder and genetic engineer.

He and his two cronies were crowded up against the stall adjacent to the door, peering at us.

"Good thing we got you covered up, Maria. Them three stooges is perverts."

She looked uncertain.

"Well, I don't *think* they'd attack you in your current circumstances," I said, wanting to get at them more than I didn't want to hurt her feelings and confuse her. I think I understand what I just said.

Then I relented. "They're the sheepaloe herders, Maria. They ain't sex perverts—'course anybody running around with sheep all night . . . Anyway, they're all college graduates, doctoral types, so whatever it is they do ain't done in public, so you're safe."

"Wyndy, you haven't stopped talking long enough

to explain," said Starvin' Marvin, shepherd number two.

"You blind?" I demanded. "This here's Superbowl LXIII."

José was beginning to appear self-conscious. So I introduced them. "José, Maria. These are the shepherds. The guy with the whiny voice, he's Bully Base. In his spare time, he fishes a lot, you can tell by his breath. The tall, skinny guy is Starvin' Marvin. The quiet one who don't speak a lot, thank God, is Crane Plash—he useta be a pilot before they took his license away."

They all made appropriate noises.

I explained about José and Maria. "So here they are," I finished, "looking for a place to fit in. I suspect the taxman from the Republic of New York is chasing 'em, but they didn't say so." Surprise ran across José's face. "You can't shit me, son, my daddy run a goat farm."

José looked accusingly at me.

But I knew the audience.

Sympathy.

"No kidding?" said Bully Base.

"Yeah. He works construction. Needs a job. And probably a place to hide out for a while."

Starvin' Marvin said, "My family's got a farm, up in Cairo, ex-Georgia, they could stay at and help work."

"Hydroponics or syrup?" I asked.

"Hydroponics. I thought you didn't know anything about water," he accused.

Maria had the baby Manuel in her arms and was crooning to him, rocking him gently.

Kinda tugged at my heartstrings, you know? Kid was nice, soothed my nerves and all. Newborns do that to me if they ain't howling like a plucked duck. Something about the miracle of life.

I wet my lips. "Ah. Maybe. Well. Perhaps if you three stooges was to back me up, maybe Maria and José and Manuel could stay here. We're always building something. And you could teach the kid how to herd sheepaloe, José could teach him to work with tools, and I . . ."

"You what?" Bully Base demanded.

"I could teach him how to get along in life."

"They'd be better off in Cairo until the heat's off them," Starvin' Marvin said. "Besides, you teaching him about life? They'd be safer digging up Atilla the Con. And you? Ancient Age?"

"Look, Marvin," I said, "I ain't gonna teach him how to read birth certificates. And I don't go about life waving mine around." Not much anyway. "It occurs to me that Manuel here," I pointed, "might like to go through life without a bar code implanted in his ass or on his palm or wherever they're fixin' to stick 'em." *I* know where they could stick their bar codes. Then it did occur to me that somebody needed to take up the cause against bar codes, computerization, transponders and all things electronic. Republics, too? Naah, too big to fight. What would I do, attack 'em with my Uzi and my copy of the Constitution? Dream on. While my tentative revolution was only one person strong, maybe I could expand it. Ah, a purpose. A fight I could sink my real teeth into. One that wouldn't call for using my Uzi. But a battle, nonetheless.

"Why don't we let them decide their own destiny?" said Crane Plash. He wore this ancient-looking pilot's leather jacket and goggles. I knew for a fact the goggles were for night vision for observing their sheepaloes —rather sheepaloe which is the plural of sheepaloe— under all conditions. While they'd genetically engineered the sheepaloe, they needed to gather a great deal of detailed information: like how and what they eat, breeding habits, herd psychology, lots of stuff. Till their data banks overfloweth. That's why they were shepherding and not guys like me.

"Gee," said José. "Maria and I just knew everything would be all right with the birth of Manuel." He paused and looked at Maria. "But we never guessed people would help us out like this. It's something we didn't think was done anymore."

"The Lord provides," Maria said.

Like hell, I thought. I said, "Here, the Bossman provides. But I think he'll see things our way."

Arpee and Oscar and Fargield and the twin sheepaloe all sat and watched like adults observing children and their babbling.

"Why don't one of you college graduates see if you can remember how to use your pocket phone and get us a doctor?" I said. *I'd* sure never carry one of them gismos. "They musta taught you something in doctor school."

I kind of hoped José and Maria and Manuel would stay. We needed some new blood around here. And a kid. Great. It'd be fun again. I didn't know if they'd fit in right away. 'Course I never had. But things did promise to be rather interesting.

The world seemed changed, just a little. And I'd never even heard of mindhopping.

It was the beginning. Me and the kid.

3: The Cell

The past was returning in broken pieces like the shards of ancient pottery archaeologists dig up. How me and Manny had ended up here in the Hub was still a mystery. Too many blank spaces.

I shook my head and surveyed my surroundings. I was lying on a genuine hospital bed in a room. No windows, one door. Recessed camera in the ceiling covered by, no doubt, unbreakable glass. A stool like dentists once used next to the bed with a regulation hospital swing-table ready to hold diabolical instruments or mind-invading chemicals or whatever they were using on me. Certainly, it hadn't been used for chow. I could tell I hadn't eaten by the IV running into my arm. Not to mention signals from my stomach allowing as how it needed solid food. I ran a hand over the stubble on my face and wished for one of those sonic sheepaloe shear things. Actually, what I really needed was a shot or twelve of good Tennessee sour mash. Kentucky stuff would do, too; after all, this shaped up to be an emergency. Looking at the blue walls, I wondered if Jack Daniels Blue Label sour mash was a secret project of the government. I hoped not.

Twisting, I saw more electronics inset in the wall behind me. Betcha nurses here were more technicians than they were healers. With my movement, a telltale pulsed a different color. I could expect some kind of visit. I was sure they could monitor my waking periods. What with the ruckus in the Administrator's office, they (whoever "they" were) might need to check on me.

The door slid open and the same doctor walked in. The door closed silently behind him. I cautioned myself to wait and see. Don't never volunteer nothing. Especially knowing you are a prisoner.

He watched my eyes tracking his every move. He stood maybe six feet tall and looked as old as I felt. He wore a uniform-blue, knee-length smock and, strangely, had a quick smile. I prefer my jailers to be grim and mean. Never trust a smiling jailer. Smiley had been in the Administrator's office, too, I remembered.

He checked a few readouts behind my head on the wall and I smelled after-shave lotion.

Before I could dodge my head, he grasped it, and with one hand he lifted my left eyelid. Then he checked blood pressure, temp gauges, pulse, that kind of thing.

"Do you know your name?" he asked smiling.

I didn't answer.

"How old are you?"

I just watched his smile.

"Born in nineteen forty-four, you are now ninety-six and your name is Pembroke Wyndham. Do you understand?"

Old as a rock. I continued to stare at him.

"Blink twice if you understand."

I couldn't resist blinking once.

He smiled wider. "Nice try, Wyndy. That trick often gets the smart ones."

Slowly, I said, "I am glad they socialized medicine."

He grinned. It was almost contagious, his engaging manner. "Your personality profile maintains its former structure."

It was hard to remember this guy was the enemy, whatever that was, and I had to fight myself to keep away from the conspirational suggestions he was obviously trying to effect.

"Who the fuck are you, where the fuck am I, and why the fuck am I here?"

"You don't remember?"

If I did, I sure as hell wasn't going to tell him.

He smiled wryly. "I need to know what you remember so I can help you."

Sure. I turned my head and wondered if I was strong enough or undrugged enough to make a break for it.

My eyes must have flicked to the door, for he said, "The door will open for me only." He paused. "It would be easier if you told me what you remember voluntarily." He emphasized the last word.

"Who was the kid?" I asked trying for information and to mislead.

"Wyndy, your actions in the Administrator's office indicate that you were fully aware—though I must admit you didn't *say* anything we could use. Other than calling us names. Which further indicates that you had sufficient mental faculties to know some of what occurred."

Now I really was mixed up. "Why are you fucking with my mind?"

His smile died and he shrugged. "It's for your own benefit."

Like hell. When somebody tells me it's for my own benefit, I start to question their motives.

"I'd like to know what effect the boy had on your memory," he said, voice turning serious. He studied me for a moment. "I can tell your awareness is higher than it has been since we began the treatments. I attribute it to the psychic energy of the boy." He pointed to the electronics behind me. "And the data bear out my supposition."

"Put your supposition where your suppository is."

"Such wit went out with the last century." He sighed. He punched a series of buttons or commands behind my head and I could visualize drugs surging into the IV tube feeding out of the console. "We'll do it the hard way."

Damn, I felt helpless. A familiar lethargy began to overcome me. Within minutes I'd be telling him exactly what he wanted to know. An anger grew in me. The emotion seemed to help and I nurtured it. Think, Wyndy, think. Get good and mad. What irritates you tremendously? Bad drivers. Nope, not enough. Bar codes. Yes. Fucking technology. Electronic revolution. American republics. Ah, this was more like it. Concentrate.

The doctor watched his dials and readouts and screens.

I jammed my mind full of information, bits and pieces that made me angry. The Electronic Revolution, the big step after the Industrial Revolution. The damn thing that led to the downfall of the Constitutional U.S.A. With the electronic explosion of the late twentieth century, the U.S.A and U.S.S.R. found themselves in a no-win situation. Their nuclear weapons were so well disguised and almost undetectable that arms control was necessary. Both sides agreed on that, no sweat. But neither side could agree on how. By then, nukes could be carried in briefcases and these were smuggled in by each country and buried or hidden all over each county by the other awaiting radio activation . . .

"Now," the doctor said, "we're almost ready. What did you remember when the boy touched your mind?" Meaning they knew he could do that thing.

. . . until some Russian bastard, a chess grand master, I believe, came up with the idea. The Soviet Union was also beset with political problems fostered by their terrible social and economic policies, they were under the threat of open revolt . . .

"Tell me, Wyndy, what happened between you and the boy?"

I felt a compulsion to speak. To audibilize. I cranked

in as much anger and bitterness into my thoughts as I could.

". . . so them commies," I said, "came up with the idea: Remove the root of the problem. It was such a surprise, such an innovative idea, that the leaders all jumped on it. The U.S.A. and the U.S.S.R. dissolved into loose federations of sovereign republics . . ."

The doctor watched me patiently.

". . . self-governing republics, established demographically so that they would never reunite. We got Cuba and they got Pakistan. They reverted to their fifteen original republics and we have eight. Amongst our American Federation, we are loosely tied together economically—the system was too ingrained to be dissolved." I managed a grin myself. "They chopped up Texas and put the parts into three different republics: *we* didn't even trust Texans. Our Republic of Dixie, Centralia, Rocky Mounts, Cincinnati, New York, New England, North Pacific, and South Pacific."

"Good history, Wyndy, but not what I'm looking for. About the boy?" He wasn't gonna say Manny's name in case I really didn't remember the kid.

"Then a professor of government at Florida State University threw in the final clincher," I intoned. "The one which would insure this new plan worked. For fifty years the fifteen Soviet republics and the eight American republics would be run under identical rules by *charter* governments selected from an acceptable pool of bids. Singapore developed 'governmental schools' and won the Dixie contract, among others. A couple of republics have selected Hong Kong charters, but no one ever chose New Zealand's bids. I wonder why? Do you know, Doctor Smiley?"

He shook his head irritably and seemed to realize his permanent smile was in place and made an effort to remove it, which failed as soon as he stopped paying attention to his facial muscles.

"But the biggie," I continued, breathing raggedly, oxygen intake up to where I might hyperventilate, "was that the political and military organizations were disbanded completely and each Republic was on its own. They overloaded with bureaucrats and the political systems in the republics grew like cancer, so much so that their seats of government sometimes are known as Fedcenters. It was a brilliant plan, for nobody, except maybe the chess master who conceived it, guessed that the politicians would not generate military arms other than police and agencies like SpecSec. Why? On accounta they didn't want to dilute their power. And armies cost money. Money already allocated for the bureaucrats, money which if diverted to a military, would lessen their power and influence . . ." Although here at the Hub I'd seen a few military, like that colonel—doubtless advisers, technical experts. Most republics maintained a small, highly monitored military cadre for two reasons: First, their space effort. Command and control and secrecy is easier with military than civilians. Also to keep the structure in place in case of emergency which might require conscription or a generating of military when some other republic or country threatened and the international safeties didn't work.

"Wyndy," the doctor whispered, "tell me about the boy."

Don't tell him! "The . . . military function, army, navy, air force, wasn't needed then. Still ain't, sorta. What with the Mexican border guarded by automatics, the unrest there is not threatening to the Rocky Mounts and South Pacific Republics. The only possible threat, China, had too many people and their military was turned inward. And the Israel-Thailand-Brazil Coalition has most of the rest of the world hesitant to become aggressive. And there is a United Nations plan which would create an international force if either the American Federation or the Soviet Federation were threatened externally."

"Wyndy," his voice compelled.

"No! . . . it cost us the fuckin' Constitution, goddamnit, an unfair trade for pansy ass Casper Milquetoasts who were afraid of their own shadow. I always been of the school of . . ." My words were just that. It was becoming difficult to concentrate. ". . . thought that when somebody invented new weapons and weapons systems, other stuff follows, other technology tags along. It's got us poised for the stars now. We wouldn't have had the Electronic Revolution without the development of increasingly sophisticated weapons and detection systems . . . the more competition, the better, I always say, but they hadda go and screw it up . . . I can prove what I say. When's the last time an enemy invader pillaged your village, destroyed your crops, burned your houses, stole all your loot, raped your women, killed your men, and took all of your children for slavery? Tell me that, Doctor. Now there ain't a lot of international tension, but because of that, we got more than our share internally. Damn well almost rather have Russian commies than the bureaucrats we traded 'em for, at least they bleed red like real men, not blue . . ."

"Wyndy," the doctor said clearly. "Enough of this talk. We have to know. Is the boy a genuine mindhopper? We have senders, receivers, espers; but they all require somebody special to communicate with. This boy may be the answer."

He'd just told me more information than I knew. A mindhopper? I must have smiled.

He acknowledged my gesture. "A trigger only. Talk to me, Wyndy. I assure you, your next treatment will erase this information from your mind."

Why not? He most assuredly had already picked my mind clean before this point. He had to know about me and Manny. Why else would they have set up that meeting in the Administrator's office? They were confirming something they suspected, running an experiment.

No. Not while I still was able to think, I wouldn't. My breath was coming fast in short gulps. His eyes went to the readouts and concern touched his face. I didn't want to be a goddamn experiment. I felt like a sheepaloe must feel. Not sure of my past, present being royally fucked up, and future about as certain and safe as a virgin in Oklahoma. Ex-Oklahoma, that is. Dizziness overcame me from the excessive breathing and I jumped on that. I breathed harder, faster, and deeper, hyperventilating until I could no longer see well and fell into unconsciousness . . . again. I dived into the miasma of blackness. They'd never get to hurt Manny through me.

It was obvious. They wanted to know what he did with his mind, how he did it, how much of it he could do, and how well he could do it. A five-year-old kid!

They wanted to use him. For the reason that mindhopping was able to unlock the chemical mind-wiping they'd done. Which made him a weapon. A tool. Something to use.

Mindhopping indeed. My mind hopped right out of there, leaving the doctor with a disgusted look etching out his permanent smile.

4: The Friendly Skies

More memory flooded into my mind this time.

I remembered standing there in the stables with a crowd of animals and people with weird names like Starvin' Marvin, Crane Plash, and Bully Base. Not to mention the new parents and Manny.

We were still arguing what to do with José, Maria, and Manny. I said, "Crane Plash is right. Why don't we let *them* have a say in their future?"

Old Crane Plash beamed. He tugged at the leather straps of his pseudo-helmet and tried to look important.

Right then, in walked Bossman and his shadow. Bossman's real name: Silas Comfort Swallow. Yep, the billionaire. He is inordinately tall, and is a tee-totaler—but not one to push his beliefs off on anybody else, or I wouldn't be working here. He has angular features and invariably wears an Abercrombie and Fitch safari suit. That safari suit has become his trade-mark and he wears it like a uniform. "Whatever *is* going on here?"

The three stooges fell imediately silent and looked at me.

"Mornin', Bossman," I said. "We got us a little problem here."

"What do you mean 'we'?" said Bossman's aide, always ubiquitously at Bossman's elbow. I liked to think of the aide as a whiny little wimp. But actually, he was thick in the shoulders and hips and had very

expressive eyes. His legit title was "Executive Assistant to Mister Swallow." His name was Lynn Oglethorpe Lium. I called him Linoleum sometimes. Well,
actually, all the time.

Everybody started explaining at once and I just
shrugged at Maria and José. They appeared to be
quite whelmed by the whole occasion.

So I gave my explanation again, this time a briefer
version sans the speculation that José and Maria were
on the run from the NY Republic taxman. "Anyway,
Bossman," I finished, "let me introduce you to José
and Maria . . . say, what is your last name, anyway?"

"Temple," said José diffidently. He stepped forward and shook Bossman's hand which seemed to
stretch too far out of the sleeve of his jacket.

"You got to be jokin'," I said. "Temple? This is
gettin' to be ridiculous." Saying the right things, I
managed to properly introduce everybody to everybody.

"Um," said Bossman, "you delivered the baby,
Wyndy?"

"Sure." I don't "sir" nobody and Bossman don't
expect it—from me.

Bossman knelt beside Maria and peered at Manny
all wrapped up. I didn't need no empathy to see that
Bossman and Maria hit it off right away. "Anybody
call a doctor?" he said mildly. When he speaks mildly,
watch out.

"Yessir," chirped Starvin' Marvin and Bully Base
together simultaneously.

"Well, where in *hell* is he?"

Nobody answered.

"Don't seem to be no problems, Bossman," I said.

"Show me your medical degree, Wyndy." His voice
was still mild.

"It's in my other pants," I shot back, and the three
stooges all took in their collective breath and Linoleum glared at me. "How about we put them up in
one of your guest cottages?"

Bossman stood. "Now somebody's thinking. Do it."

He stepped outside the stall and got on his pocket phone.

José signed on with the crew at the farm, ranch, experimental station, whatever you call it. Bossman liked "farm," so farm it was. José sometimes worked carpentry, sometimes helped the genetic engineers. He was somewhat like me: he could do damn near anything that didn't require a degree from a university. Or electronics technical stuff.

But the real surprise was Maria. Who'd ever think a little old girl from ex-WestbyGodVirginia would be a computer expert? She started off working on Bossman's PROJECT as a coordinator, but soon her talents surfaced. One day she made a suggestion, of which I could only follow the gist, to Bossman about the sheepaloe and depreciation versus total tax deduction as a business expense. See, that way he could increase his insurance on them and deduct that; but also, as a depreciated item, a sheepaloe can be written off in three years and, starting in the fourth year, become a business expense each year, not just the first. Jeez, she could make the tax code jump off the screen and do tricks. Which all led me to wonder how she and José had gotten into tax trouble up north if she was so able in that area. My guess is that she was just a quick learner and attacked her problems instead of running away from them—and had simply been following José. It was becoming obvious that she was growing into her own person, no longer the meek Mrs. José Temple.

More and more she became Bossman's accountant, from part time to full time, and less and less an on-the-spot mother.

Which, of course, led to me. Directly. The most versatile sonofabitch on the farm. See, there weren't a hell of a lot of people thereabouts could change diapers or watch a kid—to the satisfaction of the elder Temples.

Occasionally, I'd voluntarily babysat Manny on

accounta I liked the little rascal. I dunno, maybe we'd bonded together at his birth somehow. I'd go visit often, and frequently give José and Maria a break from the rigors of new parenthood. Hell, I can change a diaper with the best of them. And while diapers have technologically improved in the last fifty years, babies haven't, so you still got to change 'em.

One day when Manny was maybe six months old, I went to visit him. Manny was at the point of being weaned from breast milk to soy milk and had the colic. The Temples were permanently living in one of Bossman's guest cottages, a two-bedroom setup next to the nine hole golf course Bossman had built. Since he'd embarked on his PROJECT he was busy most of the time and no longer held big social events with people arriving from afar to share his hospitality, fiesta, and horse show. Horse breeders and buyers used to fly in all the time, but no longer. Hell, I had one of the cottages myself. Well appointed. But he'd dismissed all the help he had hired at one time to maintain them. So, in addition to doing the stables in the early morning, my job was to maintain the grounds of the cottages and the golf course. No trouble with all the automated equipment and slow-grow grass.

Anyway, I wandered over to the Temples' cottage and banged on the door. Maria called for me to come in.

Bossman was there looking cross, angular features a lot more sharp. Maria stood in front of him with a wailing Manny on her shoulder.

"Colic?" I asked.

"I don't really know, Wyndy," she said. "I'm kind of new at this mother business." She glanced nervously at Bossman.

"Call the doctor," Bossman said crossly. "I don't have the time to waste."

"It's just the colic," she said.

"But I need you now," he said.

Ah, the age-old problem. Maybe next time around

men will bear the babies and have their comeuppance. Maria had a computer access terminal here, but not all the programs and, more importantly, wasn't at Bossman's immediate beck and call. Also, it's terribly difficult to do accounting, however you do that, with a sick baby on your shoulder.

Finally, Manny saw me and squawked. I reached out and took him from Maria and he gurgled and shushed. You got to have the right touch. I started patting him low to high on his back to work out any lingering burp bubbles.

Maria's eyes brushed me gratefully.

"Good," Bossman said. "You take care of the child, Wyndy." He sounded final.

"Sure, for a little while."

"All the time," he said mildly.

"Whyn't you hire a goddamn governess, Bossman? You can afford it on the money you don't pay me." I rocked Manny on my shoulder.

"I don't want strangers here." He was speaking of possible industrial espionage concerning his PROJECT, of which the sheepaloe were only a small part.

"Everybody here was a stranger once," I pointed out. Doubtless, he'd had José and Maria investigated. Everybody who had been hired recently had been checked out. I'd been around a little longer, since before the PROJECT. Maybe he'd run a check on me, too, I don't know.

He glared at me, sighed, and said, "I will double your salary."

It occurred to me that Manny was special to him. And certainly Maria was special to him, too. On accounta while Bossman hires only the best, and them with all kinds of professional qualifications, he listens to me a lot. And trusts me, too. Sure, he knows some stuff in my past that don't need to get out in public else I'd have to kind of disappear; that kind of stuff he could hold against me. But he didn't imply a threat in that direction. Maybe it was something he knew about

José or Maria that had him worried? The more I
thought about that, the better the idea sounded, and
the more everything made sense.

Well, I didn't want to be a goddamn nursemaid,
houseboy, babysitter, whatever. So I said, "Triple my
salary," just to get out of it.

"Done."

"Oh, shit."

"Wyndy," Maria said sternly, "you are not going to
teach Manny that language."

"Damn, Maria, I . . ."

Bossman interrupted. "Maria, I want you to get that
info from the Hub computer for me . . ." His glance
at me said "Oops."

I looked from one to the other. "Don't worry, I
won't tell nobody."

Bossman stormed out. Maria shrugged and followed.

So that was part of it. Maria was so good she could
access the Fedcenter's computer system. Illegally.

Bossman's SPECIAL PROJECT:

Colonize some planet. Since they got them giant
superscope telescopes and other observation equipment up there in orbit, they can read a bar code on a
gnat's ass forty-leven light-years off. So they scientifi-
cally know where planets are and in many solar systems. Exploration of the immediate stellar neighborhood
ain't so much guessing anymore.

So Silas Comfort Swallow and a few of his megarich
buddies came up with this plan. It wasn't just an idea
any more, it was in the building stages.

They had most of the colonists picked. How? Simple. They'd committed a great amount of money to get
it off the ground, so to speak. If you want to go, what
you do is apply. But you got to have a skill they need,
like metallurgist, genetic engineer, electronic engineer,
farmer, whatever. Then you go to work on the project
and donate all your worldly goods to same. This keeps
the project solvent and, more importantly, keeps you

one hundred percent committed. I understand that there are several consortiums within the American Federation doing the same thing. The first guys there get the pick of the planets. More'n likely, a couple of the republics have their own similar projects, and, of course, the same with the Soviet Federation—though there ain't all that many rich Soviets yet to give them private enterprises attempting off-Earth colonization.

And while Bossman was filthy wealthy, and thus politically well connected, there were limits to his power. As I was to soon find out. So, he wasn't able to know exactly what, for instance, the Hub was doing about space exploration and colonization. Though rumors do get around. But those bureaucrats were protecting their own.

The big stumbling block was FTL. Nobody wanted to wait centuries, even in suspended constipation or cryogenetics or whatever they call it, to get to some far planet. So they needed a faster-than-light drive to get their ships where they were going right quickly—relatively speaking.

So across the Earth was occurring the greatest hunt since Indy Jones searched for the Holy Grail.

And there was no doubt it would be found, sooner or later. The lucky one would find it sooner. Why was it inevitable? Simple. For a hundred years schools and universities and countries have been turning out scientists and engineers. But in the last forty-plus years, there has been no war and thus scientists haven't had anything to do, so to speak. They used to work on "defense" related projects, develop same for companies like General Dynamics, Grumman, GE, Public Atomics, and so on. But no more. So legions of scientists and engineers were all working on FTL. The giant reward would make whoever came up with the answer uncountably rich. And all it would take was a key, the key, and the same legion of scientists and engineers would solve the rest of the problem swiftly. With all the resources and people dedicated to the projects, the

answer would undoubtably come. Jillions of dollars or
rubles were already betting on it to do so. Think of the
energy, the money, the manhours being expended right
then on that one problem: find the key and harness
the above and the solution to FTL would be immediate and almost anticlimactic.

Bossman's research for colonization had invented
the sheepaloe which would probably double his wealth
as soon as he allowed the genetic patent to go up for
sale. While farming the seas has staved off hunger
lately, kelp and fish certainly weren't attractive as an
only diet, and you can't very well transplant an ocean
farming ecology to another planet as easily as you can
a land based scheme.

The strange part of the PROJECT was that, while it
cost so much money, it was going to make Bossman
more wealthy from the fallout research.

So Silas Swallow was faced with a problem: two
crews and no security. Crew number one was com-
prised of the projected colonists who were getting
their act together and helping crew number two. Number two was Bossman's legion of scientists and engineers and technicians working on FTL.

He needed somewhere secure for these people to do
their jobs while he shuttled stuff into space and built
his space ship—which was already under construction
someplace up there in the sky. He needed to isolate all
these people from the rest of the world.

What he did was a stroke of genius, indicative of
how he'd made his billions.

The U.S.S. *Nimitz*. CVN 68.

No more U.S.A. and no more major military.

For scrap metal prices, Silas Swallow *bought* the
nuclear powered *Nimitz* and had it sailed off the coast
of Tampa so it would be close to his headquarters here
in Ocala and close to major manufacturing and pro-
duction of Tampa.

The *Nimitz* was mobile, had its own power, security

was simple, and it was cheaper than the land and facilities and housing would have cost.

Fully charged, the two A4W nuclear reactors could power the ship for thirteen years without refueling—and that's at sailing power, not just sitting around moored somewhere.

The aircraft carrier was designed to accommodate 6,300 men and was easily adjusted to accommodate the great deal less involved in Bossman's PROJECT. Access by boat or by chopper and tiltmotor VTOLs and a few other aircraft with short takeoff and landing requirements.

There was already a small herd of sheepaloe aboard and they were growing some of their own experimental food like a variation of amaranth.

Just a perfect setup for such a project. Not to mention they had adapted bubble technology and so there was a bubble for the ship, enclosing the whole ship, if necessary, and allowing them to environmentally control the whole thing just like the moon colony.

Me a governess. Great. At least it was during daytime only, or when Maria or José weren't available. While Maria was a fine mother, old José, he kinda lacked in those mundane domestic chores. Musta been remnants of the Latin macho. Didn't mean he was a bad guy, just meant he hadn't the patience or aptitude for dealing with babies and their problems. Maybe that's why Manny took to me, sort of a fatherly figure (all right, great-great-grandfatherly figure).

After Manny switched to soy milk for a while, the colic went away and he was into teething. Things always seemed to happen to him at night, so that when I showed up in the morning and Maria and José had to leave, poor Manny had been up half the night in pain from something or other. Babies ain't got it easy, you know. This time it was teething pains. Undaunted, I made myself a Jack Blue on the rocks; then I took his

binkie (pacifier) and dunked it in that drink until it
was right cold and gave it to him.

"Chew on that, boy," I told him.

He sucked away and the combination taste of bourbon and cold assuaged his gums within ten minutes
and we were on the way.

Holding him up in front of me, I said, "We start
your education right now, Manny. I am going to speak
to you in complex sentences some of the time; if'n I
don't, you call my attention to it. No baby talk. You
got to learn young in life that if you're gonna run with
them big dogs, you got to expect to get some of them
big fleas. That's today's lesson."

He rewarded me by spitting up undigested soy milk.
I wiped it off my shoulder.

Come morning naptime, I rocked him a while and
he failed to go to sleep. Occasionally, he'd do that;
and sometimes when he did so, he'd get a faraway
look and make baby sounds as if . . . well, it was
spooky, anyway.

So I rubbed his feet, sometimes that worked. He
didn't go to sleep. His morning nap was important to
me. That hour and a half was a nice break. I could
read or have a leisurely meal or just be by myself. So I
remembered something from one of my own first couple of children: Lena Horne. Way back when, I remembered, Lena's voice was like good bourbon: soft,
low, and easy on your ears. She'd sung the ABC song
with a flair. I'd seen it a hundred times on . . . what
was it? *Sesame Street,* that's it. Well, I gave it a
shot. My voice was a bit cranky from disuse, but
Manny got the idea. Me rocking him in a granny-
rocking chair and singing the ABC song. It was so
relaxing, when Manny fell asleep there in my lap, I
kinda dozed off, too.

I'd been a singer at one time, and it had all come
back to me. Under the alias Sandy Creek I'd done a
Willie Nelson imitation.

Nothing wrong with a morning nap, I alibied to

myself upon waking, except that some people would say I was getting old. Horseshit.

Occasionally, I'd sleep with Manny when he was having a hard time: it seemed to give him reassurance. Did I say them babies ain't got it easy? Well, it's true. A brand new world, new stuff everyday. Must be unsettling. His body changing daily, new teeth coming in, ear infections, stomach upsets at new food, new mental stimulation, maybe the start of dreaming, I don't know for sure. The strange thing: when he was disturbed and I slept with him, sometimes I felt like he was . . . articulateness escapes me . . . well, like he was deriving mental comfort as well as physical comfort. I didn't think he was telepathic, I just thought he was highly empathetic and we clicked together. Whatever, I noted there was something different about him and me. Maybe you could say we were tuned together. As we said when I was growing up, I could read his "vibrations."

One of the few governmental remnants of the old U.S.A. left in Washington, D.C., and funded by all the Republics, was the Library of Congress (along with a few other benign agencies like the Patent Office, etc.). When Manny was about twelve months old, I asked Maria if her—rather, Bossman's—computer setup could access the LOC's files. She didn't know but played with her home terminal and found it did. And the costs. I had her dig out old *Sesame Street* and *Mr. Rogers' Neighborhood* teevee shows, recorded a few hundred of 'em at high speed, and thereafter played 'em for Manny.

When he was two, he was as badass as any Terrible Two ever was—except. The incidents which mark the "terrible" parts of two were quite short and, with the empathy we'd developed by then, I could tell his mind fought the outbreaks of misbehaving. It wasn't that he knew enough to be *good*, it was just that he seemed aware that that behavior was not *him*, that the physical and mental changes he was undergoing had caused abnormal behavior from his norm. On the other hand, his outbreaks may have been worse, qualitatively speaking, because he was an intelligent kid and his mind was reaching out more, trying to accomplish more mentally and physically than his body was ready to cooperate with. I think I understand what I just said.

For example, just before he was toilet trained, he'd save up a good pee and when I laid him on his back, he'd give a "long shot" and try to hose me down. I'd dodge aside and generally say something like, "Good try, and while you're at it, learn not to pee against the wind."

I am a strong believer in liquid dynamics. I'd toss Manny in the bath or the pool and give him siphons, funnels, Tupperware, squeeze bottles—different shapes and containers with which to play. A kid can learn a lot that way, give him an engineering base and make him smarter than me who always hadda take showers when I was a kid.

Much to Maria's disgust, Manny walked first for me. I didn't tell her, knowing mothers and fathers cherish those kind of moments; but I know Maria knew. Mothers know that kind of stuff.

Surprisingly, by the time Manny was three, Maria was second only to Linoleum in Bossman's hierarchy. I guess old José felt left behind. Me, too. The consequences of her rapid rise were 1) José's resentment (the Latin macho again) and, 2) the necessity for me to take care of Manny more than ever.

We got into a daily routine of riding old Arpee around Bossman's few thousand acres. I had me a patch of illicit tobacco out in some woods I tended. While tobacco wasn't illegal, nobody grew it any more—except for a small amount by pharmaceutical companies that extracted the nicotine. Well, often I hankered for a good chew of Red Man like the old days, so I had to grow my own. Manny would play in a nearby lake and I'd watch him with half an eye (water moccasins) and weed and hoe my patch of tobacco. Took me a long time to learn to cure it right: another raid into LOC's agricultural files.

At three years and five months and eighteen days old, Manny gave up his morning nap; and, much to my surprise, I wasn't angered: we were doing too much stuff together.

When he was four, Manny could ride Arpee by himself. Of course, that horse loved Manny as much as I did. Fargield the cat moved his residence from the stables to Manny's cottage; but he still made daily forays into the stables to maintain his royal dominance over the field mice.

One problem was that there were no other children permanently on Bossman's farm. Often, children accompanied their parents who worked on the place, and Manny played with them. Or I'd take him off to fairs or carnivals in Ocala or Orlando, or to Disneyworld. But he was getting old enough now that it was time for him to have other children to play with. Maria and José didn't show any inclination to add to their family. Maybe when Manny was ready for kindergarten we'd have to arrange for playmates.

Also at four, Manny was getting quite talkative. For a kid, he did well. He had what he called his "friends" he talked to. I explained that imaginary or "pretend" friends were all right, just so long as he knew the difference between pretend and real. His response was what you would call a kid humoring an adult. "Okay, Wyndy," and he would smile.

For his fifth birthday, I arranged a surprise for him. It fell on a weekday and his parents weren't gonna do the cake and ice cream thing till that evening. So I had him during the day.

Crane Plash, the genetic engineer, was Bossman's standby pilot. Meaning he would fill in if Bossman's primary pilot got sick or couldn't make it for some reason. Crane Plash was checked out in all Bossman's aircraft: a chopper, an executive jet, and a tiltmotor turboprop cargo aircraft. Manny had expressed an interest one day when we'd rode Arpee over by the airstrip constructed about a mile from the housing complex, stables, golf course, et al. So I arranged for Crane Plash to give me and Manny a long ride.

The first thing that morning, me and Manny hopped into a golf cart, Manny driving. Without telling him where, I directed him to the strip. We parked and Crane Plash waved us over to the cargo job he was just finishing preflighting. It's a medium size British aircraft, bought by Bossman on accounta its VTOL characteristics. That is it could carry heavy loads like sheepaloe to the *Nimitz*.

Manny's eyes got real big and he grew two inches taller with excitement. "Wyndy! Can we?"

"Sure. I set it up. Happy birthday, kid."

He squeezed my hand and got real shy, clinging to my leg.

Crane Plash said, "Well, are you coming?"

Manny whooped and shouted, "Hot damn!" He ran to the aircraft.

Crane Plash looked at me. "Maria's gonna have ten pounds off your ass, Wyndy."

"What she don't know won't hurt her. You just keep that hunk of metal in the air and I'll worry about Manny's diction."

"Or whatever," he said. "Manuel, my boy, let me tell you about this thing. It's called The Iron Lady, the safest and most durable short-range cargo aircraft ever built." I followed 'em around as the pilot showed Manny the exterior and listened to him lecture. "We can take off with a quarter million pounds total weight, but you can't really get that much cargo in her. Each of the four Rolls Royce engines provide about fifty-one hundred horsepower. Cruise speed 490."

"Hey, Plash," I said, "we don't want to build one. We just want a ride."

He looked crestfallen but one look at Manny's enthusiasm got him back on course. "Sure, old man. Let's go."

We strapped in, pilot in left front, Manny in right front, me in jump seat between and just behind them.

"Regular take off or vertical?" Crane Plash asked.

"He can go straight up in the chopper," I said, figgering that like any kid Manny would love the G-forces of a rolling take off.

Plash explained he would accomplish that thing manually since we didn't have the fancy computer tie-in to air traffic control here on the farm.

Soon we were airborne with Manny trying to look everywhere at the same time.

"Where to?" the pilot asked. "We got stable air mass."

"What the hell does that mean?"

"Clear blue skies, Ancient Age."

Manny didn't answer, so I said, "How about Daytona. Manny ain't never seen the ocean, I been too busy to take him." I don't know why I said Daytona, 'cept I had some fond memories there. I could just as well have specified the Gulf coast, we were about the same distance from both.

So we did some banking and climbing and diving and Manny took everything in like he'd never get another chance. We flew to the coast and came south in the established corridor at about five hundred feet off the wide Daytona Beach beach at maybe two hundred feet altitude.

While the flight was uneventful for me, it was an eye-opener to Manny. He ate it up. We flew over ex-Florida and the Atlantic for about three hours. A few times Manny would just sit back and close his eyes as if he were dreaming.

The strange thing happened when we'd finished the flight. We were returning home sedately in the golf cart when Manny said, "We loved it, Wyndy!"

"We did?" I'd enjoyed the outing, but loved it? Naah.

I guess he thought I was asking a specific question, for he said, "Sure. My friends. I told you about them."

"Ah. Your pretend friends."

He frowned. "They're real, so there." His mouth pouted.

"The ones you talk to sometimes?"

"Yep."

"What's their names?"

"Ralph. And Kim. And Esteban. This time." He swerved the golf cart to avoid a baby turtle which crawled out from behind an ancient cypress tree at the edge of another lake.

"You talk to them all the time now?"

"Just sometimes."

"And they answer you?"

"Sure."

"You say something and they say something right away?"

He glanced up at me uneasily and kind of nodded. Like he'd broken a trust or something.

I smiled my best smile and unwrapped a wad of chewing tobacco from a sandwich baggie. I stuffed a bunch in my mouth for I had a lot to chew on. After a moment, he seemed satisfied I wasn't just another disbelieving adult. After all, I was Uncle Wyndy, wasn't I? His confidant. If anybody, he could trust me. So I didn't push it. I should have.

When we reached the golf course, he drove the cart into its recharging slot and was out, running and shouting, "Nanny nanny boo boo, you can't catch me!"

I began noticing things. Manny seemed to know stuff before he should have known it happened. He could sense emotions better than any empathetic mother. Once, I had to drive a VIP to the Hub because the weather precluded flying; when I returned, I immediately knew Manny's presence before I saw him. But my awareness of that feeling faded after a few moments and I shrugged it off.

He continued to be closemouthed about his "friends" and I didn't pursue it. Under the principle of: If you don't want to know the answer to the question, don't ask it. Nobody else even suspected Manny was any different.

Except Maria. You can't fool a mother. And she had to have been like me: afraid to know the answer and afraid to upset the idyllic existence we had here. Maria was making gobs of money, but perhaps more important to her, she was enjoying herself in her work. She was a healthy, attractive young woman. Sometimes I wished . . . well, never mind.

Maybe José noticed something, too. Certainly he was jealous of Maria's swift rise, he was jealous of my easy ability to get along with and take care of Manny. Yet he carried his own weight, working even longer hours now that he was construction foreman.

Did you ever wish you could go back, stop time? Some times are too good, you just know they can't last. Well, even though I knew that thing from being alive damn near a century, I kinda forgot it. Nothing had ever been easy for me and I should have known that you can't break a pattern like that. But, damn it, I deserved some good times. I'd paid my dues. And Manny hadn't had time to piss off the elements of the universe that kept track of those kinds of things.

5: Whangon Empty

Now there was only one piece of the puzzle left. What happened. How had Manny and I become captives here at the Hub?

But that wasn't the current problem.

The situation had changed.

They were torturing Manny.

"Wyndy!" Manny's mind-voice pleaded. He'd been crying out constantly for the last hour and intermittently for the last couple of days.

I scanned my new cell. I'd destroyed the old one, furniture and electronics, when Manny's pleas started two days ago. I knew it was two days, even though I'd had only minutes of sleep during that time. Behind unbreakable glass was the screen of a terminal in the wall, one of those with access to command and control or whatever they called it in this wing of the Hub. Doctor Smiley used it when he had occasion to visit me. Anyway, the screen was two-way and always on for them to observe me and, like most state of the art units, a readout line at the bottom showed date, time, and environmental monitoring conditions such as temperature and humidity. I watched the seconds tick off. Nothing else to watch in here. Twelve by twelve and padded. One entry: the door. And Smiley was the only visitor. Three times a day a hopper pinged and opened, and there was my food.

They had to be watching my reactions to whatever they were doing to Manny.

The kid was scared. I didn't blame him. He'd been kidnapped somehow, and removed from his comfortable environment of Silas Swallow's farm. The place he'd known from his birth. Now they were doing things to his mind. Maybe not physical torture, but probably drugs, maybe mental electronic probes, and certainly some kind of esper probing. That much I'd figured out.

Another pyschic surge hit my mind and I crouched in a corner and concentrated on seconds ticking off the screen on the far wall.

"Wyndy. I wanna go home."

"Can you hear me, kid?" I asked aloud. They'd be monitoring, but I couldn't help it.

"Wyndy?" his mind voice said again.

"It'll be okay, Manny." I made my voice reassuring, but I didn't know what my mind sent him.

"Why?" his brain wailed.

"Manny, we got something they want. I don't know what it is."

"It hurts."

"Have you let them in yet?"

"No, Wyndy." This was the best we'd communicated thus far. "But they're trying. Not like when I talk to my friends."

No longer did I believe that his "friends" were pretend friends.

Manny, God knows how, sent me a jumble and I kind of got an impression of him strapped to a bed, like I'd been earlier, with electronics stuck all over his body, especially his head. The IV out of the wall allowed 'em to keep him healthy and run whatever drugs they wanted through him. A damn five-year-old kid.

Hazy, but there, I envisioned the tall, bald guy I'd seen momentarily in the Administrator's office. He was standing next to Manny's bed and looming over Manny. An obscene presence.

I flung a defiant finger at the screen in my room. "Hang on, Manny. We'll make it somehow." Then I had an idea. "Can you shut your mind down?"

"Why?"

"That's what they want to see, kid. You're special. They want that. Don't give it to 'em." Manny's connection was so strong, I realized I hadn't been vocalizing. Or maybe it was the practice.

"Oh, it's okay." He drifted away. In a moment he came back stronger. "I don't think they can hear me."

"Like your friends can hear you?"

"Right. Like Esteban and Kim. I've been talking to them." His mind-voice faded and returned again. "I just talked to Ralph."

"And?" I prompted.

"We just talked."

"Yeah, Manny." I knew damn well that indicators and recorders were going crazy—Manny was giving them what they wanted. Why were they doing things this way? Why not simply ask Manny to show them? Surely had they solicited his—or our—cooperation first, we might have even volunteered. Of course, they might have done that thing, I just couldn't remember. On the other hand, maybe whatever they were into was so secret that they didn't want us to know—but then they could have simply lied and tricked us into cooperation without telling the real reason. Although, it did occur to me that once you get a five year old's dander up, he probably won't ever cooperate. Maybe that's why we were in this situation.

Through our connection, I could feel the insidious fingers of mental pressure mounting. "Wyndy. It's them again!"

"Who?"

"I'ontno," he answered forlornly.

Baldy, or somebody, up there with Manny was an accomplished esper. And was invading Manny's mind.

"Fight them, Manny," I said, speaking aloud involuntarily. "Don't let them in."

He was clinging to me for support. But if he broke the connection, he could be mentally stronger and withstand their assault better. I started to explain that to him—but then it would put him in a dilemma. He'd have to make a decision he wasn't capable of making rationally.

"Manny, hear me?"

"Yes, Wyndy." He was scared and confused, kinda like a baby bunny in a wolves' lair.

"When it gets too bad, shut your mind down. Don't think. Just build a wall and keep them out." I wished I had the mental agility to loan him some of my psychic energy for his own defenses.

I must have transmitted that thought, for he responded. "Ralph is helping me." I remembered now: Ralph was in a place called London. Sure. London. And he "talked funny." The last piece of the puzzle was there in front of me, tantalizing me. But even if I remembered, it wouldn't help Manny right now.

The others: Kim was in Singapore, and she talked funny, too. As did Esteban, who lived in a tiny village I could only remember was on a mountainside I'd guessed to be in the north of Spain. There were a handful of others.

The mental pressure on Manny became unbearable for me, and I felt him whimpering. "Close your mind, Manny."

"I can't. When I do, it hurts more."

"Goddamnit!" Aloud this time. I got to my feet, frustration overwhelming me. They were hurting Manny. I ran at the door, leaped into the air, and lashed out with my good foot. The padding absorbed the blow without a trace, and I fell and rolled to spare my bad leg. If Manny could move, the physical exercise might help divert his mind.

Diversion.

"Manny!"

He didn't respond for a moment, then just a simple undecipherable query.

"Remember *Sesame Street*? Lena Horne?"

Mental affirmation.

"The ABC song, Manny. Sing with me. Now."

His interest piqued, the connection became stronger.

"A B C," I started, and he joined about the LMNOP part where we always rushed through it. I found I was singing at the top of my voice. We finished together, "Now I know my ABCs, won't you sing along with me."

I had his attention. "Again," I shouted and sang. We were together on that one. "Faster this time," I demanded, putting as much command into my thoughts as I could. Ten minutes later, we were still going strong. Lena Horne would've been proud of us. I'd mimicked Grover, Oscar the Grouch, Big Bird, and Bert and Ernie.

After the hundredth time or so, I asked, "How's it goin', kid?"

"Better, Wyndy. It don't hurt as much."

"Doesn't," I replied automatically. "How about a few verses of 'Rockabye Baby'?" From there we went into repetitive nursery rhymes. Then Manny commed he wanted to do "Home On the Range" and "Happy Trails." Pressure on him lessened and I went into my Willie Nelson act, some of which I'd sung to him while riding together on Arpee. Manny joined in where he could remember, if not, he picked up the melody and rhythm.

By the clock, two hours, thirty-three minutes and eight seconds later, they quit the assault on Manny's mind and he fell asleep, exhausted.

Me, too—

—only to be awakened an hour later by another assault. We went into our act again. I taught Manny a few old songs that had repetitive patterns, like "The Long Black Veil," and "Seven Spanish Angels." Lefty

Frizzel, Willy Nelson, and Ray Charles were better than us, but what the hell.

This went on for thirty hours, on and off. I knew *I* couldn't hold out much longer. I only hoped that exhaustion-induced sleep would be sufficient to thwart Baldy's probing.

At the thirty-hour mark, I knew we'd lost. They weren't gonna quit until they got what they wanted—and I no longer cared a damn bit about whatever that was. I was building a hatred within me, a murderous hatred. The anger again helped sustain me. I could only wonder at the power of Manny's mind to remain sane through this ordeal. I had ninety years of trial and travail, etc, to prepare for this. He had nothing but five years of happy kidhood.

I collapsed and couldn't even recall Lena Horne's face any longer. It was like I was in a cloud with that goddamn time and temperature line glowing through the fog. It was the only concrete thing in this room I could use for a focal point, except my navel . . .

"Wyndy—help me . . . please? It hurts . . ."

I felt his pain and couldn't do anything. Utter frustration.

WHANGON EMPTY

It pulled me slightly out of my semi-conscious state. What the hell?

The screen. Date time temp line interrupted only a flicker.

Again. A fraction of a second.

Right. Time it. Five seconds, flicker.

Concentrate. Now. Five seconds. Again.

W-HANG ON-EMPTY

Sure. Wyndy—hang on. Empty? A simple code telling me everything. MT. Maria Temple didn't want to use anything that could be traced to her or Bossman. They were working on springing us—or rescue. Maria had wormed into the Hub's computer system and found a way to communicate.

I perked right up and made to tell Manny—then I

debated whether to give the kid false hope or not. Maria or Bossman couldn't possibly know what was going on here, what they were doing to me and especially Manny. Could they know? Naah. They might suspect, after all how often does a government kidnap a five year old?

Manny was groping for my help. Pressure mounted again. He'd never last—though I wasn't certain if capitulation to Baldy and his project wouldn't be an easier choice than fighting. What could we lose?

"Manny?"

He barely acknowledged me.

"Your mother, Manny. She sent me a message. She told us to hang on."

His mind soared. Them five year olds are like that. And Manny certainly loved his momma.

I couldn't ignore the burst of enthusiasm and hope Manny shot my way. "Yeah, we're gonna get out of here, somehow, soon. Your mother and Bossman are working on it."

And Manuel Temple fell asleep, a deep sleep, ignoring the probes, and we lost our connection. I knew if they went after him again, he had enough strength to wake me up for help.

I slumped right there watching W-HANG ON-EMPTY, and fell asleep while humming Lena's "Stormy Weather" and remembered the rest of the puzzle.

6: The Unfriendly Skies

They came for Maria and José Temple on a dark and windy day. My memory was sharp. Clouds had boiled off the Gulf all morning and rain threatened. I was mowing the ninth fairway when the SpecSec chopper swooped out of the sky like an owl after a field mouse; it landed heavily on the helipad as if to assert its own strength. I expected a squad of troops to storm off and fan out.

Nope. Two men climbed out and casually looked around. They spotted the walkway to Bossman's imposing residence and followed it.

Manny was riding beside me controlling the height of the laser cutter, following the contour of the ground on a screen and operating the joystick as if he were at an arcade. "I have to go to Momma," he said. His voice was tense.

"Right. Kill the cutter." I turned off the vacuum and swung the mower around and high-speeded toward the house. We parked at the walkway and hurried along. Before we reached the door, José jogged past us appearing worried. His tan work clothes were soaked in sweat and his hair disheveled.

Manny glanced at me apprehensively as José brushed by and I just shrugged.

When we got to the reception room, the entire cast was already there and in place. Bossman concerned, scowl on face. The two SS guys grim faced, but speaking matter-of-factly. José angry, waving his arms, hair on his forehead flopping around with his abrupt movements. Maria's face hard, then momentarily softening when she saw Manny. He went to her and she put her arm around his shoulders.

The gist of it all was that the Temple family was required to go to the Hub for an extradition hearing. The Republic of New York had requested their return for tax violations.

How had they found the Temples? Bossman's employee records? Possibly. Computers somewhere always sifting through data and names and numbers? My own opinion was that, because of Bossman's PROJECT, the biggies in the Hub had us under constant surveillance and had checked out José and Maria. They found a discrepancy somewhere and further investigation revealed José's propensity for not paying taxes.

But José and Maria were small fish, not worth a chopper and two SpecSecs. Why, then? Because of the Bossman and his position and political clout. Maybe. On the other hand, perhaps somebody at the Hub thought they had found a lever, something they could use to manipulate Bossman. Maybe they were sending a signal to him. Too many possibilities, so I paid attention.

"No!" José almost shouted and waved his hands some more. "Leave us alone," he said as he swung around. I smelled alcohol on his breath. Not one to miss my own nip now and then, I ignored it.

"José," Maria said. Her eyes and voice were trying to warn him and calm him at the same time. She clutched Manny closer to her. Her body language, which probably only me and maybe Bossman could read right then, showed she was really worried.

Could the Hub officials have discovered her infiltration into their computer system? That would certainly give her cause for alarm. In that case, this was only a ruse to get her away from Bossman's protection and find out what she'd done for him. This was getting complicated.

". . . sorry, sir, just following orders," said one of the SS.

"And they must return with you right now?" Bossman asked mildly.

"Yes, Mr. Swallow."

"Perhaps you would extend *me* a courtesy?" Bossman looked at the guy evenly, but it was more of a statement than a question. He didn't wait for a response. "I find I have some business at the Hub. I shall personally escort my employees to their hearing. We can take my chopper so that you won't have to provide return transportation once this error is straightened out."

The senior SpecSec guy was quick on his feet. "Certainly, sir. I would extend you also the courtesy of myself as a guide and escort. There is room in your chopper; I admired it on our landing."

Playing his role, Bossman said, "Your presence would be welcome; I always have trouble finding my way around in that maze."

"I am not," José said pointing at the two of them, "a side of meat to be discussed and disposed of without notice . . ." His anger died as he saw Maria staring at him. "Rather, we are not items . . ."

Bossman ignored him and turned to me. "Wyndy, get Crane Plash for me, please."

"Sure." Usually I got a small shot of pleasure when other people used nicknames I'd invented. Not this time. I was busy figuring how I was gonna get on that chopper myself.

It was easy. I just got into the copilot's seat before any of them boarded.

When we sailed into the Hub's airspace, Crane Plash turned to me and said, "Always a learning experience, this flying about the Hub." The SS man came forward and gave him a code. The pilot nodded and spoke softly into his mike for clearance. As we landed, I could tell it was a special landing area, not public access. Crane Plash spoke softly, as if to himself. "Simple date-time code. Anybody with a computer and radio access to these frequencies could figure it out."

If only we hadn't brought Manny, everything would still be all right. Maria was worried, José mad as hell; but Manny picked right up on their emotions. Doubtless, he thought they were all gonna be deported to New York and thrown in the slammer. His mind must have been in high gear and splashing mental waves all over the goddamn place. Adding to his apprehension was the cavernous hearing room, where an imposing official sat behind a large desk affair well above floor level, obviously designed to contribute to the overall effect on those coming before the "court." Hell, I was tempted to be awed myself, but my natural dislike of authority prevented this; I simply growled and sat on the edge of a nearby table, eliciting a couple of nasty looks at my breach of etiquette.

The official, whose face reminded me of a brick, was crisp and efficient, consulting his terminal only occasionally.

Bossman took the lead and spoke in behalf of the Temples. They established that José and Maria had committed no crimes in our republic and had dutifully paid their taxes: withholding will get you every time.

As they began the extradition phase, a side door swished open and Baldy rushed in, followed by a very thin black woman and a hunchbacked, sunbrowned man. Looking back now, with the return of memory, Baldy was the same Baldy as would direct the mental experiment in the Administrator's office.

Brickface glared at the interruption, awaiting an explanation. Baldy and his two followers surveyed us and their gazes locked in on Manny. Manny entwined his arm in Maria's dress and jammed up against her looking like he wanted to cry.

Abruptly, Baldy and his two sidekicks turned and left.

Bossman resumed negotiating and in a few minutes, Brickface held up his hand. "A moment." He read something off his terminal, tapped a query or something, and sighed. "Mr. Swallow, may I propose a solution?"

Bossman nodded.

"I propose that if you were to guarantee payment of back taxes and interest, it might be that I could convince my counterpart in New York to accept a fine in lieu of, ah, rehabilitative incarceration service." I think he meant jail.

Bossman nodded, obviously wondering at this sudden turn. Maria looked at José with hope on her face. José glowered. He was getting a lot of practice glowering.

Silas Swallow must have realized what I had: it was a hook. They, the nameless Hub officials somewhere pulling the strings, had got their hooks into him and his operation. He'd have a big IOU to pay off. His immediate acquiescence signaled Maria's—and maybe José's—value to him.

What happened next was what I'd guessed. Bossman punched in his code and transferred fifty-odd grand to New York, and the Temple family was released pending New York's agreement. "Paperwork and approval take time, you know?" Brickface said.

The whole thing smelled worse than a dead possum. And Bossman knew it and could do nothing about it.

Unhampered, we returned immediately to the farm outside Ocala.

Nothing happened for six days. But I was uneasy. I imagined far more overflights of choppers than usual, more odd vehicles driving around the perimeter of Bossman's domain, too many "I was lost and just turned on this road" people.

Manny was initially happy over the seemingly easy disposal of the problem. Then he became cranky and his eyes showed something was bothering him. "Headaches," he explained.

On the sixth day following our visit to the Hub, Manny and I were returning from a ride on old Arpee when it happened.

Arpee was sweating from the workout and we were all tired. Manny sat behind me with his hands around my waist. We were heading for the stables when half a dozen choppers came droning over in formation. Four of them split, heading for the compass points and stopped and hovered in the air. The last two choppers dived for the helipad and performed a military landing. This time troops poured out of both of them, rushing to surround Bossman's residence and fanning out through the cottages.

Arpee whinnied at the sudden noise and unexpected movement. He danced some and I had to rein him in. Manny instinctively tightened his grip around my waist. Maria and Bossman appeared on the balcony of his upstairs office suite.

My mind was assessing the situation when Baldy and his two companions, the black woman and the hunchback, came down the troop ramp of the first chopper. Baldy paused at the top of the ramp, looked around, spotted us immediately, and flung his arm out and pointed directly at us. His other hand snatched a radio from his belt and he spoke into it.

Now, I can't read lips, but I couldn't mistake what Baldy said into the mike: "There he is!"

And Baldy didn't mean me.

Manny blasted me with my first experience of a surge of psychic fear. I couldn't mistake that, either.

I could see Maria's hand go to her mouth as she, too, realized whom they were after. Person to person, non-esper type, I was more attuned to Maria than I'd been to anyone in the last forty or sixty years—maybe more so than anyone other than my first wife Becky— rather Rebecca. Both Maria and I knew they were after Manny—and we both suspected why.

Her arm lashed out with an imperious gesture directed solely at me. *Run!*

My heels were already slamming into Arpee's ribs.

Troops were turning their heads in our direction and officers beginning to shout orders.

Arpee squealed like a kicked dog and leaped ten feet ahead and hit the ground at a full gallop. I ducked my head like I'd seen jockeys do and kicked him again into a dead run. Manny was holding on like a tick on a dog.

We angled away toward the back of Bossman's property, tearing up great globs of slow-grow out of the eighth green and ninth approach. We leaped a water hazard and I glanced back. Weapons were training on us, but I thought we were far enough from effective range. Not one of the weapons I saw was lethal: they were all variations of stun guns.

Arpee was laboring after half a mile. Over the pounding of his hooves I could hear the noise of the four airborne choppers converging on our position. One buzzed us as we headed for an area of trees and foliage. Fortunately, there were few gunships around these days; they only had troop ships with which to chase us down.

Another chopper braved a giant old oak we dodged beneath. He pulled up suddenly to avoid it and spoiled the aim of a gunner hanging out a hatch. That surprised gunner dropped his stun gun. I cut a hard right and Arpee gallantly obeyed but his timing was off. Poor old bastard was really breathing raggedly.

We raced along at the edge of the trees. Another chopper swung alongside of us, propwash blowing dust and leaves all about and whipping us with limbs. Another gunner leaned out and took careful aim. I jerked the reins to the left and we ran right under the chopper. That damn pilot was too intent on following us and broke left, too. I caught a glimpse of a second chopper charging in and swung Arpee back toward the trees.

I didn't see the two choppers collide there in midair, but I heard them. It sounded like a convention of garbage trucks all throwing dempsy dumpsters at one another. The resultant fireball missed us, but the force of the explosion and the heat wave washed over us. It scared another mile an hour into old Arpee.

We pounded down a trail into the woods and darted out into a small clearing. Arpee's hooves tore up my tobacco patch like a tornado. We skirted the edge of a swamp and came out onto pasture land scattering a gaggle of sheepaloe.

Arpee was struggling now. All his sensory imputs must have been telling him to panic, but his desire was much stronger than his old body. Manny's face was pressed into my back like a bad spring in an old pickup.

I had no time to think, only time to react. Reminded me of a few battles, especially in Thailand. I needed my Uzi. I could take out a couple of unsuspecting choppers.

Arpee stumbled and I guided him onto a gravel road toward the rear of the property. The sun was obscured by smoke from the two dead choppers.

Arpee slowed and I gasped for breath in sympathy with him.

Another chopper came in low. I glanced at it and saw two gunners, both with weapons already trained on us, no doubt firing already. Mercilessly, I hauled in on the reins and Arpee's head came up and around, drenching me with lather as he tried to stop.

The chopper overshot and I kicked the horse into motion again. There wasn't any real cover for maybe half a mile. Sheepaloe were running around the pasture like heads with their chickens cut off. I would have reversed back into the tree cover we'd just left if the chopper had not been coming back at us and heading in that direction. I tried to direct us right at the chopper's nose so the gunners wouldn't have a good shot, but the pilot swung sideways toward us. I could see the strapped-in gunner's hand white on the trigger of his stunner.

A great spray of foam-flecked blood spewed from Arpee's mouth as something within him gave. My legs felt slabs of his muscles tremble and slacken.

Then Manny cried out and my body began tingling. I'll swear to my dying day that I could spot the invisible laser sight-dot on Arpee's head right between his laid-back ears. At the laboring run, Arpee just went forward and down. I've never heard a horse's legs break before or since in my life, but that one time was enough. *Crack crack* went his two front legs almost simultaneously, sounding like Paul Bunyon ripping great limbs off giant redwoods.

I kicked loose of the stirrups and hit the ground with my arms outstretched, too conscious of Manny still clinging to my back. I couldn't roll like I should have to land safely, but I managed to spring a somersault with my hands which jammed my arms into my shoulder sockets with tremendous force. Next I hit with my feet and tried to run to maintain balance, but I pitched forward on my face just like Arpee had just done.

The chopper was still overhead and its blades were blowing the sweat off my brow. My body tingled again and I knew the gunner had me at max range. Manny's arms relaxed—he must have taken full brunt of the stun gun's blast. It was sweeping over us again and I rolled to avoid its rays. I felt strangely weak but managed to scramble to my feet.

I snatched up Manny and stumbled off, skirting Arpee. Blood was oozing from his mouth and nostrils and both his legs were askew like bent coat hangers. He looked pleadingly at me, surprisingly not making a sound. I had no time for regret. Propwash knocked me down and I rolled backward dodging the stun gun again. Damn things didn't tear up spurts of ground like legitimate weapons so that you know the direction of fire, traverse and all that technical stuff.

On my feet again, no time to settle Manny somewhere comfortable, I carried him cradled in my arms. I ran ten feet one way and zigzagged just like the old days. My body realized before my mind did that my bad leg wasn't working right. Time takes its toll on age. I reversed and headed for a sheepaloe wallow, feeling like a cowboy running from Indians.

That damn chopper was tenacious. He swept in slow, angling sideways so the gunner had a better field of fire and the bastard did that thing. Tingling, stronger this time. My mind was still running, but my legs weren't.

Manny was slipping from my arms no matter what I told my arms to do. My bad leg gave out first and I simply crumbled there in the sheepaloe pasture.

Manny tumbled out in front of me and came to a rest. I stretched for him like a first baseman but couldn't reach him.

Manny's mind touched mine once more and he was gone and I tried to climb to my feet and nothing worked and I tried to breathe and blood from a smashed nose choked me and I tried to turn my head to see what the hell I was going to do and my head wouldn't obey me and my brain kind of forgot what I was trying to do and tingling . . .

7: The Maze

When I woke in the cell, I couldn't tell if Manny was awake or not. Which meant they weren't assaulting his mind right now. Strangely, I found myself more rested than I would have thought. I would need that rest.

The second thing I did was stare at the time and temp line on the inset screen. Maria was playing it safer this time: every ten seconds a letter. To an unaware observer, the message line only seemed to electronically flicker.

S . . . O . . . O . . . N

Something was up.

"I'm hungry, damnit. How about some chow?" They'd be monitoring me.

While waiting, I paced and thought, getting the kinks out of my bad leg and my mind at the same time. I found I could actually breathe through my abused nose.

The significance of Maria's message told me several things. The most important was that somehow she'd identified my exact location. Maria and Bossman wouldn't chance some sharp-eyed Fedcenter lackey intercepting her messages to me, so the message was obviously appearing on my screen only. So maybe they had Manny pinpointed also. More importantly, they had some plan. Maria couldn't do anything on her own; it had to be done with Bossman's resources.

And all of the above meant that any legal course of action was out: they wouldn't chance the messages if they could spring Manny and me legitimately through governmental channels—or even using Bossman's economic and political clout.

The delivery chute pinged and I lifted the trap door and found a tray. Surprisingly for institutional food, it was good. Chicken, rice, spring peas, bread, butter.

"How about a package of Red Man?" My spirits must have been higher than I thought.

While I ate, something important occurred to me. Maria and Bossman. Bossman didn't have to put his good offices on the line for Maria's child. Well, I discounted the fact that he might be concerned with me. Silas Comfort Swallow had a lot to lose. All for the child of an employee. Was Manny somehow valuable to Bossman—maybe his PROJECT—in some capacity? Or, more likely, was Maria that important to him and his various operations including the PROJECT? Or, and most likely, was Maria personally more important to him? He'd been a widower for many years; and Maria had been working closely with him for at least five years. There just might be something between them, anywhere from totally platonic to real, true love.

S . . . T . . . A . . . N . . . D . . B . . . Y

I looked about for a weapon. No such luck. No bed posts, no nothing.

STANDBY was coming at five-second intervals now, telling me it would be a lot sooner than later.

The time line told me it was 0234 hours and the seconds ticked along. I dumped the unfortunately plastic tray into the chute and dropped to the bed pretending to try to return to sleep. No use alerting the bad guys. I felt anticipation at the coming action. What was to be my role? Since they obviously couldn't communicate in this manner with Manny, their plan might be that I would be the key to retrieving the kid.

All right, I wasn't gonna leave here without him, anyway.

Which still didn't explain what *I* was doing here. Did they think Manny's mental tricks could somehow be linked to me? Not very likely. And they wouldn't be all that happy with me after losing two choppers and crews because of me. If the Hub officials weren't concerned with the mutual affinity between Manny and me, why else? Why hadn't I been taken to task (read prosecuted) for attempting escape, resisting arrest, with violence and mayhem, etc.? Was it because of my obvious relationship to the Administrator?

My third wife had been one Nancy Li Smith-Hyde. We'd had a daughter whom I'd lost track of after Nancy had divorced me. That was before the wars in Thailand, which kind of intervened in my life like a Berlin Wall. I'd had one life before them, and seemingly after the wars, started over. The Administrator could be a grandchild, great-granddaughter, or niece. Something like that. And it had taken the current circumstances to pry loose the resemblance to Amber Lee-Smith and the possible familial relationship.

I was thinking about Nancy and our life in Los Angeles where I was running my own lawn mower repair shop mostly changing rings and doing valve jobs on Briggs and Stratton three-and-a-half-horsepower engines, sharpening blades, doing tune-ups, and the like, doing it for cash when the customer would agree (cash: the customer didn't pay sales tax, I didn't write a ticket and declare it on my taxes and account sheet and everybody profited except the tax guys) until some jerk who wasn't happy with my work turned me in. It all went downhill from there with Nancy . . .

The screen blanked and a schematic I guessed was my portion of the Hub appeared. A green W indicated, obviously, my current location. A red line surged along a route through corridors and floors like an out-of-control ancient mercury thermometer. Any kid familiar with complex video games could have followed the track and solved the game in seconds; me, it took a little longer, but my military memory came back and clicked into position. The red line stopped and a green script M appeared. Manny's location.

While memorizing the route, it occurred to me that Silas Comfort Swallow might just be flexing his own muscle. While he wouldn't let this action be traced to him, it would be obvious that he had had something to do with it. Maybe he was telling the Administrator that the Hub need oughta beware of who they messed with.

That schematic disappeared and the escape route appeared. From Manny's room to . . . ah, got it . . . the SpecSec helipad we'd used when we first went to the deportation hearing.

In thirty seconds that map was gone and the entire screen flashed NOW. As I moved to the door, I saw the screen return to normal dark with the time and temp line back in place.

I touched the plate and nothing happened. I grasped the protective fabric and pulled and the damn door slid open. There was a short hallway leading to a brightly lighted area. I hurried that way. Not three in the morning and nobody about here.

A control center, empty of people, full of view screens and ubiquitous clipboards. How come it was so easy? Quickly, I checked and found the screen for my room; she must be running a tape of me sleeping. Where were the guards? Technicians? Nurses? Probably only one or two on duty and Maria most likely had faked something on instruments or screens of another room to get the monitors over there. I snatched a smock from a hook and pulled it over my institutional pajamas.

Following the schematic in my head, I took the emergency stairs up three flights. Manny's area wasn't too far away; it stood to reason that they accomplished all their nefarious operations in one wing of the Hub, colocating most of them for security purposes.

When I peeked into the corridor from the emergency exit, a guard with a stun gun ran past and didn't notice me.

Something, or somebody, had triggered an alarm.

"Wyndy!" Manny's mind screamed into mine, startling me.

"Yeah, kid." I paused, figuring what to do next.

"What's going on?"

"I'm coming to get you, Manny, get ready."

"There was shooting somewhere."

"Don't worry, I'm coming, kid."

So Bossman and Maria had an alternate plan in case I was not able to contribute—or didn't make it that far. And shooting meant a projectile weapon, not a stun gun or one of them new laser rifles.

Boots clumping, one pair, so I leaned against the wall in the corridor and made like I was wiping my face with a corner of the smock.

An SS guard hurried by, rifle at ready, concern on his young face.

"Hey, what's going on?" I asked.

He brushed past, more aware of the importance of his own function right now, ignoring my query.

I hurried after him. "The patients all right?" I demanded. He was traveling in the right direction.

"Clear the area," he shouted over his shoulder. I continued following him.

I smelled it before I saw it.

Cooked human flesh gives off a stench that has a way of landing on your tongue so that you think you can taste it.

We ran out into a big central control area just like the one which had been monitoring me. Two guards and two technicians were standing looking over a body on the floor on the far side of one of the two C-shaped consoles. None of them looked too healthy, for their faces were contorted in horror. One tech turned and vomited into a corner waste chute.

The man on the floor was wearing a jumpsuit. His

left side, about where the kidney is located, was scorched, obviously by a laser shot, and the beam had traveled across his lower pelvis. He looked at me.

His unshaven face looked like someone had twisted the excess skin in a vise, he was in so much pain.

José Temple moved his mouth dryly, his eyes burning into mine, and said, "It was all I had left I could do for her . . .them, Wyndy."

His outstretched hand was but a few inches from my own Uzi. I guess Bossman knew where I hid it.

A dead guard lay on the other side of my Uzi.

The guards were looking at me strangely now, recognition that I didn't belong dawning on their faces.

One alert fellow even started swinging his weapon to bear on me. But I was already bending over to retrieve my Uzi, so I swiveled on my bad leg and lashed out with my good one, feeling my bare toes crush into his throat satisfactorily. Hurt my toes, too; too long outa practice. I came up shaking the strap out of the way and shot the other SS man in the middle of his face. The guard I'd followed twisted and screamed as 9-mm rounds ripped him apart. It would have been foolish and timewasting to take a stun gun and put the technicians out. So, acting on that premise and the fact that they had possibly contributed to torturing Manny, my anger and I shot both them dead.

"Wyndy?"

José's eyes were cloudy and haunted and I don't think he could see me. "Yeah, José?"

"Tell Maria . . . for me . . ." He breathed shallowly, trying to regain lost air.

I didn't have time for a death scene. "Tell her what?"

"I still cared for her. The drinking, the accusations . . . you see, I was no longer *the* man in her eyes. You see?"

"Yeah." I paused. Time was running out. "I think you were. You are here, are you not?"

He seemed to smile. "I am. You brought Manuel

into this life, Wyndy. I charge you with . . ." His voice just trailed off and he was dead. A final cloudiness shut out the haunted look in his eyes.

"I will tell her you went out as a man, José." I stepped over his body to the main console. One glassed-in section was labeled EMERGENCY ONLY. With the stock of my Uzi, I smashed the glass and hit a switch under the words SECURITY ALL UNLOCK.

"Wyndy, help!" Manny's mind shouted.

Ignoring Manny for a moment, I turned José's body over to get to the satchel scrunched beneath his body. Ammo clips, good. The rest of the clip in the Uzi I sprayed over the electronics stations. Then I trotted down a corridor to Manny's room, kicked open the door and went in low.

The sunbrowned hunchback was there, lifting Manny out of the bed. Apparently, he'd already disconnected all the IVs and electronic leads. I shot him three times in the hump and he dropped Manny back on the bed and whirled on me. I could tell he tried to strike me in the mind, for Manny screamed, and I felt some small trickle, a mental equivalent to the stun gun on my body, but it did not affect me. His hump and bent-over posture had misled me, for he was a huge man. He pushed a bedside table at me and I had to dance out of the way he was so quick. Then he was on me before I could bring the Uzi to bear on him again.

I just let his momentum bowl us over, pitching him over my head with my legs, and as he flipped past, I busted his skull with the butt of the weapon. I didn't know whether or not I'd killed him, but I didn't have time to do an autopsy.

Manny was helping me up. "Get me *out* of here!" he said, face strained, breath sour. His face was gaunt and no longer looked five years old. The bastards.

"Let's go, kid," I said and turned and glanced out the door. "Still clear."

"More are coming, I feel them."

I hustled out the door and Manny followed.

"They were trying to do things to my mind," he said.

"Yeah, but I don't know why," I said, worrying how to get Manny past José's body.

"My daddy is dead," Manny said.

"I know."

"He died like a man."

Kid didn't sound like a five year old, either.

"And we ain't gonna waste his sacrifice." I urged him around the consoles in the central control room so that he couldn't see José. I was hearing noises seemingly from everywhere. Alarms, shouts, electronic beeps, metallic sounds. We ran down an adjoining corridor, one which had no doors opening onto it, giving me hope that it was a good exitway.

At the end of the corridor stood a pair of security doors, one wing of which slammed open as we reached them. I shoved Manny against the wall and let two security guards run through before I shot them.

Manny slipped to the floor. Poor kid was exhausted. They had put him through a hell of an ordeal. Not me. The old, familiar adrenaline pushed through me, heightening my awareness, sharpening my reactions, honing my automatic responses. I lifted him roughly and tossed him over my shoulder. The strap on my Uzi I snuggled around my fist to hold my grip on the weapon.

I went carefully through the doors into another corridor, up an emergency stairs exit, and out into a more public area. Up an escalator scattering cleanup crews and maybe food service people, around a giant atrium, dodging aside when feeling the tingle of a stun gun. I slid under the cover of a marble bench and located a roving guard who was training his stun gun on the bench. I scooted forward and shot his legs out from under him. The Uzi sounded strangely flat in that open place. The guard's screams were piercing.

Lunging up and balancing Manny on my shoulder, I heard the sounds of activity from behind us. Needing a diversion, I leaned over the rail of the landing and looked below. The atrium continued down maybe three stories. I shot out some of the glass on the floor below and tossed the still screaming guard down, where he hit and lay still. Good as I could do.

I ran down a ramp and almost shot three ancient black women, obviously a cleanup crew. They were clustered around the back of one of those janitor robots, one of them probing inside a panel with a hairpin. Nothing changes, does it? I tried to put a finger to my lips to tell them to be quiet, but found I had none to spare. They simply stared at us wide-eyed.

Then we were out a recognized door and onto the SpecSec helipad.

8: Crane Plash

There were two bodies immediately outside, courtesy, more than likely, of José. José, who had spoken against war and fighting. A José who was no longer the innocent young man—tax evasion not counting against guilt or innocence. A José who had changed gradually over the last five years. Somehow, I'd always think of him as I saw him there in the stables, hovering protectively over Maria in labor.

A chopper was running in place on one of the spots and I almost shot Crane Plash before I recognized him.

I smelled fuel. The air was full of it and I coughed.

Crane Plash gestured frantically. I ran to him and his chopper, a Hub VIP bird. I handed Manny to him and he tossed the kid inside with little caution for injury. As I climbed in, Crane Plash handed me a signal flare gun. "Fire this when we get airborne." He indicated growing pools of fuel from all of the ten or twelve SpecSec and VIP choppers on the helipad. He'd been busy.

Yet he did not move to the cockpit. Then understanding reached him. "José?" he asked softly.

"He didn't make it," I said and hosed off about a ten-round burst at the doors we'd just come through as they had opened with several men running through them.

Crane Plash spoke not another word, but scrambled

to his seat and I had to grab the chopper's frame to keep from falling out as the craft lurched. The Uzi banged hard against my bad leg as I juggled it and the flare gun. I cocked the flare pistol as the chopper's blades revved to max, and fired underneath one of the other choppers when we swooped off the roof. There was a slight pause and then an audible whoosh as the fuel ignited. I stumbled back into the body of the chopper only vaguely aware of the flames leaping beneath another and another chopper on the helipad. No explosion came for about twenty seconds, but by then we were out of the danger zone and skimming over the intersection of Highways 10 and 75.

Crane Plash hugged the ground, probably using that terrain following gear.

I strapped the unconscious Manny into one of them fancy VIP seats and went forward and joined the pilot. "Thanks," I said.

He was intent on instruments, his face buried in the HUD, or Heads Up Display. He had a piece of paper in his teeth. He indicated for me to take it.

When I did that thing and looked at it, I saw there were two long numbers.

"The first number," he said as his hands flew over the controls, "is a secret account number of Mr. Swallow. Use it, it won't be traced. The second one is a hopefully secure access to his computer system. Maria will monitor it."

Well, that answered that. We were on the run. We couldn't return to Ocala and the farm.

"Memorize them and destroy the paper."

"Where are we going?"

"Atlanta. There is a car waiting with safe papers and an altered transponder. They shouldn't be able to trace you for a few hours."

"Then we're on our own?"

He pulled the stick back and the chopper gained altitude. He looked at me. "Yeah, you're on your own." His eyes were tired but alert. "Mr. Swallow and

Maria trust you, Wyndy. Had it been anybody else, well . . . SpecSec's gonna be all over the farm like stink on shit and no way can Maria evade surveillance."

"Are you involved too?"

"Yeah, but I got a cover story that will stand up."

"All right." I thought for a moment. "It also means the Federales will be monitoring each person who boards the *Nimitz*." The ship wouldn't be safe for us.

"Correct, good buddy," he said. "And Bossman doesn't want to chance a search by fugitive warrant."

I nodded, though he couldn't see me.

"How is Manuel?"

"Beat."

"Mr. Swallow—and Maria—want to know what they were doing to you in the Hub."

"I don't know rightly. But once I can talk to Manny, I might can figure it out. They had him electronically monitored and were, I think, trying to evaluate the extent of his mental capacity."

"Esper?" he asked, surprised.

"Something like that. But he is more. Tell them there is a baldheaded bastard who seems to be in charge, has the power. He has what I figger to be a couple of assistants, one a black woman and another, who might be dead, a hunchback."

"Maria says she needs some key to get into their information system to retrieve enough to understand."

"You mean an access code or something?"

"You got it, Wyndy."

"I'll see if Manny noticed anything."

The pilot turned back and dropped altitude and shoved his face back into the HUD.

"Oh, yeah, something else," I said. "The Administrator. She's my great-granddaughter or niece or something." I paused, thinking. "It took a close look at her for me to guess Amber Lee-Smith is one of my ancestors."

"Descendants."

"Whatever. I shoulda paid more attention to the

media when that Singapore crew got the charter government contract, but I wasn't too happy with the way things were going, anyway . . ."

His head turned to me and stared at my face for long seconds. "Will she help?"

"No," I said decisively. "That wife and I did not part amiably. Amber'd probably like to fry my gizzard. She knew who I was and yet apparently okayed their experiments on us."

"Oh, shit." He adjusted the HUD closer to his postion. "Us?"

"Yeah, somehow, I was part of the experiment. Maybe it's as simple as Manny and me think-talking and the Administrator hopes it is genetic and can learn how to do so herself."

"You know what you are saying?"

"Yeah." My voice was bitter. "We're not only just escaping from some illegal, secret government project, one which we might could wiggle out of, but we got the top level of the Hub government on our ass."

"Succinctly put. Mr. Swallow wants his hands clean."

"The PROJECT?"

"Yep. Nothing must interfere."

"Then why is he involved now?"

He banked to the right and said, "I don't know. We can bury the connection so far, but not much more. Maybe he feels loyal to you, Ancient Age."

"Like hell," I said. "You know damn well that he'd trust me to escape on my own eventually."

"There's that."

"And how is he gonna hide José's body?"

Crane Plash shrugged. "José is—was—the kid's father. It's only natural he would be involved. Independent action."

For a while I brooded in silence, making and discarding plans.

"Wyndy, I'm gonna have to tell Maria about José—or Mr. Swallow is."

"Tell her that José died without pain and that his

last words were of her and Manny. He held them off until I arrived. Machismo, that's the word for it." Embellished a bit, but close to what happened. And Maria would be comforted by the fact that José thought he had gone out with macho. I hoped it would be enough.

"All right, Wyndy, if that's what you say. Listen, Mr. Swallow told me to tell you he's sorry, but . . ."

My mind had been working overtime. I knew what he was going to say and didn't want to make it any easier. "You talking long-term?"

"Yep. He can't help. Too much riding on it. You got plenty money in that buried account."

"How much?"

"One hundred grand interest a year."

At least a million dollars. Bossman was still loyal. Me and Manny could live on that. "Maria knows she can't come near us for a long, long time, doesn't she?"

He nodded grimly, face still buried. "It's killing her." His jaws clenched and unclenched. "Bossman and her know. They know she will lead them to you and sign her own son's death warrant."

"Maybe worse," I said.

"What?"

"Never mind. I'll contact her when I can through her infosystem. Maybe in a couple of years, we can sneak together or something."

"Look, Wyndy, Maria ain't one to leave her child alone—even with you. Anything you and Manny can come up with, get her the info so she can work on the problem."

He was trying to tell me something by repeating himself. "You're repeating yourself, Plash, say what you mean."

He glanced out of the HUD at me. "I'm loyal to Mr. Swallow."

"C'mon, you know me, buddy."

"I do that," he said finally. "Manny's capture devastated her. José turned alkie and they fought. He couldn't handle her authority and position with Mr. Swallow. Mr. Swallow, I think, would like to marry her—now that she is ah, available." Jesus, the poor bastard must be in love with her. Five years. The pilot continued. "I don't know whether she returns Mr. Swallow's affection or not; but it is obvious that she owes the well-being of her child, maybe even his very life, to Mr. Swallow and his resources. And will continue to be in his debt."

Now I was beginning to understand. All Maria wanted was her son and his safety. But she was trapped in a web just as me and Manny were. And those two webs were mutually exclusive. God damn. Life ain't fair, is it? The only solution I could see right then was for somebody, namely me, to go out and kill a goodly number of the top officials of our republic, including one of my descendants. Which would probably complicate matters more, not to mention putting me on a course for certain death.

Crane Plash must have been following the same train of logic. "Bitch of a problem, ain't it?"

I didn't answer. To solve it, we had Silas Comfort Swallow and his resources; Maria and her brilliance and, more importantly, that mother-drive; and we had me. Not to mention Manny and some kind of unusual esper ability. Come to think of it, all that cut down the odds against us right handsomely.

"We'll survive," I said curtly. I swung the copilot's HUD to my face. "Punch me up some maps on here, Plash." I studied hard until we came to the outskirts of Atlanta.

CP had jungle fatigue jumpsuits for us, all the rage, don't you know? Our institutional jammies would have been noticed even in this age of nostalgia fashion.

The largest McDonald's in the world is in Atlanta and has its own helipad. It was crowded at breakfast. We ate and I joked with Crane Plash. "Gonna be McSheepaloe burgers here soon, boy." McDonald's Mercantile Emporium covered a few hundred acres and sold everything from cheese and soyburgers to cars and electronics and kneewarmers.

The car was in the parking lot. Along with clothing for both of us and a bunch of cash. The car was an Indy car replica, befitting our position as wealthy.

Manny had not said a word since I explained our problem. Except: "I'm not going to see Momma, am I?"

"Not right now, kid. We're on the lam."

"Always the dramatics," Plash said and climbed into another car. "They're counting on you, Ancient Age," he said.

I dressed formally, drove downtown thanking traffic engineers for finally solving the Atlanta traffic probem, and went alone into a ritzy jewelry store. They obligingly checked my balance, something over a million dollars, and sold me ten diamonds worth nine hundred thousand. We drove to Savannah and, still playing the rich man, chartered a small jet for Merida, Yucatan, where we chartered a yacht for Havana. In Havana, the persons we had been—using Bossman's provided documents—disappeared. Not that I didn't trust the papers and all, it's just that I didn't trust 'em. A good investigator might be able to follow our trail. An old fisherman took us to Andros Island where we hired another boat, no names of course, for Nassau. In Nassau, I sold the diamonds and put the money into an account that I'd had open for decades, under the name of Sandy Creek.

In Nassau, I bought one of them new bubble-craft, a boatlike thing which was encased in that super thin, indestructible plastic offshoot, which could close up in a bubble for hours on end and ride out any storm, rain shower, or opaque to protect from sun. It was the perfect thing for us amateur sailors, what with infallible electronic guidance and all. It occurred to me that space travel had indeed contributed, despite the naysayers, to the human condition. There was a whole new field of science now, commonly called "bubble physics" with its natural companion, "bubble engineering." They hadda develop it for the moon colony before they could learn to tunnel properly up there. Even Bossman had a state-of-the-art bubble on the *Nimitz*.

We set sail for Daytona one fine morning. It was my intention to set up life as legitimate as possible. Sandy Creek had been a resident of Daytona Beach for years—I'd had to do something with my salaries and money over the years. Long life has its bennies: I already owned an entire floor of a fancy condominium. Twelve units. There was a business account and a personal account that I'd seen to it had enough activity, albeit not very periodic, which we could use comfortably with no questions by the banking authorities. I planned to set up residence in one of the condo units as a well-off widower with his small son.

We drifted through the islands for a while—Manny loved the no-fault sailing, boating, motoring, whatever the nautical types call it. I kept him busy and the slow pace and sea and sun seemed to help reconcile him to the death of his father and to the fact that his world was no longer the same.

We were discussing names. Manny had the autopilot off and was spinning the wheel, slewing us about within the parameters the boat's governor allowed.

And he was arguing with me. "I can't call you Daddy," he said.

Well, I was afraid of that. Maybe because of the age difference, people wouldn't remark too much on that breach of father-son etiquette. I gave in. "Okay, Sandy will do, I suppose. But you gotta choose you a name, too."

"I am Manuel."

"We been through that, kid. It's too obvious. Which makes it dangerous."

His face scrunched up. "I like my name!"

"Yeah, it's what your momma named you, all right, but . . ." Uh oh. Shouldn't have mentioned Maria.

His face scrunched up worse. "I want to see my momma."

"We get set up nice and fancy, Manny, and maybe we can arrange it."

"Promise?"

"Cross my heart, hope to die, stick a pin in my eye, and call in the FBI." Though the fibby was long gone.

"Larry Jim," he said.

"What?"

"Larry Jim. That's the name I want."

"Oh, sure. Um, how'd you come up with that one?"

"Two of my friends. Those are their names."

"Yeah? Which friends?"

He glanced furtively at me, spun the wheel again, and the bubble seemed to stretch to accommodate the maneuver. "My friends."

"The ones you talk to with your mind?"

He nodded.

"How many friends you got you can talk to like that?"

"Some."

"Manny, tell me."

"Larry Jim," he corrected.

"Sure, kid. Look, we got to figger this out. Them bad guys at the Hub captured us and done things to us and we gotta know why so we can fix things up and get back to normal, see?"

"I don't know how many. I never counted."

"More than five?"

"Sure."

"More than ten?"

"Yes." He twisted the wheel again and I had to juggle to keep from spilling my beer.

"Damnit, Manny, quit that. Snap on the autopilot and come over here and sit down and let's talk."

He did that thing and the bubble-boat swung about 120 degrees to return to the proper course. "You're not 'posed to say 'damnit,' Wyndy."

"Call me Sandy."

He sat down with a soda pop. He was wearing a bathing suit and had taken to the sun, sea, and wind well. I could tell the relaxed pace had begun to have an effect on his weakened condition from the ordeal at the Hub.

"We gotta talk about your friends and your ordeal at the Hub, so we can understand it and maybe have some information to tell your mother so she can snoop and find out what the hell is going on."

"Gee, Wyndy . . . Sandy, I dunno . . ."

"They killed your father, Manny."

His face fell and he seemed to curl up within himself. It was a cruel thing to say, but I needed some method to reach him. He'd set his soda pop down and was hugging his knees to his chest.

"Okay, Sandy. What do you want to know?"

9: Tiny Bubbles

"**S**peak to me, then, Manny Larry Jim. You talk to friends using your mind, right?"

"Yes, Sandy Creek." He giggled. "Funny name."

"Sure, kid. Let me tell you something here. Other than rumors I've never seen substantiated, about the only kind of espers there are are those who can mind-talk between themselves at short range." At his blank look, I said. "What I mean is, espers are people who can talk with their minds. Okay?" He nodded. I continued. "Substantiated means proved. And these people can only mind-talk to each other when they are real close. Maybe in the same room. Except I suspect there are a few at the Hub, and maybe elsewhere, whose mind-talk range is a little farther. For instance, my best guess is that when we went to the Hub the first time for the deportation hearing, that Baldy and his two henchmen—henchpeople, that is—picked up something of your mind, your transmissions. I don't know if they can read them or not, but . . ."

"Only if I want 'em to," Manny said.

"Good. Now we're getting someplace. But from what you've told me, your mind-talk is not limited to line of sight or geography or anything. That is," I amended quickly, "you can mind-talk a long way."

"Sure. I know where Singapore is and London and stuff."

"And you communicate with your friends there?"

"Yep."

"How many, total?"

He thought for a moment. "Maybe twenty."

Twenty children in the world with a technique unmeasured. A new and higher class of esper.

Manny unwound his arms from his knees. "Some of my friends know a few others than we all talk to."

I nodded. The numbers were growing. Though eventually, they'd reach all of each other, the new class esper. Suppose somebody in authority had figured that out and was trying to understand it and could locate those children and . . . use them, use their ability? Use their technique. I felt I was getting closer.

"Are you ready to talk about what happened in the Hub?"

"Yes." Meek, very meek. I didn't like Baldy and cronies more than I didn't like 'em before. I hoped the hunchback had died.

"If it'll make you feel better, Larry Jim, the hunchback is probably dead."

"No, he's not. He didn't die."

"Oh. You know?"

"I felt his mind before we left."

Damn. Next time . . .

"All right, Larry Jim Creek, what did they do to you?" I already knew most of it.

"They . . . they had me in a bed and I couldn't move and they had wires and stuff on my head and body and tubes into my arms and stuff and they were recording stuff from them and they tried to get into my mind sometimes from right there in front of me and sometimes from someplace else there in the Hub."

"And you fought them off."

"Yes. They . . . they tried to hurt me."

I didn't know that their purpose had been to inflict pain. I suspected Baldy and them were trying everything they could think of with little regard for Manny and the health of his mind. The sonofabitches.

"Can you think of anything they said or your mind heard them think that would help us?" I asked.

He looked at me blankly.

"Did they mention, say, a project name?"

He shook his head.

"Did they discuss what they were doing in front of you?"

He shook his head again. Smart operators as Baldy and his compadres seemed to be, they wouldn't. If for no other reason than scientific method.

"Do you know their names?"

"Doctor Hodgkins."

"Baldy's name is Dr. Hodgkins?"

"Yes."

"Named after a disease, no doubt."

"What?"

"Nothing, kid. How about the other two?"

"The black lady's name was Janine something or other."

"Good. And the hunchback?" Don't let it be Quasimodo or whatever that was.

"Mr. Rodney."

"Were there any others?"

"Besides the regular nurses and stuff?"

"Right." This was like digging for gold—a lot of work with only occasional results.

"A couple, maybe close by, but I never saw them. They tried to get at me together."

"And they all were able to talk with their minds?"

"Yes, Wyndy."

"But not near as well as you can."

"Yes, Wyndy." I could tell he didn't want to talk any more. The memories could not have been pleasant.

It was difficult, but I wrenched my thoughts away from what had happened. Manny still seemed mesmerized by the episode. To get his mind off that, I dug into a locker there in the cockpit. "I got you a present, Larry Jim, one I forgot to give you before."

That got his attention. Five year olds ain't changed

in ninety years and maybe longer. I tossed the package to him.

"Wow!" he said as he opened the bag. "Underwear? That's not a present . . . oh, wow!"

A ten-pack of Scooby Doo underwear and a couple pair of Garfield swimming trunks. Some things never change, either. The twentieth century's contribution to art.

Manny immediately changed into a pair of Garfield trunks and paraded around as if on display. At least it had gotten his mind off his troubles.

So Hodgkins and company had accidentally discovered that Manny had extraordinary powers. They'd sold somebody high in power on the necessity of exploring Manny's ability. Likely the Administrator. They knew they couldn't get him legally, so they took him illegally and covered it up. Then, during their experiments, they had monitored him physiologically with medical instruments and equipment. And probably mentally with the rest of their espers. The "attacks" he, and later he and I, had fought must have been efforts to penetrate his mind and get him to communicate to them what he knew, what he could do, and how he could do it. I doubted that Hodgkins and his crew had the ability to read minds. They could probably send and receive to each other at short distances; and they had developed sort of a gang-mind energy they used to try to pry into Manny's brain. I'd also bet that they didn't know whether Manny's ability was a result of some physical difference within his brain or some inborn mental difference.

Me neither.

Hell, I wasn't articulate enough to explain what I already knew, much less hypothesize technically what the deal was.

I decided the sun was too bright and opaqued the bubble. The opaquing came from a function designed into the moon bubble to shield them from deadly solar rays. I don't understand technology, much less technology on the molecular level.

Thinking of the bubble, I couldn't help but burst out in song: "Tiny bubbles," I sang, "make me warm all over." With apologies to Don Ho.

Manny giggled and joined me on the refrain. Then he broke into my rendition. "That's it! Tiny Bubbles. That'll be the name of our boat."

"Fine with me, kid. The *Nimitz* don't gotta worry about its literary license."

Manny ignored the last. He'd learned by now to disregard my obscure humor.

As we neared the coast of ex-Florida, I thought more and more about our circumstances. I was approaching it wrong: we were going to be a nonagenarian and a five year old living together, albeit as father and son. Too obvious. And, I suspected, there probably weren't a hell of a lot of children living in that condo for Manny to play with. That wouldn't be disappearance, that'd be "on display."

So I made a decision and programmed *Tiny Bubbles'* computer for Ft. Lauderdale.

We parked, or whatever it is you do with boats, at Bahia Mar for a few days. I explained to Manny what I was going to do and he didn't like it.

"It's part of our cover," I told him.

That night I donned my Willie Nelson-type persona of Sandy Creek. It meant braiding my hair into pig tails, using a headband, with jeans, an old shirt, and canvas deck shoes. I'd grown the obligatory beard-stubble the last week or so on the trip. Because of my age, the stubble was the requisite white and gray. Sandy Creek, when in Daytona, to support himself—namely me in my Sandy Creek disguise—frequented bars with an old guitar and sang for tips. There were a lot of us these days, dipping into the nostalgic times past, impersonating past and famous singers. It provided a minimum and sometimes higher living. Elvis was the biggie. Ten or twelve in every town. Willie

Nelson, Springsteen, and maybe Stevie Wonder next. Ray Charles, Lena Horne, Johnny Cash, Dolly Parton, Jolson, Roy Rogers, Buddy Holly, Hank Williams, and Frank Sinatra to a lesser degree. All with readily identifiable looks and singing styles. A perfect way to blend in with nightlife—nightlife being the least tracked by government computers and such. Most of these impersonators were transient, which was another benefit and helped explain Sandy Creek's intermittent activities in Daytona.

After I'd put Manny to bed on the bubble-boat, I left and cruised the bars. Manny was safe: takes an industrial laser to break into one of them bubbles. Also, what with the new and harsher government and the proliferation of technology, our republic had very little crime. Pembroke Wyndham was probably a statistic all by himself.

For a week, I went from bar to bar at night. In the daytime, I took Manny to museums, boat shows, movies, the beach. But my real work was at night.

Finally, I found the right one. Her. A government-inspected whore. Broward County inspected, that is. Many places had legalized prostitution and drugs like pot and all. Showed the governments had become more concerned with tax dollars than before: always searching for new sources of revenue.

Winsome was her name. Her last name didn't matter because she was fixin' to become Mrs. Sandy Creek. Her qualifications were that I liked her, and that she was of mixed Jamaican and Cuban heritage—the café au lait skin which could account for Manny being *our* son. Other requirements Winsome filled: she was pretty, not beautiful, but pretty; she was tired of her prostitute life and wanted someone to support her for a while; we were sexually compatible; she was wise enough not to ask too many questions; and she had a son by a Caucasian who was six years old. Her son's name was Zell. Where she'd dug that one up, I'll never know. At any rate, it would give Manny the brother he never had. I hoped they would get along.

Winsome's face was finely chiseled and her expressive eyes recalled to me the beauty of the islands. She was maybe five eight with jet black hair. Her mouth twitched when she smiled. A hundred years or so ago, when I turned eighteen, I'd learned that beauty was a function of character, not looks and/or profile. However, it *was* necessary that my companion be attractive— the more so the better. Specifically, people would look at her and not me and Manny.

I brought Winsome and Zell aboard one night about two in the morning. Of course, Manny was up waiting for me. When I introduced them, I expected Manny to query me through his mind, but he didn't. He seemed quite apprehensive. And why not? His world had been destroyed. I was the only person, the only thing, which linked him to his former life, and now I'd changed the rules. There were two new people he had to contend with. And we maintained the facade of Sandy Creek and his son, Larry Jim.

Now we were four.

Zell, if anything, was more quiet, more reserved than any of us.

I paid up and we slunk out of Bahia Mar under the cover of darkness, just from habit. I didn't need anybody to see the old man and the kid leaving with a woman and another kid.

Winsome broke the ice first. While I ain't a bad cook, she was great. As we toiled north on the intracoastal waterway toward Daytona, she made an effort to win "Larry Jim" over. No slouch, she. Cuban chicken and yellow rice quickly became Larry Jim's favorite dish. And I knew that Zell and Larry Jim were getting along when they both appeared on deck one day, each wearing one of Manny's Garfield swimming suits. Looking at them, they could easily be mistaken for brothers, especially if Manny stayed nut-brown as he was from the sun.

I knew the whole thing would probably work when one day, maybe about Vero Beach on the inland waterway, Manny snuck up behind Winsome and went "Boo!" and she wasn't expecting it and turned around and swatted his butt.

Something I'd never done, but something that Manny occasionally needed, the little devil.

"Wyndy!" Manny screamed into my mind.

I came around the cockpit and looked inquisitively at him.

"Did you see that?"

"You needed to be taken down a peg or two, your highness," I thought at him.

He pouted and sulked, but the kind of person he was, he got over it soon enough and he and Zell went swimming with a herd of manatees we encountered.

The manatee had been saved largely through the efforts of one person: Jimmy Buffett. I hoisted a margarita to his memory. Governments had finally helped when they discovered it was much cheaper to have manatees eating the channel-choking water hyacinth and lilies than spending money to clear 'em.

Winsome and I sat on the cabin cowling sipping frozen margaritas and watching the kids.

"He adjusts, no?" she asked.

"Yeah. But it's healthier for him. He ain't had a momma for a while. And the life we lead, he hasn't had much discipline."

"He needs school," Winsome said.

"Yeah, I been thinking about that."

"Maybe we should settle somewhere for a while. Zell should also be sent to school."

"We can tie in with the computer below. There's lots of schools that operate like that."

"Poof!" she said and snapped her fingers. "Is not worth anything. Children must be with other children."

"It's worth considering," I said truthfully, letting her think I tended to agree with her. Actually, it's what I wanted from her. I wanted it to be her idea. I'd

led her to believe, initially, that I wanted companion-
ship, longer than just temporary, without obligations,
and a mother for my child. No doubt she suspected we
were maybe running from something, more than likely
"Larry Jim's" mother. Whatever, it served my purposes.

She put her hand on my knee. "Think seriously,
Sandy."

She had a nice way of persuasion. And I knew I'd
chosen right, for she was pushing for the right stuff:
kids and values. Not high living and an easy life. In
this she reminded me of Maria Temple, I thought
guiltily.

"Well," I said, "I've always been partial to Daytona. I've worked there before and could support us
for a while."

"Okay by me, Sandy." Her quick and knowing hands
massaged my neck and shoulders. One thing about me
and my age: a bit gnarled, but my looks, while not
handsome in the least, were sort of ageless. I coulda
been anywhere from fifty up. I doubt she guessed how
old I really was. Especially since I'd proved how *young*
I was. Also, that agelessness contributed to the genu-
ineness of my Willie Nelson impersonation. And the
physical labor of running the bubble-boat all over the
western Atlantic had hardened me and taken some of
the worry out of my face and my bearing. Quite con-
vincing a disguise, if I do say so myself.

Winsome brought us a batch of frozen daiquiris, the
kind she made from that highly spiced Jamaican rum,
and sat down and leaned her back against my shoulder. "I am comfortable, you know?"

"Yeah, me, too." It was a lazy time, a fun time, a
hiatus between that haunted always-looking-over-your-
shoulder time and the time to come.

After a while, Winsome took the braids out and my
pigtails became one large ponytail. As she was doing
this, the kids swam back to the bubble-boat yelling.

"Last one aboard is a dumb-ass," Manny shouted.

They fought over the ladder and Manny won and climbed up dripping.

Zell was right behind him. "Damnit, Larry Jim, you cheated."

"Nuh uh." Manny grinned.

Winsome bent over and whispered in my ear, "Sandy Creek, you are in trouble."

"Next person on this boat who cusses," I said loudly, "don't get no ice cream for a week."

"And he does get a paddling," Winsome added.

"Sandy, too?" Zell wanted to know.

"That is correct," Winsome said with finality.

Damn, it don't take married life long to get down to the nitty-gritty.

10: Spelling Bee

"**D**amn it, Winsome, why did you let them do it?" I couldn't contain my anger.

She blinked, obviously calculating whether to use tears or logic on me. Logic won. "I did not think there would be anything wrong with it." She paused. "And what *is* wrong with Larry Jim and Zell entering a spelling bee? They were the best spellers in their home-rooms and they were so happy that they each won their grade level competition . . ."

Two years had passed. Zell was now in third grade, Manny in second.

"Sandy, do not evade me. What did I do wrong?"

I'd been gone for a week, no questions allowed about my trip—except Manny knew what I'd been doing and where I'd been.

"Here's what is wrong!" I almost shouted and waved the damn newspaper in her face. At least Manny should have known better.

Winsome gave me a flabbergasted look. "Poof. The color in the pictures is bad. Besides, they were so proud, so happy."

Right there in the local section of the Volusia County weekly was an entire page of kids' pictures. Spelling Bee winners by grade level from all the schools. Manny, second row center.

I tossed the paper aside. Was this it?

"Sandy, I know . . . you are not who you say you

are, okay? I do not argue. You have given my son and me a life, a living for which to be thankful. And I am. But . . . it was all so innocent. I did not think . . ."

"Yeah, you didn't think." I made an effort to control myself. My voice was becoming dangerously brutal. I picked up the paper again and stared at Manny's picture. He was clearly recognizable. "Larry Jim Creek, Second Grade, Shores Elementary." But then again he was just another kid amongst other children. Would someone recognize him? Did the Hub have data processors going through all the local papers for whatever reason, synthesizing and sifting? I knew most bigwigs had rooms full of clerks cutting out clippings, monitoring televideo, paying attention to what was going on everywhere within their purview. Would some bright young up-and-comer see Manny's picture and expose us? Well, the first thing I'd know of it would be blue-suited SS guys surrounding us.

I went into the kitchen and poured myself a double jigger of Jack Daniels Blue Label.

Two years earlier we'd come into Daytona on the bubble-craft. I'd bought a house in a middle income neighborhood full of kids and schools and we'd set up housekeeping. To keep my cover, I'd been singing in bars, honky-tonks, and some nightclubs, doing my Willie Nelson imitation. My voice was close to Texas nasal twang and it was a good impersonation.

Occasionally, when Willie wore out his welcome, I'd fallen back on automobile repairing. I was a mechanic first. Everywhere in the republics on this continent, automobiles were electric with those life time batteries which last maybe five years. While the air is cleaner, performance has suffered.

However, in Daytona, there were several museums dedicated to the old days. The Daytona 500 and Speedweek. They still ran the 500, but with electric cars. Imagine that. Anyway, a couple of the museums, they maintained ancient cars in original condition for display and parades and the like. '57 Chevies, '56

T-Birds, a Carroll Shelby Cobra, a '66 Mustang, a 1908 Mercedes GP, old Packards and Hudsons and Corvettes and Model-As, '63 GTOs, and so on. And while the countryside was replete with electronic engineers, there weren't many auto mechanics. So I had a job whenever I wanted. Even when I wasn't working for a museum, they called me for solutions to problems, even though they had the tech data. Made me happy this high-tech society couldn't run without us low-tech guys. Gave me a warm glow.

So we were getting along fine there for two years. Manny and Zell went to school just like regular kids. Winsome kept house in a parody of olden times. I worked. We'd attended the 500, which used to be the greatest sporting event on Earth, two years running. I was able to monitor the rental management agency which handled my condos and was satisfied with their performance.

Winsome and I were compatible. Which led me to believe I should have taken this route instead of marrying all or most of my previous wives—it made for a less complicated relationship. Manny and Zell were becoming brothers. Everything was going well. But that is when I start worrying. When things go well, watch out. It falls under the old "Too Good To Last" axiom. Manny lobbied me to arrange a meeting with Maria, or somehow get her here to live with us.

His pressure on me made me realize something deep one day: Manny's dream was for Maria to escape the Hub's surveillance and come over here and marry me and I would be his father and he'd have his real mother, not some substitute. No matter how much he liked Winsome. I think, also, that way down inside of him, he was jealous of me and Winsome when it could have been me and Maria—and him. Which caused me to think, to reevaluate what I felt for whom. I suppressed those feelings. What good would they do?

After about six months, I'd taken a trip, disguised of course, to Orlando and booked a hotel room. I used the room's computer to access Maria through Bossman's system with the secret code number Crane Plash had given me. Maria must have been frantic to hear from us.

Our communication was circumspect, though if anybody monitored it, it was obvious who was talking and about what.

After scrambling and code translation, I had to wait for her to come on line.

W—HOW IS HE?

Manny, of course.

WELL. SENDS HIS LOVE.

ME, TOO. OH, ME, TOO. TELL ME MORE.

HE LOOKS FINE. GROWING LIKE A HYDROPONIC TOMATO. ACADEMIC DEVELOPMENT HIGHER THAN NORM, BUT AM KEEPING HIM WITH AGE GROUP AS HE IS NOT DEVELOPMENTALLY HIGHER THAN NORM.

Which was true. Manny might even be a genius, academically speaking, but his physical growth, dexterity, and coordination were average and some of the manual skills, such as coloring and handwriting, were slightly below norm. Didn't bother me. Hell, when I went to elementary school, I never even had those subjects. If you could print well enough for someone to read, they passed you. Might have accounted for my GED.

DOES HE HAVE PLAYMATES?

ROGER. PLENTY. HE FITS IN WELL SOCIALLY.

I AM HAPPY, THEN.

ARE YOU, M? We weren't fooling anybody with these initials.

YES. SS IS VERY UNDERSTANDING.

YOU STILL WORK SAME POSITION?

YES, THOUGH LINOLEUM NOT HAPPY WITH MY ADVICE TO SS ALL TIME. PROJECT ADVANCING RAPIDLY. NASA SHUTTLE CON-

TRACT BUILDING A SHIP IN EARTH ORBIT
PROGRESSING.

HAVE THEY SOLVED THE FINAL PROBLEM?
I asked, referring to the FTL drive.

LIKE ALL OTHER ASPIRANTS, WE STILL
NEED KEY, BUT SS OPTIMISTIC.

I wished she would stop calling him $S.

WERE YOU AND M ABLE TO PROVIDE KEY
OR CODE TO OTHER PROBLEM?

NEGATIVE. WHAT VERBALLY REPORTED
TO YOU VIA OUR DRIVER REMAINS OUR
ONLY CLUE. I hoped Crane Plash had told them
what I'd said about our incarceration and the experi-
ments on me and Manny. NAMES: BALDY IS
DR HODGKINS, MAY HIS DISEASE CONSUME
HIM.

ASSUME YOUR REMARKS AS BLACK HU-
MOR.

ROGER. ALSO HUNCHBACK NAMED MR ROD-
NEY. WOMAN NAMED JANINE, LAST NAME
UNKNOWN. M REPORTS SEVERAL OTHERS
PRESENT, THOUGH NEVER VISUALLY SEEN.

OK. WILL RUN THAT INFO THROUGH MILL
AND SEE WHAT I CAN COME UP WITH. PAIN-
FULLY SLIM FOR MUCH OF A CHANCE.

UNFORTUNATELY.

ARE YOU HOLDING UP, W?

ROGER. FEEL YOUNGER THAN IN YEARS.

I WISH I WISH I WERE WITH YOU BOTH.

(Me, too.) HANG IN THERE.

THANK YOU FOR TAKING CARE OF MY SON.

MY PLEASURE. TIME'S UP. WILL CONTACT
YOU AGAIN. LOVE, W.

TELL M I LOVE HIM AND THINK OF HIM
ALL THE TIME.

ROG. BYE.

I severed the connection and called up the room
service menu. I ordered an extensive meal to lull them

in case I was being monitored, which I doubted, and rose and walked out the door, went downstairs, got on my bike, and rode the bike paths from Orlando back to Daytona. The forty-five miles took only three hours. I'd always been in good physical condition from manual labor, now I was in better shape than in years. My bad leg was much better for it, too. This generation was worse than the jogging generation of fifty years ago. There were more bike paths than roads, seemed like. However, it did provide me with a convenient, aerobic, low-profile transportation method.

Other times, months apart, I'd contacted Maria from Tampa, Disneyworld, and Palm Beach. While she'd gotten into some of the Hub's personnel files and reviewed data on Hodgkins and his team, she'd found nothing to use in extricating Manny and me and her and Bossman from our mutually exclusive webs.

Now this time I'd just returned from Jacksonville where our communication was fruitless as usual.

Maria's last line added pressure to me and to our situation: DAMNIT, WYNDY, I WANT MY SON. No longer were we using the subterfuge of name initials.

I'd had no answer for her.

"Sandy? Sandy?" Winsome's voice called me back.

"Sorry, Winsome, my mind wandered."

She'd come into the kitchen behind me. There were tears in her eyes. "You are not who you claim to be. You are mysterious and take mysterious trips. You have more money than you could possibly expect to have. You tell me nothing and yet you expect me to do the right thing all the time with no guidelines. Have I not done everything you wished? Have I not been a good mate for you? How do I rate your anger?" She batted her eyelids for effect. That rich copper-gold like a Monarch butterfly.

I looked at her and sighed. I tried to fold her into my arms, but she dodged aside. "Look, Winsome, I'm sorry. But honest, I can't tell you. It wouldn't do you any good to know and might even cause you harm."

She looked at me dangerously. "You endanger Zell?" Her first thought was for her kid. Well, I couldn't argue with that.

"Not if we keep a low profile."

"Shit, Sandy, what I am going to do?"

"Yeah. I got the same problem."

We moved into an uneasy truce. Yet I was torn. Should Manny and I go on the run again? The smart answer would be yes. But that would mean disrupting Manny's schooling. It would mean deserting Winsome and Zell—and the longer we stayed together, the more danger they would be in if and when we were discovered.

Damn! I realized that I was fully expecting to be caught.

The next day, I put the house and the bubble-craft in Winsome's name. At least, if we had to make a quick break for freedom, she'd have something. She could sell the boat and get a job and be financially solvent.

Would the SS hurt Winsome and Zell? Probably not. She could simply tell the truth and with a lie detector they'd know it as the truth and not take out their frustration on her. Or so I hoped.

So I discussed it with Winsome. We were sitting on the front porch drinking beer and watching Zell and Manny and some neighborhood children play soccer in the middle of the street. "Winsome?"

She looked at me expectantly.

"If they ever come to you with questions, answer them truthfully. You have nothing to hide and everything to gain. And if they come to you, hiding any of the truth will not matter, for they will know who we really are. Do you understand?"

She jerked her head in a sharp nod. Who are 'they'?"

"Authorities." I sipped and thought. She was alarmed. To ameliorate this, I said, "I have signed the house and the boat over to you. The paperwork is in my desk and properly recorded."

"You are thinking of leaving us, me and Zell, are you not?" Her eyes were steady but I thought her chin might have trembled a bit.

"We might have to." I drank half of my beer.

She lay back, head hanging over the back of the lawn chair, eyes closed, face tense, cheek muscles drawn tight over delicate bones. "I like this life, Sandy. Being a housewife is fun. I do not think I love you— yet. You are too secretive. But I have a past, too. I am learning to care about you—a lot. You have been a decent husband and father—and a more than excellent provider. I do not wish anything to change." She just stopped talking. Maybe she felt she purged herself of whatever she was thinking—or resigned herself to her current circumstances.

Well, hell. Now I was worried about her, too. One of the reasons I'd searched out and picked a hooker for this job was that I thought she would be tough enough to roll with the punches and, all things being equal, be someone I wouldn't have to worry about their welfare when we disappeared.

For disappear we must. Inevitably, the SS, the federales, the authorities would close in. Probably doing so right at that moment.

So now Winsome and Zell were caught in a web all their own. The pressure on me mounted. I could feel it, feel my own web tightening.

Manny fell down out there in the street and skinned his knee right next to the injury he'd suffered when he crashed his bike into a clump of palmetto.

It occurred to me to disappear now, sever the connection so that later it would not be so bad for all of us. And, possibly, if we left before we were discovered, it might keep Winsome and Zell from being connected to us. On the other hand, Manny and Zell were like brothers; it would be terrible to uproot Manny again.

Zell. In some ways he was a strange kid, a more modern kid than Manny would ever be. He had his own computer. Manny generally disdained technology outside of school requirements. Sometimes we'd take *Tiny Bubbles* down the intracoastal waterway to the Kennedy Space Center outside Titusville and watch 'em launch NASA shuttles. Zell was fascinated; Manny only mildly interested. The contrasts of their interests amazed me and made their brotherlike relationship more odd.

I decided to stick it out. Terrible forces attacked my mind. Was I doing the right thing?

That night, I took Manny for a walk and explained our problem. Frankly, I don't think he wanted to worry about it; after all, that was my job. He'd reconciled himself to this existence and was actually enjoying it—even the routine of it was reassuring to him.

"Manny," I said as we walked down the sidewalk, "the way I understand it, you can mind-talk only to others with similar abilities, and to people with whom you have a great affinity at relatively short distance."

"Yes, Sandy," he said snottily, reminding me to call him Larry Jim. "I could talk to Momma, I think, if we were close to her." His telepathic abilities were expanding slightly with age, but not growing as fast as he was physically. Which might be a clue or something to his higher class ability.

"But you cannot read minds or anything like that, correct?"

"Yep."

"Remember at the Hub? You warned me of guards heading our way?"

"Yep. I can sense strong presences, especially those of danger. It's sensing only. No words or thoughts or nothing like that."

"As I suspected." Probably a direct consequence of his telepathic abilities. "What I had in mind, Larry Jim, was to ask you to be alert. I'm worried about that picture in the newspaper. You should have known better. Irregardless, do you think you could sort of scan around with your mind periodically and tell if any of them blue-suited jerks are after us and closing in?"

"Sure. Last week you said the word was 'disregard-less.' "

"Whatever."

I think I slept better that night for knowing Manny was playing mental sentry.

But all my planning and scheming went for naught.

11: '57 Chevy

That specific day, I was working at the Speedway Museum. On a '57 Chevy. Black with white roof. In 1957, Chevy changed the displacement of their engines from 265 to 283 cubic inches. And this one was bored out and had all the racing additions. Not to mention dual dipsticks, high speed floor mats, and high performance mudflaps.

The plaque in front of the car read:

ONETIME BOOTLEG CAR OF JUNIOR JOHNSON. JUNIOR WON 50 OF 311 GRAND NATIONAL STOCK CAR RACES AND WAS CALLED "THE LAST GREAT AMERICAN HERO" BY WRITER TOM WOLFE.

Well, I didn't remember who Tom Wolfe was but I knew well who Junior was and doubted he had run moonshine in this '57 Chevy on accounta he was already out of the federal prison at Chillicothe by 1957. He'd been arrested at his father's still for manufacturing nontax-paid whiskey. Aw. Somebody lost some taxes. Us drinkers been paying more than our freight since Christ was a corporal. Junior even won the Daytona 500 in 1960; it said so on another plaque somewhere here in the museum. Neat guy, Junior Johnson: outran feds for a while, like I was doing, and then won the biggest race of 'em all, the Daytona 500, which I'd never do but had always dreamed of doing. Eventually, Ronald Reagan had pardoned Junior. I doubted that Amber Lee-Smith would do me a similar courtesy.

I was tinkering with the fifty gallon-plus moonshine tank someone had installed in the trunk when Winsome called.

Her face in the televiewer was pure panic.

"Sandy?"

I turned on the picture for her to see me and her face softened to one of worry. "What's wrong?" I asked, dread seeping though me like the plague.

Her mouth moved and she had to calm herself. "I never watch it, but I was outside and our neighbor, Dora?"

"Go ahead, Winsome." My voice was commanding.

"She watches that Public Awareness Station, channel two-fourteen?"

"What the hell is that?"

"Among other things, they show pictures of missing children."

She didn't have to tell me the rest. Somebody at the Hub had stumbled upon a brilliant idea.

"There was a photograph of Larry Jim," she said miserably.

I forced myself to be casual. "Probably a mistake, Winsome. I never kidnapped nobody. Let me watch it and see when it comes on again. I'll check it out and let you know when I get home tonight."

"It will be okay, Sandy?"

"Sure, love. No sweat. Look, I got to get back to work, okay?"

She looked happier. She didn't want things to change.

"Okay, dear. I am going to fix your favorite—prime rib—tonight, all right?"

"Sure." She was scared I'd skip town. "That's pretty expensive. If it ain't rare, I'm stopping at McDonald's."

"You can afford it," she said saucily. "And I will use litmus paper instead of a meat thermometer. See you tonight?" She needed reassurance.

"Yeah." Like hell.

Pulling the televiewer over to the black and white '57 Chevy, I switched to televideo mode and channel 214 and watched them flip through photographs and statistics of missing children and some lost wives and husbands and fathers and mothers. People pick up and go sometimes. Just ask me.

As I waited for the right photograph to come along, I worked furiously and thought faster. No doubt Manny's photo would pop up. Goddamn do-gooders and their special televideo channels. If it was Manny, someone would turn us in. How long had the spot been running? Were the authorities even now on their way?

Damn! I scraped knuckles as I wielded a large Ford wrench.

In twenty minutes I had the moonshine tank lines changed to larger lines and connected with the gas tank. Now the Chevy had maybe an eighty-plus gallon capacity; though by volume shine probably ain't the same as gasoline, it sometimes tastes the same.

Our getaway car was almost ready. It was a plan I'd had in mind since I started working there. I always have contingency plans. I had several real-motor cars tucked here and there about Daytona.

Then Manny's photo popped up. I had the sound turned down and didn't bother to watch any more. It was a photo they must have taken in the Hub and he looked pale and wan as they say, whatever wan is. Now he was maybe three years older and filled out and sun-exposed, etc. But the startling resemblance was there.

I flicked the set off and wheeled it back to its place. I walked casually over to the office and told the curator of the museum I was going to gas up the '57 Chevy and take her for a test drive. He shrugged his okay. It wasn't unusual for me to do that thing. Mechanic that I was, they let me do whatever I wanted, they were so thankful for me working there. In these days of computer-controlled cars, grand theft auto was virtually unknown. But one more minor charge wasn't going to bother me.

There was some gas already in her tank, but I wheeled the car out back and pumped seventy-eight gallons into the two tanks, thankful for the single filler valve. Of course, the car was in top shape; I'd worked on it hadn't I?

During all this I was frantically shouting mentally for Manny. Either we were too far apart, or he wasn't paying attention.

Casual would explain every movement I made. But there wasn't one wasted movement. Soon I was driving off the museum's lot and heading for Shores Elementary School.

One thing about this decade. They're really into nostalgia. One of the manifestations was the preponderance of singer impersonations. Another was the resurgence of contact sports. In fashion, people were dressed any way they pleased: jungle fatigues, cowboy like Roy and Dale, gaudy Hawaiian, twenties mobster, ad nauseum. The biggest was automobiles. Sure, they were all battery-run electric machines with a top end of maybe seventy mph. But the high-tech boys had perfected plastic. For a couple hundred bucks extra, you could special order any body style you wanted for your electric car. Computer operated molds quickly reproduced whatever you requested. All had the same insides, but different exteriors. And '57 Chevies were popular. One of the reasons I'd had this car ready. I also had two or three others prepared I could have just as easily taken.

As I drove, I passed old Cadillacs, a '63 and a half slant-back Ford, T-Birds, Mustangs, De Sotos, Dusenbergs, a 1903 Hispano-Suiza, a Top Fuel Dragster with "Big Daddy" stenciled on the side, a Formula 1 replica, and so on. Me and my '57 Chevy were not out of place. Another bennie: since this car was a museum display and an antique, nobody had bothered to install, or required the installation of, a computer with their goddamn transponders.

While some of the antique car aficionados ran tapes

through outside speakers of original engine noise to simulate exactly their car's supposed sounds, I had installed a baffle system in the regular exhaust-muffler system of the Chevy. This made it appear more like one of them plastic electric cars.

And I wasn't worried about gasoline. Batteries are great to run cars on, but heavy equipment and farm tractors and so on still require petroleum fuel. So it was available.

I goosed the accelerator, downshifted, and did a four-wheel slide around a corner as a test. Worked fine. It was a column shift. I wished for a four-on-the-floor Hurst, but you can't have everything.

My mind was still hollering for Manny. I wanted to speed, but I maintained the proper limit, observing all traffic rules.

"Wyndy? What's wrong?"

"Manny?"

"Got you, Wyndy. Tell me what's wrong. I'm in the middle of math problems."

"Kid, they might be on to us. I want you to do exactly as I say."

"Oh, shit."

"Don't talk—think—like that. Listen. Escape Plan One. Ask to be excused for a bathroom break. Go out the back of the school to the rear fence. I'll be waiting. Do not, repeat, do not go out the front or past the office or anything. If somebody starts to chase you, run like hell. I'll be there in five minutes."

"Just like we practiced?"

"You got the drill, kid."

He didn't respond. We'd paced out an exercise in case this ever happened. There was a six-foot chain link fence any kid could climb which bordered on a small spur road leading from a housing subdivision.

Then he came back to me. "What about Zell? Can he come, too?"

"No."

"But Sandy . . ."

"Do it, Manny. No more Sandy and Larry Jim.'

"Can I tell him good-bye?"

"No. Just get up and walk out."

"Okay." His mind-voice was meek and scared.

I took a chance and wheeled across a fried fish place, and snuck in the back way of a McDonald's Emporium. One good thing about high-tech is they got bank machines everywhere. Quickly, I drew out as much cash as the thing would allow, quite a lot considering my account. I wasn't worried about discovery now. The authorities would be moving to capture us, not monitoring banking activities. My one worry fell aside when I got the money: they hadn't put a hold on the account. Maybe they didn't want to prematurely warn us.

When I pulled up, Manny was already climbing over the fence sobbing and gulping air. Kid broke my fuckin' heart. He'd gotten comfortable with his life again and here we were turning his world upside down again, changing the rules again. Goddamn.

He dove in through the open window. While most stock cars back in the old days had their doors welded shut or were body cast without doors, this one remained authentic. Doors and windows and everything. Just like factory stock. Museums sometimes disregard origins in their quest for authenticity. I headed for 95 which was a superhighway running up and down the coast from below Miami to Washington or some god-damn foreign place.

Manny continued to cry as he snapped on his seat belts. "Wyndy. I saw Zell."

Damn.

"I just looked in the door of his room and sort of waved and he knew there was something wrong and sort of waved back and I started crying and couldn't stop."

Empathetic, that was Manny all right.

"Well, I'll tell you one goddamn thing, Manuel Temple. They done fucked with us for the last time. Ain't nobody ever fucked with Pembroke Wyndham as much as they fucked with me and goddamn if I ain't gonna start fucking with them now, by God. You got my word, son. We're on the offense now. Them mother-fuckers ain't gonna know what hit them."

Manny was quiet now, staring at me and surprised at the vehemence of my outburst. Not like me to lose my temper, especially when in action—which, in effect, we were now.

"I'll tell you another goddamn thing. We're gonna see your mother, too. Maybe not right away, but soon. You got my solemn word on that."

He brightened perceptively. "Can we? Really?"

"Honest injun."

We hit 95 and I surged the Chevy up the ramp and to the legal 70 mph and slotted us among several of those giant trucks with their convoys of trailers.

Manny was quiet and while I wanted to plan, my mind wouldn't let me forget that we were deserting Winsome and Zell. What would Winsome think? She was sharp and would know the score as soon as Zell returned home from school without Larry Jim.

While I couldn't deny that what I was doing would hurt Winsome and her son, at least I'd set them up to where they were financially well-off. She wouldn't have to be a prostitute again. Her kid was ensconced in a fine educational system. If she could weather the SpecSec storm, she'd come out ahead.

"Manny?"

"Yes, Wyndy?"

"Did you sense any danger as you were leaving school?"

"No," voice small and lost.

Good. Maybe they weren't on to us yet. If we were lucky, we'd have a decent headstart.

I continued driving north.

On the run again.

12: The Lion's Den

Anger can sustain you only so long. I planned and drove. That old '57 ran real fine, purred like a nympho in heat. I was convinced we could outrun anything on the ground. But what concerned me, always, was stuff we couldn't outrun: radios, choppers, roadblocks.

In Jacksonville, I went into a bank and opened a safety deposit box I'd already had prepared for just such an emergency. IDs and cash. ID which would stand casual scrutiny. One of several sets purchased in Nassau with Bossman's money. Other sets and cash I'd stashed in other safety deposit boxes throughout the state, specifically each time I'd taken a trip to contact Maria. We bought some camping gear in case we didn't want to stop at motels—while our ID was good enough, all such businesses might be on the lookout for a man and a boy. That night we continued our trip, me with an idea of reconnoitering, Manny simply sitting in a stupor. Poor uprooted kid. We headed west on 10 and in no time we entered the outskirts of Lake City where the Hub towered over the landscape and the intersection of 10 and 75.

At a truckers' motel, I registered for one night as a man with a wife, three children, and a mother-in-law. Fortunately, motel clerks still don't have to personally count their customers. And who would expect us to register that many people? At least our double room was spacious. And with computers and transponders in cars, it's no longer necessary to have license tags on your vehicle—which made us indistinguishable from every other '57 Chevy on the road. Additionally, I was giving a lot of thought to a paint job.

Anyway, who would think of looking for us near the Hub?

In the morning we went to Mac's Steak House, sign of the golden arches, for breakfast. We got our food and ate in the car. Ain't nostalgia great?

"Manny," I said, "let's talk. The way I figger it, we got only one chance of gettin' out of our fix: we gotta find out what's going on and why. And we are going to solve that mystery. We been on the run too long. I'm sick of it. How about you?"

He smiled and quoted me. "I'm sick and tired of being sick and tired." Kids love cute clichés.

"To do all this, we got to find the key I've been talking about. We need some key term, code, numbers, something from Baldy Hodgkins and his cronies so that we can give it to your mother and she can dig it out of their computer." I looked at him directly. "Fine so far?"

He nodded apprehensively. He knew what was coming.

"Look, kid, I don't wanna do this to you, but I see no other way." Actually, there was another way. Kidnap and interrogate Baldy or one of his aides. However, the danger and problems involved in that scheme were exponentially greater than the one I'd settled on.

He nodded again, this time more apprehensively.

"You got to monitor thought waves, whatever it is you do, till we get that clue." I paused. He'd known it was coming. "The question is, Manny, can you intercept their think-talking without them knowing you are there?"

"I'ontno," voice small and meek.

"They talk together like that, right?"

"Sure." He glanced at me. "I know them well enough to pick them up."

Too bad Manny couldn't read minds, else we could snatch what we wanted and make a hasty departure. There was trauma associated with the Hub and Manny was reluctant and I didn't blame him. "We have a lot of time, Manny. You can sort of slide into it."

"Okay."

"Give it a try right now."

"Now?"

"Now, Manny. Let's find out."

He slumped back and closed his eyes. I toyed with the column shift.

After a few minutes, he sat up. "Nothing."

"Nothing because they ain't transmitting? Or because we're too far away? Or maybe because there's too much activity here at McDonald's?"

"I'ontno."

We were maybe five miles from the Hub so I drove back to the motel and we went inside. I had Manny lie down and went into the other room myself. Perhaps comfort and silence and no distractions would help.

Nothing.

We tried on and off all day in case they simply weren't conversing mentally with each other.

Nothing.

The next day, I drove us around the perimeter roads circling the Hub. Manny concentrated.

"Sometimes something tickles my mind," he said, "but . . ."

He didn't have to finish. He didn't want to have to go into the Hub itself. Well, me neither.

The effort was telling on him. The energy and concentration tired him out, so I called off the search for the rest of that day and we drove up into the country-side of ex-Georgia, did some searching and, two hours after nightfall, liberated sixty gallons of gas from a couple of road repair vehicles—two of which were not diesel powered—parked alongside a road. Used what used to be called an Oklahoma credit card, namely a length of garden hose.

I let Manny sleep late and fed him a good meal.

We drove to the Hub and parked in the public lots. Manny tried again.

Later, he shook his head. "Hints of mind-talking, but nothing . . ."

"Too much ferroconcrete and electronics, kid. Let's take a walk."

We walked around outside. There were little parks, fountains, areas full of flowers and grass and trees that management always puts in when they want good window dressing. On a park bench in the looming shadow of one of the many-storied towers, Manny tried again.

"Careful, son, I don't want them to discover us more than I want to find what we're looking for."

"Huh? Oh." He'd been with me long enough for me not to have to translate a perfectly good English sentence.

After an hour, he shook his head. Instead of speaking, he thought at me, "Nothing, wh . . ."

"No!" I said immediately aloud. "Don't take the chance."

"Sorry, Wyndy. I get a bare whisper now and then. Nothing solid."

"Well, back to the old computer graphics-design program."

"Huh?"

"A play on old terms, son."

We had to penetrate the Hub itself. I didn't like it and I knew Manny was dreading the experience. Compounding our problem was that we were exposing ourselves to recognition. The Hub contained some people who had seen us and would recognize us; a small number admittedly, but it still wasn't something I wanted to chance.

Two days later, we were in a third-floor cafeteria in the central section of the Hub eating lunch. I had a crew cut and was wearing Teamsters' coveralls, not unusual, and was clean shaven with darkened eyebrows. It took a conscious effort not to limp on my bad leg. Manny was dressed, much to his disguHas a girl, in slacks, a blouse, and a wig. He kept licking his strawberry lip gloss off.

"Close, Wyndy, close," he whispered. Later, "They've stopped their mind-talk. I couldn't make it out anyway."

One more day and we were up two floors in a public access library which actually had books in addition to computer cubicles. Manny sat against a cubicle wall, and I toyed with the computer, ostensibly filling out forms for a business license as a commercial fisherman.

"I got 'em!" he whispered hoarsely.

"Don't get caught," I said unnecessarily while wondering why I hadn't thought of this a couple of years earlier. Maybe for the same reason that they hadn't thought of putting Manny's photograph on the missing children network until they did. A lesson in there somewhere about being creative.

Anticipation sometimes works to your disadvantage. Manny monitored their mind-talking for an hour or so, but it was desultory, day-to-day business he overheard. Nothing we could use. The only thing we learned for sure was that the hunchback, Mr. Rodney, was alive and well. I wondered if his hump still had my slugs in it. The physiology of humps on hunchbacks wadn't my strong suit.

Manny tired easily so we went back to the motel. While much of motel cleanups nowadays is mechanical, they'll still give you a ten percent discount if you're staying longer than a week and agree to make up your own beds and stuff like that. We did that thing. Saved having maids, etc., snooping around and finding that most of the suitcases for six people were empty.

The next few days in the library, we were disguised differently. Me as a visiting professor from the University of Miami doing research in real books on the manatee for a paper (funded by the Jimmy Buffett

Memorial Foundation). Manny looked older and passed as my assistant.

People came and went in the library and I was becoming concerned over the fact that the longer we stayed, the greater our chance of discovery. But what choice did we have? The people who might recognize us even through our disguises were a couple of doctors, technicians, SS guys, and Baldy and his crew, none very likely to visit the library—especially the section with shelves of books like a geometric forest.

And Manny was showing the effects of tension, concentration, and energy expenditure. He was pale and listless and exhibited little of that child energy and enthusiasm.

One evening, we stayed late, past the great exodus of workers with whom we generally mingled to help hide us from possible discovery. Manny's face became animated and I had to hold myself from interrupting him to find out what the hell was going on.

Then: "Sonny's Bar-B-Q. They all ate lunch there as usual and liked it." Well, I'd eaten at Sonny's and they *were* good. So now I knew to avoid the Sonny's in Lake City. Memory of which made my mouth water: extensive salad bar and best real-pit smoked chicken you'll find. Ribs okay, too.

"A technical discussion," he whispered. "Brain growth spurts." He closed his eyes and concentrated. His lips moved and I had to lean close to even hear him. "Concrete operational." Nothing for a moment. My hand was poised over my notebook, waiting. "Epstein . . . brain mass . . . Epstein again . . . a name— Hollingsworth . . . Piaget . . ."

This last I had to guess at spelling. Apparently, mind-talk is phonetic like mouth-talk.

". . . growth spurt . . . neurons . . . preoperational . . ."

He opened his eyes and they were haunted. "Wyndy, I'm tired. It's so hard making sure they don't, um, feel me there."

"Yeah, I know, kid. But this is the first time we've

got them talking about it. Give it another try, okay? Maybe you can get enough so we don't have to come back."

"Yes, Wyndy." He leaned back again.

I glanced around. Nobody near as we were in a corner I'd selected for not being in a convenient line of travel.

"Myelinate. Incoming stimuli. Temporal lobe. Learning tasks. Myelination. Spurts and plateaus. Epstein and Brandeis University . . ." His face changed to one of horror. He stood up and jerked his head in panic right and left.

I dragged him back to his seat. "Disconnect, Manny," I ordered, though he probably already had.

He opened his eyes. "I . . . I think I forgot to protect . . . they stopped. Mr. Rodney, I think, sensed me. They know somebody was snooping . . ."

"Right, kid. We just get up and walk out like we're going for a cup of coffee." I tucked my notebook into a pocket and hustled us out the door. As we went past the desk, I said aloud, "Coffee's going to taste good right now." I thought then that if we ever extracted ourselves from this mess, I'd still have paranoia for years, always looking over my shoulder and covering every move I made with an attempt at normalcy.

We went down escalators to the public exit concourse. My eyes were strained like a fighter pilot's looking for bogies. I had one eye open for blue-uniformed SS guys, another peeled for camera monitors, and a third frantically watching for someone I'd recognize who in turn might recognize us.

Quietly, I cautioned Manny. "It would be nice for you to put one of them alert-us-sentry programs into your mind, or whatever it is you do, but don't chance it. They might be tuned in, waiting for something like that."

He nodded and stumbled after me. I didn't know if Hodgkins and crew were capable of that type of mental function, but I didn't want to find out the hard way.

The minutes dragged by. We were walking down the public concourse, banks of exit doors just ahead of us, when I casually glanced behind us. Five blue suits were trotting this way, armed, going to the doors to check IDs. I calculated their arrival time with ours and the convergence was obvious. I stretched my stride and egged Manny on. I checked my watch and swore. "Damnit, we'll be late. Hurry up!"

Manny caught the concern in my voice and didn't argue.

I could feel five hot breaths breathing down my figurative neck. Only a couple, male and female, was ahead of us now. We had maybe a hundred feet to go. Seventy-five. Fifty. I could hear the rhythmic thump of five pairs of boots triple-timing it toward the doors. The couple went through the doors and I knew we weren't gonna make it.

"Hey!" I shouted. "Bill. Gloria. Wait for us. C'mon," I said to Manny and waved my arm at Bill and Gloria who couldn't hear or see us because they were already outside. "Wait up," I shouted for effect.

We ran slowly, and Manny even whistled at Bill and Gloria.

We reached the doors and I flung one open and hollered, "Bill!" again. "There they go," I said loudly and leaped outside, Manny following. As the door closed, I saw the SS troop stop inside. Were we safe?

Not yet, I'd have bet. One thing in our favor: after work hours at the Hub, a giant monstrosity of architecture, and hopefully not enough SS to cover every possible exit and search the premises, too.

The parking lot was not entirely vacant, but maybe eighty percent so. In the Chevy, I accelerated quickly, speeding and illegally crossing the pavement not using the marked lanes. I figured a traffic ticket wasn't as bad as capture. On the other hand, I could be calling attention to us. Well, it was a judgment call which paid off. We funneled onto a major highway leaving the parking lot of the Hub as little motorized vehicles with SS guys appeared at the lighted parking lot exits, dropping a guard off at each one. Had we been taking the underground subwalks between Lake City and the Hub like many workers, we'd have been trapped.

One thing about this fugitive business I'd learned: always carry what you want to take with you if you got to cut and run. Well, we'd done that thing and I headed for 10 west and we didn't stop for eight hours until we got to Pensacola.

13: Keys

There followed a couple of weeks of the aimless driving I'd termed "Escape and Evasion." Always that haunted feeling, looking over your shoulder, scrutinizing everybody you meet, always alone, Manny and me, the routine of day-to-day life in Daytona a growing regret.

In Pensacola, I'd transmitted everything Manny had learned to Maria and her electronic toys.

Right now we were sitting under several mammoth sheepaloe in the back of an eighteen wheeler. Maria had said that she'd solved the problem, in so many obfuscated words on a screen, and wanted a meeting. We had Bossman's approval, so I knew it must be important. Since they were obviously watching Maria, we would go to her.

Bossman had selected the Hillsborough County Fair, which used to be known as a State Fair before Florida became ex-Florida, for the first public showing of his sheepaloe. We'd simply snuck onto the truck on the evening of the last day of the fair. Under the feed-grain bin was a false bottom which we struggled into.

Maybe three hours up 75 to Ocala and over to the farm. Smelly hours. Starvin' Marvin and Bully Base were in the cab, having been the display crew. We had not communicated, other than knuckle-knock replying to a casual kick on the bin to let them know we were there.

A series of jolts, backing and forwarding, told us we were at Silas Swallow's farm, and soon the truck was backed up to the stables.

The rear doors opened and somebody pulled the ramp down. We stayed in the bin while they herded a couple of the beasts off.

"Wyndy?" Marvin's voice came softly. "Come on out."

We crawled out and saw several sheepaloe still in the truck.

Marvin grabbed my hand and shook it. "Good to see you, old-timer. Boy, you sure have changed," he said admiringly as he looked me up and down. "Doesn't seem to be anybody about, but you never know. Each of you exit between two sheepaloe in case they have an infrared scanner."

"Right."

We did that, me first, then Manny. Once we were inside, we didn't have to worry.

"Into Arpee's old stall," Bully Base said.

Damn. I hadn't forgotten Arpee's valiant effort. In vain. May there be a horse heaven and he the chief stud.

Of course, Maria was there. Manny ran into her arms and she sort of folded him up. No tears. But we'd probably need to tape Manny's ribs.

Diplomatically, I didn't stay. I went into the storeroom and rooted around until I found my rat-holed bottle of Jack Daniels Blue Label. Starvin' Marvin, Bully Base, and I shared a few shots straight from the neck of the bottle.

Starvin' Marvin, whom I'd appellated with that moniker, drank long and deep. He fit his nickname: long and lanky, stereotyped sunken cheeks to match, always hitching up his pants, an engaging smile when he spoke. Bully Base, who fished all the time when not on duty, taller and gaunter, big, sweeping mustache, recessed eyes, and always wore a fishing hat with lures

and hooks and all that fishing paraphernalia stuck in
it. Bully Base drank only sparingly.

"Crane Plash told us a little of what happened at the
Hub, Wyndy," said Marvin. "He spoke of pyrotech-
nics and the like." He hesitated. "And we worked
with José some; he was a good guy."

Marvin was prompting me for the full story.

The booze tasted smooth and hit the spot a few
times. That spot ought to be pickled by now. "Non-
violent José Temple," I mused. "Who'd have believed
him capable of that."

"What?" demanded Bully Base.

It occurred to me that they were not only personally
interested, but they'd been directed to report to
Bossman. "The pilot stayed with a chopper he'd stolen,
kept it running on the SS and VIP chopper pad. He
also opened fuel drain valves of all the other choppers
there and was sitting in a lake of fuel when I got there.
Amazing a spark off his chopper didn't ignite the
whole thing."

"And?" Marvin prompted.

"On liftoff, I fired a signal flare into the fuel. Instant Fourth of July."

"How about José?" asked Bully Base.

"He made it to where they had Manny," I said
slowly. "How, I don't know. Part stealth, part bravery
under fire. I got there a couple minutes after he did.
Took three of 'em out with him. He had them diverted
and off guard. I mopped up."

"That's how it was?" Marvin said seriously.

"Yep. I got Manny and we made it to the chopper
and you know the rest."

Marvin glanced at Bully Base, then back to me.
"All right, Wyndy. You done good. I shall so report."

"Make sure that the man has continued my salary
all this time, too," I said, thinking of it for the first
time. "At the triple rate we'd agreed on."

"Seems to me," Marvin said with a grin, "there

"And you know how all this comes about?" I asked to get away from an uncomfortable subject.

Maria rustled her papers. "The break came when you provided the names Manuel overheard at the Hub. Epstein specifically, though some of the other info would have led me eventually to the same data. I simply read everything I could about and by Epstein looking, not for data, but for key words. I plugged them into the computer which rifled all the computer storage at the Hub for programs using those words as code or recalls. Herman T. Epstein was a professor of biophysics at Brandeis University about a century ago, give or take, who developed theories of learning based on brain growth. It does so in spurts and plateaus."

"I always thought you were born with the maximum number of brain cells," I said, "and only lost 'em as you got older." Though, under that concept, I'd have none left by now. Not notice much difference, before now and currently, some would say.

"Correct," she said. "By the age of eighteen months you have almost all the brain cells you ever will have. But these cells expand, form routes, patterns, ever more complex. Neurons, dendrites, axons. Epstein found that there are brain growth stages which," she flipped a page and read an underlined section, "give quote a functional increase in the intelligence of children end quote."

"Big deal," I said. "All of us go through it. So what?"

Marvin said, "Listen, Wyndy. Epstein identified five stages of brain growth. The first occurs at the age of three to ten months. He terms it sensorimotor. A child reacts to his environment perceptually."

"So what's new? They still pee in their pants and gotta be changed."

"The second stage," Marvin said haughtilly, "is called preoperational. From two to four years. Language and symbols used to relate to objects."

I nodded, suddenly understanding. During that time

period of Manny's life, I'd been the primary one in his life, unconsciously contributing to his development. I recalled some of the things we'd done then. It fit. "And the other stages?"

"Six to eight years," he continued, "the world changes, and things in it, and the child learns to deal with that. Called concrete operational. The next stage, termed formal operational, stretches generally from age ten to twelve. Here they become able to reason in different manners and can have abstract thought. The fifth, and final stage, goes from fourteen to sixteen plus. Distinguished from the previous stage in that a child develops creative problem solving."

"What does all this mean," I demanded, taking a swig right from the bottle.

"We don't know, exactly, yet," Maria said. "Manuel might have a sixth and as yet unidentified stage, which will occur after the others, or has occurred simultaneously with the others."

Manny's eyes were glassy and he was on the verge of falling asleep in his mother's lap when ancient Fargield the cat sauntered in and went past me with a minor brush and leaped into Manny's lap. Soon Manny was scratching behind the cat's ears and the cat was purring and eying a piece of chicken.

And I didn't know if I wanted to know what all this was going to mean to Manny.

"See here, Wyndy," Bully Base said nasally, "we suspect Manuel has gone through those stages *without* the plateaus in between the brain growth spurts."

Maria nodded. "There was speculation in Dr. Hodgkins' personal notes he'd left in memory. But Hodgkins never knew the extent of Manuel's ability. He guessed at some of it . . . that's why they . . ."

"Kidnapped him and done what they did to him," I said to save her some trouble.

She nodded. "The breakthrough came when I plugged in one of Epstein's terms, phrenoblysis, which is a Greek word referring to the mind swelling or spurting.

Hodgkins had used the word as a retrieval code. From there it was a small matter of gathering information."

"Any more chicken?" Marvin asked.

Maria dug out another hot dish from the picnic basket. I grabbed it and took a breast before Marvin could finish it all off.

"Some more things you might like to know," Maria said. "The two- to four-year-old stage is primarily important in auditory training and language recovery. Epstein supposed that when children are in a fast stage of brain growth, the intellectual input, if deep enough and novel enough, will really affect them later on. Stimulus, the right kind, is powerfully important."

"Like when I was his governess?" I mumbled.

Maria only nodded her head imperceptively at me.

Bully Base said, "After puberty is when a child gets empathy, or more of it. But we suspect that somewhere in there Manuel has gotten his personal insight a lot earlier."

"Manny is terribly empathetic," I said.

"Right," he said. "The prefrontal cortex is suppposed to be the base for evolutionary development . . ."

"Cut the crap," I said. "You're trying to tell me Manny is a step or something ahead in human evolution?"

"Yep," said Marvin with a mouth full of potato salad, "we think so. He skipped his plateaus thus far, more or less, though his body grows on as a normal child will."

"Which explains why he's slightly clumsy and doesn't do his seatwork in school as well as his classmates." Keeping "on task" his teachers called it.

Marvin's head bobbed up and down. "Good chicken, Maria." He eyed a leg and chomped into it.

"How?" I asked. "Or do I want to know?"

"Myelination," Bully Base said.

"What the hell is that?"

"A fatty coating the brain produces. It insulates and provides nourishment to the axons. Myelination jacks up the speed and increases the intensity of the neural signal fibers—which, among other things, connect one hemisphere of the brain to the other." His face twisted in disbelief as Marvin picked up two muffins and squirted butter into them.

"I don't want to know no more," I said. "You gonna cut into Manny's head to see what makes him tick?"

"That's what they did to Albert Einstein," Marvin said while shaking a pepper shaker over a spoonful of Jello.

"They cut into his head?" I wanted to know. This was interesting.

"They took his brain out before they buried him," Bully Base clarified. "Inordinate myelination."

"And Manny's the same?"

"We don't know," Maria said. "It's possible. But perhaps he is developing a talent different from Einstein's theoretical grasp."

"Now it's beginning to make sense," I said. Manny was fast asleep, his head in Maria's lap, and his hand on Fargield's back. "Einstein's myelination led to his genius; Manny's—and probably that of his mind-talk friends—is making him an empathetic genius and a communicator they can't beat with electronics."

"Close enough," said Marvin.

"What's the bottom line?" I asked. "And say it in English."

Maria ran her hand through her son's hair. "Manuel is a mindhopper. A new kind of esper. He may be a part of human development or evolution. It may be that he and his friends are freaks. But it is as if nature engineered his talent to unlock the techniques of FTL. He just might be an advanced human in terms of evolution." She paused and looked above her at their ceiling. "Those at the Hub were trying to discover how his talent could be applied to many things, FTL especially, weapons research, and if the talent is transferable, say genetically."

"Maria, you're not telling me that you're gonna bolt

Manny into a space ship and plug a computer into him and go faster than light?"

"Wyndy," she said softly. "Manuel is my son, remember?"

"Sorry. Lost my head."

"Not unusual," Marvin muttered. I glared at him.

"We are going to take him to the *Nimitz*," Maria said, "where there are scientists and engineers and mathematicians and theoreticians who can help use Manuel to solve the problem."

"You ain't taking Manny away from me," I said, voice hot.

"He's *my* son," said Maria, fire coming into her eyes and voice.

"I'm going with him, then," I said.

"No, you're not," Bossman said and pushed into the door.

Marvin lurched to his feet spilling crumbs and wiping his fingers on his pants.

Maria said, "Good evening, Silas."

He nodded to her.

"Like hell. I am going with him," I said, not rising, but taking a swig from the bottle of Jack Blue.

"You know what your job is, Wyndy," Bossman said.

Damn right I knew. I didn't want to know. I didn't want to do it any more.

Bossman's voice became milder than normal. "The Hub wants FTL in the worse way. They won't share it, either. They want Manuel Temple. It's in their files Maria swiped. No effort spared. If they suspect we have the child at the PROJECT, they will send in troops to get him. We can hide him there. It is not unusual for Maria and me to go to the aircraft carrier so now his mother can visit him. It would be more difficult for us all if you were around gathering attention."

I drank again. "So my job is to act as a goddamn decoy while the scientists and techs tear Manny apart."

"Yes to the former, no to the latter," he said. He glanced at Maria. "You have preserved him to this point, Wyndy. None other could have done so. You have our appreciation. And eternal gratitude. However, the job is not finished. You must continue on as before to insure the boy's safety at the PROJECT."

"Shit." I picked up an ear of corn and crunched down on it, thankful that I still had the original issue of my own teeth. "How long?"

Silas Comfort Swallow shrugged. "Until we solve the theoretical and mechanical problems involved with FTL so that those in the Hub no longer have cause to want the boy."

"What's in it for me?"

"Wyndy!" exclaimed Maria shocked.

Bossman glared at me. He knew goddamn well what I meant. That I knew well where my loyalties and obligations were, but I was tired of my current role. And especially I didn't want them to take Manny away from me. A quick look at Maria told me that she understood now; of course she would, she'd been forcibly separated from him for damn near three years.

My voice harsh, I spoke slowly. The two genetic engineers looked at me like I was the very devil. "Above and beyond, you know that, Silas. That's me. I done bought you three years so far and now you want more. How many?"

He shook his head.

"I ain't gettin' no younger," I said, voice still hammering at him. "With all your money, can you buy what I can give you?"

"Perhaps," he said.

"And jeopardize your friggin' PROJECT, too."

He nodded. "What do you want." He said the words, not asked.

"A seat on the bus, if Maria and Manny's going."

Maria was looking back and forth between Bossman and me. "What on Earth?"

"It is what I figured," Bossman said. "All adults are

required to be married and accompanied by their spouse."

"I already got a wife."

Maria shot me a startled look. Hell, she'd known I'd picked up a temporary wife.

"One who fills an established personnel slot." Bossman knew he had me. Winsome might fill some slot on their space ship; however, since she had no academic credentials, it would be difficult. Of course, I'd have the same problem.

"I'll figger it out. Yes or no?"

Maria was staring at Bossman. She understood now. A tear made its way down her face like a surfer down a giant wave. "Please, Silas?"

"All right," he said.

Marvin piped up. "We'll probably need somebody to clean up after the sheepaloe on the ship."

"You bring your own shovel then, buddy," I said. "I'm done shoveling shit."

Bossman nodded. "Agreed."

"Agreed," I said and took a drink of sour mash. "Sealed with a drink." I handed Bossman the bottle. He wasn't a drinker and I was curious as to what he would do. He touched the bottle to his lips and handed it back. Hell, that was good enough for me. "Make sure they stock plenty of this for me."

He grinned knowingly at me and I knew not only wouldn't there be any booze on the space ship, but that I'd become rich distilling and selling my own alcohol. I rubbed my mental hands.

If I lived through this. Which all masked some of my other motivations. Federations, republics, plastic cars without motors, bar codes. It didn't take much to think of the giant old oak in every new office plaza or housing development or ultramodern shopping mall, the oak which nobody pays attention to, but they don't cut it down. It stands right there in the midst of ferroconcrete, glass, bubbles, and plastic, no use to itself or to anybody, simply a reminder of things past.

Sidewalks and streets are routed around it. It only serves to give a little shade, a little protection when needed. Just like me. But unlike me, them poor old trees don't get the opportunity to hop on a space ship and go someplace else. If all this worked, not only would we be gone to some far-off solar system to start over, but the very fact of the doing would change the face of this world, no doubt for the better. Not to mention that I wasn't letting Maria and Manny go anywhere without me.

"A decoy," I mused. "You are aware, Bossman, that in order to do that job correctly, to mislead them, I must be seen occasionally, which increases the chances of my being captured. Which increases the chance of your PROJECT being compromised when they torture out of me what Maria and the engineers just told me."

"I know that," Bossman responded.

"I don't," Maria said.

"Maria," I said. "I have to surface. I have to have them see me, chase me, be hot on my tail. Otherwise, their attention will shift here and to the PROJECT."

"But it is not safe."

"It will make it safer at the PROJECT for Manny," I said.

"Must it come down to that?" Her eyes were pleading. Almost made me feel good and, at the same time, sorry for myself.

"Yeah," I said. "But I'm a professional at it. Nobody could do it as good as me. Ask Silas."

Her eyes did and he said, "Wyndy is correct, my dear."

Well, I wouldn't bet a counterfeit three dollar bill on my chances. "Then it's settled. I'll be on my way shortly. I'd recommend that when our little mindhopper here wakes up, that somebody have him tell his friends wherever they are to lay low until you-all solve the final riddle."

"Good idea," Bossman said, voice approving. The SOB had already written me off. He reminded me of the jerk who'd introduced me to my sixth wife, may he have intestinal worms through eternity.

The worst part of it was that I knew I'd miss Manny tremendously, like the loss of a limb, only more so. But I'd been around long enough to know that doing something constructive would compensate.

Like chasing down the Administrator and finding out what the hell she had against me.

I smiled at the prospect of action. "If you'll let me have enough cash for the road, I'll get going. There's a hell of a lot of federales out there who need to go on a wild goose chase or three."

15: Escape and Evasion?

I left the farm before Manny woke. No way I wanted to go through a parting scene. It was bad enough leaving Maria. They snuck me onto Bossman's chopper and soon Crane Plash was lifting off.

"Where to, Wyndy?"

"Back toward Tampa. I left my car there." And some hidden cash—though I was fairly rolling in green, my favorite color, by now. Which thought was an anachronism in itself—like me—because money was color coded; however, the big bills were still mint green.

He flew the proper directed air corridor until the last minute when he told ATC he spotted a fire on the ground and was dropping down to investigate. Whereupon I stepped out and waved and he was gone.

I trudged to the nearest shopping center, and believe me Tampa is full of them, stole a bike and was soon off to the fairgrounds where I'd left the '57 Chevy. Before dawn, I was at a marina where I broke the lock off a pump and stole enough gas to fill the tank.

To avoid a connection between me and Bossman's sheepaloe display at the Hilsborough County Fair outside of Tampa, I headed for Sarasota before instigating my plan.

A spoonful of silver nitrate mixed in with a bottle of Coppertone suntan oil and applied over my exposed skin turned me into a black man. It would wash and wear off in four or five days; but *nobody* was looking for a black Pembroke Wyndham—all they wanted was a haole.

Out on Siesta Key, I wandered down the beach and finally went to the house on stilts over by Big Pass which was a museum. It had belonged to John D. MacDonald, the writer, and was where he wrote most of his Travis McGee stories. The attendant handed me a brochure which said more visitors came here than to any of Ernest Hemingway's houses. John D. had my vote, too. For a while I wandered around looking at real books, movie posters, plaques, typewriters, desks, manuscripts, and so on. People came and went.

On leaving, I asked the door attendant, "Did you see that old man and kid?"

Of course he was busy and probably didn't remember anybody who came in. He kind of rolled his eyes and shrugged, trying to be polite, but not sure of what I was getting at.

Tugging my hat down over my eyes, I said, "No big deal. Kid just looked familiar."

He handed a pamphlet to a family and I faded out.

Two hours later, I was back on the mainland and stopped at a Publix supermarket. I found a televiewer and called the cops, not turning on the picture.

"Hey, I seen 'at kid, the one on the teevee?"

"What kid, mister? Would you turn on the picture, please?"

"I'm 'fraid o' trouble. I jest wanna do my duty. 'At kid, the missin' one, name of Temptate or sumpin', ya know?"

"Where?" Cop's voice was bored, thought he was dealing with a drunk. Which was okay. By the time they got it all figured out, the trail would be cold.

"Ona beach, over by Mr. Mac's house."

"Yeah?"

"Goddamn, officer. You ain't all that interested, I

ain't gonna friggin' bother no more." I snapped the disconnect switch.

They'd run it through the computer, no rush. Then some SS guy would jump into it on accounta they must have it flagged in the system somehow. Then they'd start checking up and down the beach and find the attendent who wouldn't remember me, or might recall a black man, but would remember somebody mentioning something about a kid. Corroboration.

By that time I'd be in Naples, a couple of hours south of Sarasota.

In Naples, I went to ground for a couple of weeks. During that time, I punched in the Sarasota area do-gooder channel on a televideo and there was this picture of Manny. And two of me. One of me was from when I was captive in the Hub. Christ, did I look old. The other, a computer sketch overlay of the first photo, doubtless garnered from interviews in Daytona, in my Willie Nelson guise. Because of my recently, and necessarily, shortened hair, I had to go to a costume shop to buy a wig. Willie Nelson was ever popular. Must be a lot of bald women over in China what with providing all that real hair.

Didn't take me long to make myself up as Willie Nelson again. Looked more like my picture. It was harder looking old. A few touches here and there with makeup pencils, squint a lot, grow the stubble.

Found a giant continuous fleamarket and bought me a wheelchair, an old-fashioned one with a big battery motor on it.

The next day I was back to Sarasota and cruising Sarasota Square Mall in the wheelchair as a paraplegic, blanket, shawl, the whole bit.

After a while, I motored into a special handicapped stall in Maas Brothers' men's room. While the chair was equipped for such purposes, nobody ever questions handicapped people going to the bathroom. When no one else was in there, I rose from the wheelchair and crawled under the stall door in my Pembroke Wyndham/Willie Nelson outfit.

Unconcernedly, I strolled around trying to get noticed. Damn people were minding their own business. At a corner standup, I ate a slice of pizza and had a glass of beer.

Finally, I browsed through Walden's Tapes & Disks getting madder and madder. Nobody was paying attention. Or maybe they didn't watch the do-gooder channel either. Wandering through racks of tapes, disks, electronics games, stylos, and so on, I had to make myself conspicuous. So I asked the clerk to let me run through the "OTHERWORLDS" catalog on her machine. She looked at me like, "What are you, some kind of a weirdo, or what?", but said, "Yes, sir."

"Young lady, I'll thank you not to be snotty with me. Hell, I been a member of 'OTHERWORLDS' club for sixty years, on and off." Jeez, what I gotta do, wave a flag at these people?

Don't know what her gripe was, hell, everything in the store was automated, just one clerk in case of emergencies or for people like me who come in saying, "Say. Do you got that book about war? Don't remember the title or the author or the publisher, but I seen a interview with one of them outa New York cable . . ."

You can tell. When they purposefully don't look at you, something is wrong. This clerk didn't want to look at me any longer—recognition made her eyes furtive. I took my time scanning the catalog on the screen, watching out of the corner of my eye in case she hit some kind of emergency button. Nope. She'd call security when I wasn't standing right next to her. Reckon you don't handle "murderers" like shoplifters.

Thanking her, I shook my head, "Nothin' new anymore, is there?" and walked slowly out and joined the throngs feeding into Maas Brothers. Into the GENTLEMEN, waiting for a guy to finish, just doing my business. He left and swiftly I tore off the wig, forced

the handicapped stall door open and was in my wheelchair and under my blanket and shawl in a snap. Even
quicker, I wheeled out. As I went out the large main
entrance, I noted several hard-eyed guys striding alertly
around the store. Uniformed security wouldn't be far
behind.

In five minutes, I was heading for 75 and Tampa.
The old '57 Chevy rolled along as if she wasn't almost
older than me. We blew past a 1999 Winston Special,
one of the nicer cars of the times, and a 2020 De
Soto-Hudson which also caught my eye.

Eight weeks later, in Tampa, I pulled the same
trick. This time I let them see me leave and cops
chased me down Buffalo Avenue. I outran them all
and hit the 4, 275, and 75 exchanges so they didn't
know which way I went. Soon I was speeding north on
75 heading for Orlando or maybe Disneyworld they
would think. Doubtless they had computers searching
through the traffic, trying to figure out through each
automobile's own computer-transponder who to stop.
If you ain't got a computer's transponder broadcasting
to their laser readers under the road, they can't find
you.

A month later, they actually chased me on a highway out of Orlando. I outran them of course, so they
turned off *all* the cars via general command and all
vehicles started coasting down. When I ran over the
place where it happened, I didn't stop. I kept going,
dodging cars coasting to a stop, and scatted off on a
feeder road. It would take them a few minutes to trace
me. I pulled behind a warehouse and peeled off the
large sheets of stick-on plastic. Earlier, I'd repainted
the Chevy yellow on the bottom, black on the top;
tacky, yes, but certainly not black on bottom and
white on top any longer. Then I'd covered the new
paint job with stick-on plastic sheets mimicking the
original paint scheme.

I had several more appearances such as these planned
at a leisurely pace when I realized that somebody was

gonna figure it out. How could I stay out of sight for three years plus and now I was stumbling around like an amateur and couldn't not avoid discovery? And how come they were always seeing me and not me and the kid? And how come we were still in our kind and gentle republic? How come I wasn't hiding out in the mountains someplace or the desert or Mexico or the warrens of giant cities like San Antonio or Dallas?

What I needed was a kid. And to be seen heading the hell out of ex-Florida.

In Jacksonville, I bought a bike with one of them battery-run motors they got for lazy cyclists, took it apart and got it in the car. I drove to Atlanta and put the bike together, and locked it at the McDonald's Emporium we'd visited right after the breakout at the Hub.

Then I drove downtown, busted my ass to get recognized and chased, and made an almost fatal error. The bigger the city, the more responsive are the local gendarmes. And the better equipped. Namely, your basic '57 Chevy can't outrun a chopper. On the other hand, what with all the bridges and interchanges and buildings and all, choppers can't really land on your roof and stop you.

But they can hover high enough to keep you in their sight and direct an ever-growing ground posse to box you in and capture you.

I came blasting off Peachtree onto the combined 75 and 85, shot south heading for the mammoth intersections of 75, 85, 20, and 285, not to mention several access roads and local arteries. This series of cloverleafs and over- and underpasses helped confuse the chopper. But he was sharp: he simply sat up there and waited. Guess he figured I had to come out somewhere.

Well, he was right.

I went whipping west on 20, took the Jackson Parkway and they thought they had me. I was traveling flat out, maybe 130 miles an hour in traffic, goosing the accelerator and stomping the brakes better than any goddamn computer could ever figure out.

Of course, I was working on an idea, always having contingency plans ready. Jackson Parkway wound through some tall trees as I recalled. I felt the authorities were closing in; they had to be herding me carefully, setting up roadblocks, getting enough troops and covering all the local roads.

I jumped the curb of the Parkway, dug up sections of a park cutting though to a smaller street, and burned rubber heading for my destination. I might have bought another minute or two. Right then I was paralleling Jackson so I knew I was going the correct way.

Unfortunately, the bridge over the Chattahoochee River was in the open. So I came screaming onto it, a local-type bridge, two lanes, maybe a hundred yards long, at ninety. There was some other traffic, not much, but enough to complicate my plans.

Ostensibly I swerved to avoid another car. Actually, I was pumping accelerator, brakes, and double-clutching all simultaneously while downshifting. All of this resulted in a howling four-wheel slide. Rubber smoke outraced me and clogged my nostrils. People looked, of course. That screeching tire noise is one of the scariest attention getters of all time, probably atavistically replacing the roar of Tyrannosaurus Rex.

Just like it was choreographed, the right side of the yellow-black '57 Chevy smashed through the bridge railing and the car toppled off the bridge.

As the right side of the car became its leading edge, I got a knee on the driver's window frame. The car continued to roll over, left side tires catching on the ruined bridge railing causing the poor old Chevy to begin a flip. I allowed that motion to contribute to my push-off and I hit the water feet first before the car did, hoping, of course, that my acrobatics had not been witnessed.

It would take 'em a while to drag it out and search for me when they didn't find me in the car. I, of course, left some mudstained boy's clothing along with mine and a few other telltales in the back seat. Might fool 'em.

Soon I was pedaling through the back country of ex-Georgia heading south again. I thought maybe I should lay low for several months and then the next time I surfaced, it would be with a genuine kid, proving we were still together and on the run.

16: "Through your eyes I have seen the blood on your hands."

It was raining when I pedaled into Daytona. So, not looking anything like my previous Willie Nelson persona, I rode by Winsome's house. No sign of 'em—nor of any watchers, though electronics are more reliable.

Taking a small chance, I rode over to the marina where the bubble-craft had been moored when we'd left. It was there in the same slip. I waited for a particularly nasty squall to blow in off the ocean; under its cover, I punched in the old combination to the boat and, thank God, it worked. Soon I was hidden in the cabin below decks.

The first thing I did was execute a special program on the craft's computer. No one had changed any programs or added others. *Tiny's* navaids were all tied together in system, which allowed my special program to run a certain unusual combination of electronics equipment which told me that there were no *active* eavesdropping devices on board. Of course, state of the art and all, computer-directed, long range, directional monitoring equipment don't register. But that's a gamble. And whoever uses it has to be able to justify the enormous expense.

The second thing I did was to locate all the parts to my Uzi, which were scattered in different places about the boat, and put 'em together.

Then I bathed and robbed the pantry. Whenever *I* set up a pantry and stock it, there is always booze.

Heaven Hill is a nice bourbon made in Bardstown, which is in Nelson County in what used to be called Kentucky. I'd been on the run a long time, or so it seemed, and it was restful to lie on a bunk with a tumbler of Heaven Hill on my chest, listen to the rain beat on the bubble, and rock with the waves. Neat. Nostalgia. Fun. R and R.

Here and there within the boat was dust. It never ceased to amaze me how that bubble could keep water out but not dust. 'Course, I knew it was just dust which had settled, me not having told the computer to run the airconditioning program which would have filtered the air.

The computer combination to the bubble-boat being the same and the dust and everything all meant that Winsome had neither sold nor used the craft. A pity, for it was costing her money—if nothing else, in interest or dividends she could be getting from investing the boat's sale price.

A flood of guilt hit me then. Winsome. I hadn't checked up on her and Zell during all my travels. Of course, her televiewer was certain to be monitored, her mail opened and read, and possibly her house might be under human and/or electronic surveillance.

Were she and Zell still here? Or were they nonpaying guests of the SS someplace?

As I slipped off to sleep in the familiar surroundings, I again felt the guilt. Hell, I hadn't felt this bad about most of my wives, much less a whore who'd been paid well for the chance she'd taken by signing on with me and Manny.

No matter, I still felt guilty. More so, considering what I had planned.

I slept well into the afternoon, so I rested and ate and drank that day away, too. Didn't want to chance leaving the bubble-boat during the day. I planned.

It took me a while to come up with an acceptable plan, but finally I did so.

Fortunately, there was an encyclopedia disk for the computer. I sucked out the section on armadillos and cut it down to about four hundred words. What I had left would fit on one printed page. And while I consider plagiarism a crime right behind rape and ahead of pillage and plunder, it would be only one of the lesser charges against me. The computer printed about thirty "information" sheets on armadillos. For instance, not a lot of people know they came out of Mexico into the U.S. of A. about 1840 or so. They have some things in common with man: they mate face to face and are the only other animal which can catch leprosy. And their worst natural enemy is the car, on accounta one of their strange habits: when frightened suddenly, an armadillo jumps straight up into the air. Which causes impacts with auto bumpers, grilles, and headlights.

I went to bed early and rose and was out of the bubble-boat before dawn carrying the information sheets and a gunnysack—one of my last ones. Gunnysacks are almost extinct, just like me. Tooling around on my bike, I found a series of open fields back on the mainland. Nowadays, armadillos are like bullshit: everywhere. I dug around in a few burrows until I had a dozen baby armadillos, skin like pliable leather, not yet hardening into armor. Generally, a litter is four; in fact I've never seen otherwise.

With the armadillos and info sheets in the gunnysack, I cruised over to my old neighborhood. I looked different now. Short hair, part of my scalp shaved over my left ear and a dirty bandage affixed thereto. The kind of thing people stare at and remember instead of your face.

I walked down our old street knocking on doors and trying to sell armadillos. Of course, no one was interested. But the role fit; an itinerant drunk trying to con up the price of a drink or two. To conceal my limp, I had to walk like I had a terrible case of hemorrhoids going. And I threw in a fake Spanish accent too, no? Nobody recognized me.

House after house, I would hand out a free "information" sheet on armadillos and try to sell the babies for five bucks. When turned down, I would drop my price all the way to a dollar. I'd hit ten or twelve houses before I got to ours.

I punched the announcer button and found that I was actually nervous. I'd know soon whether Winsome was here or in the slammer. Not needing any complications, I'd chosen time and day so that Zell would be in school.

"What is it?" the speaker said. Winsome's voice. Shit hot.

Like any good salesman, I didn't answer and did turn my back to the camera eye next to the speaker.

After a moment, she opened the door. She was dressed casually, skimpy two-piece, and had a dishtowel over her arm. The sight really affected me, especially in the "if things were only different" section of my brain.

"Well?" she demanded impatiently.

"Señora, por favor, armadillo?" I held out one of the little critters in the palm of my hand.

Winsome's eyes were squinting at me, and her face was scrunched up as if trying to make sense out of something she didn't understand but knew she should.

"Five dollars."

Her eyes narrowed even more. "You?" Her voice was quizzical.

I held up one of the info sheets, on the back of which I'd written: DON'T GIVE ME AWAY. PLAY ALONG.

She didn't even glance at it. "You sonofabitch," she said, clipped accent making it sound cute.

Frantically, I pointed at the sheet. Finally, she read it and looked up at me. "What do you want?"

"You buy armadillo?" I folded the paper to the next

line I'd written: ARE YOU UNDER ANY KIND OF SURVEILLANCE?

She shrugged, eyes still inordinately staring at me. "I have no use for an armadillo."

"Four bucks, señora." I couldn't take the chance of electronic listening devices. Quickly, I scribbled on the sheet: MEET ME TONIGHT AT THE BOAT.

"Why would I want to buy an armadillo?" she asked again. "I once had a pig in a poke and it did me no good."

I winced. "Two dollars for two armadillos, special price for you, lady."

"Just a moment," she said and disappeared. Shortly she was back. "No armadillos. But here is two dollars anyway." She gave me the bill and closed the door in my face.

As I tucked the bill into my pocket, I read on the face: MAYBE. YOU SOB.

I worked the rest of the street and got another two dollars and a "traveler's cup" of coffee.

That night I was uncomfortably settled on top of a van in the marina parking lot at the far end under a tree where I shouldn't be noticed.

At eleven, I recognized Winsome's car as she drove up and parked. She got out and walked down toward the dock. Once on the wooden planking, she stopped and looked back as if to check whether she'd been followed or not.

Which was why I was where I was.

After a moment, she went on to our slip. Remnants of yesterday's storms were gusts of wind and it blew her hair quite appealingly.

In a half an hour, I gave up and went out to the boat. I punched the combination and stepped through the bubble-joint and went down to the cabin.

Where Winsome turned in her seat and arched an eyebrow or three at me. She was drinking coffee. Uh oh, serious, no booze.

"Well, Sandy," she said and sipped coffee.

I went to the coffee pot and poured me one. "The name is Wyndy."

"Yes, I know. I have done what you wanted and have been paid for my services. I also have paid a price. What is it you want now?"

She wasn't gonna be easy to convince to help me one more time. "Um, how's Zell?"

"Heartbroken. He lost a brother recently. And a friend—he thought. He also lost a lot of innocence when the Special Security grilled him."

Upon a closer look, Winsome was different. She'd lost weight. Her nails were bitten down to the quick. It wasn't difficult to imagine shadows under her eyes. "It hasn't been easy for you, has it?"

Her gaze was penetrating, fierce. "There is that."

Something lay there between us heavy with the force of accusation.

"Damn, Winsome. I'm sorry." I shook my head.

"You're sorry?" she demanded, amazed.

"Yes, damnit. I'm sorry." I got mad. "Winsome, you signed on. The liaison was beneficial to you and Zell. Not to mention financially. Hell, invested properly, you won't have to work again." She started to say something, but I held up my hand. "Yes, I know I put you at risk. I said I was sorry. I made a judgment that your risk—and Zell's—was worth the possible price . . ."

Her head snapped around, eyes flashing. "Then I horribly misjudged you, Sandy Creek."

I shook my head. "However you want to look at it, Winsome. Manny has some secret locked up in his head. Larry Jim, that is. The government of our fair republic had kidnapped him—and me—and was engaged in torturing him in an effort to extract that secret. With the active participation of the Administrator."

"What secret?" Her voice said that she didn't quite believe me.

I tossed a mental coin and told her. "I'm not really sure exactly what it is, Winsome, but they say that if they can figure out how his brain works in a special mode, they can use that knowledge to develop faster-than-light travel."

Her body language told me that her skepticism was rising.

"Scientists in the Hub were forcing it out of him and it was killing him, Winsome. He didn't even know he had something that special and they were ripping the thoughts right out of his mind. Hell, I doubt I will understand the esoteric biophysics or mental jitterbug when and if they ever figger it out."

"You are telling me Larry Jim was a prisoner of the Administrator right there in the Hub? And was tortured?"

"He and I both. But we escaped."

"Through your eyes I have seen the blood on your hands." She paused. "You are not Larry Jim's father then. What of his mother?"

"A woman who has lost her husband to this madness," I said. "He was killed trying to rescue us from our captivity in the Hub. Manuel's mother has been separated from her child for those many years."

She nodded. As a mother, she could relate to that. "Her name?"

"Maria Temple."

"Ah. She is the one you are in love with."

We locked eyes and I sat down heavily. Never even having been tasted, the coffee in the cup splashed out. It felt like the hot coffee had been poured on my skull and underneath my scalp. I knew how Custer felt when the realization hit him that no reinforcements were coming.

And I understood a few things that I hadn't quite understood about myself before.

"You are surprised I know?" Her face was slack.

I nodded numbly.

She shrugged. "Women know these things. Think

you that I was not able to have you fall in love with me did not tell me more than words could? And after all my efforts. Well, Wyndy-Sandy, I tried for the years we had together. If your heart was not elsewhere, well . . . things might have been different. Will you tell me about it?"

I did that thing. From the beginning.

In the middle of the telling, she interrupted. "Just exactly how *old* are you?"

"Old enough to have a smallpox scar." I exposed my arm.

When I finished, she said, "It did not escape me that you are a very capable man. Which made it more difficult for me when you left without warning. That really hurt."

"No choice, do you see that now?"

She nodded wearily. "Knowledge now is not even scant comfort then."

She talked weird like me sometimes.

"Tell me about when they came."

Her voice was flat. "It was hours after we talked on the televiewer. I had the prime rib fixed special for you. Even though Zell had come home alone and crying. I had hoped. . . well, I hoped . . . but I knew you and Manuel were gone." She stared down at her coffee cup and twisted it around and around, flipping her thumb over the handle when it went by.

SS surrounded the neighborhood, choppers overhead like angry flies on a carcass. Apparently they'd waited as long as they could for Manny and me to come home. Maybe that bit of hesitation saved us.

They'd taken Winsome and Zell off to the Hub, less than an hour by chopper.

She and Zell had told all they knew about me and Manny, just like I'd instructed Winsome to so do. Drugs, hypnosis, electronic lie detectors, all convinced the SS that Winsome and Zell were telling the truth. While unpleasant and certainly inconvenient, their experience in no way matched the ordeal Manny and I'd gone through. Thanks for small blessings.

Somewhere in her story, I'd poured us some Heaven Hill bourbon. As she finished talking, I refilled our cups.

Her face was still expressionless and her words came out tired. "Why do you return here, Wyndy? You have to know there is some kind of monitoring of our house if you and Manuel are as important as things make you seem. Why? Why tear apart our lives again?"

Christ, I felt bad. I felt like I just backed over my own kid in the driveway. "I need Zell."

That got her attention.

"He could pass for Manny at a distance, and I must maintain the ruse that both he and I are still on the loose."

"There are other children all over who could pass for him." She looked at me expectantly. "Why, Wyndy?"

"Maybe I wanted to see how you were doing," I snapped.

A faint smile this time. We were beginning to understand each other once again. "You wish to 'borrow' my son Zell. Is this before or after you take on the entire SS, all local police, and *the* Administrator personally?"

"Before."

"Besides danger and risk, what does Zell get out of it? And what is in it for me?" Her mouth twitched at the corners.

"You remind me of me," I said. "You know that?"

17: Zell

When we'd lived here with Winsome and Zell, I'd had a paranoia of being discovered. Consequently, I had about thirty alternate plans for escape and most of the logistics set in place to support those plans.

Daytona being special, one of the few places which had in various museums and auto shows old time cars which needed to be maintained. To support this, there was a giant graveyard of dead compression engine automobiles. Elsewhere, these had been melted down for their metal and thus recycled. But in Daytona, there was always a possibility of needing parts or body styles or something.

However, near the Atlantic, old metal tends to rust. So they put all the old junked cars in one four-square-mile area inland and erected a giant bubble to cover it from the elements. They called it "The Auto Graveyard." While the place wasn't temperature or humidity controlled like the moon bubble, the autos deteriorated a lot less than they normally would.

Not to mention some smart joker charges two bucks for a tour of the place, nostalgia and all that. Pays for itself. Tens of thousands of wrecked or discarded cars. Wonderful.

In section H-44. Me having prior access as a mechanic. I had another car ready. 1958 Plymouth Fury. High tail fins. Used to be red, now faded to pink. License tags, front and rear, read: CHRISTINE.

I chose this particular car because it was a popular one on the highways today. Only they were plastic replicas with batteries versus motors.

Thanks, Stephen, I said silently as I slipped into the front seat. At least nobody had cannibalized from it. Of course, I'd hid it in back after fixing it up into running condition. Under the dash was a circuit breaker, which I flipped, allowing the ignition system to complete its own circuit. I also appreciated the fact that batteries, even twelve volt ones, are good for many years nowadays without any maintenance.

Making sure there weren't any people around, I headed for a feeder road through this graveyard of the twentieth century, then I wheeled into the central parking lot along with everybody else, and nonchalantly got out and went on a tour. When that was over, I simply drove off with the other vehicles, only mine was metal and engine, not plastic and battery.

Paying attention on the way to the rendezvous, I saw two other Christines.

I picked up Zell while he was walking home from school.

He hopped in and glared at me.

"Hello, Zell."

"Hello, Sandy."

"Wyndy. The name is Pembroke Wyndham."

"Oh." He sat, strapped in, and faced forward, hands folded in his lap.

"Did your mother brief you."

"Yes." Reluctance in his voice? Some, but mostly disapproval.

"Thanks for helping me out, Zell."

"Sure." He hadn't looked at me other than while climbing in the car.

"I know it's not easy for you, but I don't think there will be any real danger."

"Fuck the danger." Petulant and angry.

Now *he* sounded like me.

"That's a start," I said, heading south, staying with

the traffic and returning a wave from a driver of another Christine. I decided to appeal to his kid's sense of what was right and other esoteric stuff like intrigue and adventure. "With your help, I'm gonna flimflam the Administrator of our fair republic and strike a blow for freedom and free enterprise at the same time. Not to mention getting even with them for what they done to Manny—Larry Jim—and me and your mother."

"I care?" His face was hard. Maybe he wasn't really acting. Nope, not at all.

"Zell, by now you know that a man's gotta do what a man's gotta do." Hit him with clichés, couldn't hurt.

"You certainly do what you do, ne'mind who gets hurt."

"Zell, I'm sorry."

"Sure."

"I really care for your mother. And you."

He finally glanced at me. "Yeah?"

I remained silent.

"Then why. . . ?" His eyes told me that he wanted to be convinced.

"Awright, Zell, I ain't gonna shit you any more. They want Manny. He's special."

"I know."

Well, I guess kids can't keep secrets from each other.

"If they catch him, they will rip his brain out. From the inside."

His face scrunched up. He must be fighting some inner battle. "But you hurt my mom!"

How the hell was I supposed to answer that? "I hurt me, too, son. I did what you accuse me of. Why? My judgment. I placed Manny's safety and well-being above mine and your mother's—and consequently, yours. That's why we got together in the first place. Me and Manny were on the lam, see?"

"You don't gotta embellish for me."

"Where'd you learn that word?" I wanted to know.

"Spelling bee," he said, and a few tears edged out of his eyes. Hell, I missed the good old days, too.

"Anyway, we were on the run and I found a convenient and effective method of hiding us. That's it. That there were people hurt, I accept the blame. But no one was killed."

"People have died?"

"No, Zell," I said, voice harsh. "Killed. Many."

"By you?"

"Yeah. Your mother didn't tell you what a big badass I am?"

He giggled a little. "Nope. She never said anything bad about you—Wyndy."

Which made me feel like I'd just accidentally drowned a bag full of kittens. And was standing there in the water staring at the gunnysack dripping water and realizing I didn't wanta and it was too late.

But Zell had sat back and seemed to be more relaxed. I briefed him on his role.

In Orlando, chosen because it was a giant population center, we stopped at a public booth.

I turned on the video this time. As I spoke, Zell, his back to me and the televiewer, stepped in and out of the picture as if he were pacing and acting as the lookout. Easily he could have been mistaken for Manny.

I called the Hub operator.

"Administrator's office, please."

Which gave me another operator. Obviously I wasn't authorized or I'd know the number code. "What's the purpose of your call?"

"SpecSec business, jack. Move your ass."

Which gave me still another level of operator. "Your business?" She was obviously SpecSec.

"None of yours, sister. Put me through your channels to the Administrator's office."

"Look, mister, if you are smart enough to get this far to me, you know then that I cannot do so without coded authorization."

"Tell them that it involves Hodgkins' project."

"Standby one, please."

Which got me to the Administrator's secretary I remembered. He didn't recognize me. Of course, I'd changed. Although I was wearing a Willie Nelson wig to cover my partially shaved head. On the disguise principle that it's easier to remove a wig to instigate your disguise than it is to put one on.

"Give me the Administrator please."

"Your name?"

"Phillip Marlowe."

"Purpose of call?"

"Hodgkins' project."

"I can connect you with an assistant or somebody else, but not the Administrator." His eyes flicked aside and I knew the call was being traced. Maybe it was automatic. Maybe not.

"Look, bub. Here's the deal. I'll call back. By then you'll know who I am and the Administrator will know why I'm calling. I want to be put through immediately to her. Got it?"

He nodded and started to say something, and I disconnected. They'd play the tape of the call and figure it out quickly.

That would hold them for a while.

I took Zell back to Daytona and dropped him off. "I'll need your help maybe once or twice again, Zell."

"Sure, no sweat. It was fun." He closed the door and leaned back inside. "Wyndy?"

"Yeah?"

"Will you see Manuel?"

"Not for a while."

"Oh. Tell him hi, if you do."

Under a false name, I rented a truck and drove the highways. An eighteen wheeler with sleeping accommodations. At inspection and weighing stations, I was simply going home or returning to home base empty.

But I could park at night-stops and highway rest stops and blend in. I wished I had thought of this earlier as it avoided the traps of motels and so on—

although an old man and a kid would have been rather conspicuous.

Twelve days later, I found a public booth in Miami which was observable from a number of different positions. I taped a message for the Administrator to be sent off six hours hence during the height of rush hour. The machine was to dial the Hub, and I would ask for the Administrator's office, Wyndham calling, yes, I'll hold. I tried to sound natural, figuring they'd keep me on hold till they could trace the call. There are certain bennies to hi-tech.

At five that afternoon, I was standing on a bridge over a canal with ten or twelve ex-Haitians, cane pole hanging over, line in the water, two blocks west of the public booth which had transmitted my call. At five. At five oh three, choppers and cop cars swarmed in.

"I knew it," I mumbled.

"Whot, mon?" The speaker was tall and gaunt.

I indicated the mess of cops. "Must be somebody didn't park in the slot right, huh, mon?"

He grunted. "Fuggin' coppers." He jerked up a scrawny catfish and made a face.

I didn't catch any fish. And Miami won't soon forget the traffic jam.

Two weeks later, I took a chance and accessed Maria's computer code.

HOW'S THE TIME FRAME?

She wasn't there to answer, so I checked back later and there was a message.

GETTING CLOSER.

Which meant I still had too much time to kill so I made my activities more leisurely. Frankly, I was tired of this crap. Not exhausted. Just sick and tired of being sick and tired. Manny, I missed Manny.

Another couple of weeks. A recorded call to the Administrator. "This is Wyndham. I am trying to come up with a safe method for me to have a conversation with Amber Lee-Smith. I will contact you again when I have worked out the arrangements."

I was pretty sure such tricks as calling from one station and having a second transfer the call would be traceable. I could go overseas to Jamaica or Brazil or Mexico and make the call, but they still might get me—and I didn't want to expose myself foolishly at borders this late in the game. I was down to considering personally dangerous schemes like hijacking the Administrator's chopper, or sneaking into her office at night—since I knew the secret code for the bubblevator at the Hub to the Administrator's office level. None of these things had that just right feel.

A go-between? If so, who? And how could I find someone trustworthy? Answer: I couldn't. Anybody connected with Silas Swallow would endanger his PROJECT and thus Manny and Maria. And I'd been out of circulation too long and had no friends other than . . . Winsome. Winsome? Nah. Put her in too much danger. Expose her one more time and she'd likely get burned. Or would she?

And all this speculation made me mad. All my plans were too complicated. When scheming, I'd learned, the best plan is the simplest plan.

One of my main concerns was becoming a major worry. Silas Swallow's PROJECT was nearing completion. Which gave me what we used to call time frame compression; I was running out of time. However, all this served my purpose as a decoy.

I decided. A simple plan but, some would say, audacious. The audacity of the plan should surprise the opposition sufficiently to allow me to get away with it. I hoped.

One last time, me and Christine picked up Zell. I drove up to Jacksonville and taped a message on the televiewer to be transmitted in twenty-four hours.

Again, Zell bounced around behind me, just within view of the camera's eye, acting like a second-rate lookout at a bank robbery. Willie Sutton wouldn't have approved, but what the hell. Theatrics improves the product, I always say.

"This is Wyndham for the Administrator. I wish to have a face-to-face meeting with you. To indicate your willingness, place a personal ad in the Tallahassee *Republican*, next Saturday. Quote, Sandy, meeting agreed, end quote. Then I will phone you with time and place." This latter was merely to keep up a front and mislead, but it was an expected item, so I included it. And of course I wouldn't be anywhere near Tallahassee. I'd get a copy in St. Pete or someplace.

As we drove out of Jax for Daytona, I told Zell, "More 'n likely, this was the last time I'll need you, son. You've saved me a lot of time."

He looked surprised and, in his widened eyes, I saw his mother's. "We won't see you again." His voice was a statement.

"Beats me, kid."

"I won't see Manuel again."

I shrugged.

"Are you going on the spaceship, too?" I could sense the jealousy in his voice. Well, he'd always been hi-tech. I remembered his enthusiasm when I'd taken him and Manny to the Kennedy Space Center for tours and such.

I felt a sense of loss. "I didn't know if I would or not, Zell, but I arranged it—if in fact it all comes about."

"That is real interesting," his voice came out sarcastic and superior like only children can do.

"Whatcha mean, kid?"

"I have been reading and watching about Mr. Swallow's building of a spaceship in orbit and monitoring its progress. They're about the most ahead in that race in all the American Republics."

"And?" I prompted.

"What I cannot figure out is how."

"Please explain." I was becoming uneasy. A young kid was making me so by his lecturing and superior knowledge.

"The ship's about all built, they just need to put in the engines, right?"

I hadn't been keeping up with it. "So what?"

"You told me they needed Manuel's help to design an FTL drive."

"I know all this."

Another Christine drove by and the driver waved. Christ, I was in a Christine Fraternity and didn't know it. (Or was it sorority?) I'd spent a lot of my time juggling Christine and the eighteen wheeler up and down the state. I could have put Christine inside the trailer, and did so on infrequent occasions, but that was dangerous if stopped for routine or random truck inspections.

"How come then, Wyndy, they come to design and build a ship, a spaceship, any kind of ship, or any kind of transportation, without taking into account fuel, engines, stresses, shielding, stuff like that?"

That sat in my mind like rotten fish in your belly. I couldn't think of any kind of transport which wasn't built around its engine, sails, whatever. What I said, in a carefully calm voice, was, "What do you make of it, Zell?" It occurred to me that kids were a lot smarter these days than they used to be. I kind of hoped my parents had said that thing at one time or the other, but somehow I doubted it.

"I don't know, Wyndy. I kind of go along with the experts."

"What do they say?" I needed to be a dentist to get anything out of this kid.

"One theory is that Mr. Silas already has an FTL and is keeping it secret till the last minute."

"Then why'd they need Manny?" I asked.

"Yeah. I thought about that. But the experts quoted in public don't know about him and all."

"Right. So that discounts that theory. What's the others?"

"The only logical one left, which makes sense to me, is that they had an idea of what they were doing and Manuel is the last link. From the design, it tells me that in their new FTL drive, they might need only maneuvering engines for normal space operations. Maybe like to get far enough away from the gravity of planets and moons and stuff before going FTL." Zell looked right smug about his technical knowledge.

"You look right smug," I said. "You been reading again?"

"You remember you were the one who made me join the Walden OTHERWORLDS CLUB?"

"Awright, awright. Big deal."

"Wyndy?"

"Yeah, kid?"

Came the bomb: "Would you take me with you?" His voice trembled, was hopeful and scared all at the same time.

"What?" My brilliant rejoinder.

"Maybe you think you owe me for helping out?" he said hopefully. "And my mother, too, she helped before." Said grudgingly as if embarrassed to bring the subject up.

Since I didn't know what to say, I didn't say it for a change. I tried to change the subject. "What about your mother, Zell? She might miss you. She might not want you to go."

His face fell. "I'ontno." Just like Manny.

Which made me feel like a loving mother who is forced to leave her baby in a basket on the church steps.

Goddamn, life ain't easy.

He looked at me, face pleading, anticipation dripping from his eyes.

"Hell, kid. I ain't in charge. I jest shovel shit and drive cars. I flat-ass don't know."

His face fell and the baby in the basket froze to death before the padre found it.

18: The Man and the Disease

"More coffee?" the waitress asked pointedly. I was taking up a four-person picnic table. You can do that if you get to the restaurant early like I'd been doing.

"Yeah, sure," I said, wanting to snap back at her but not wanting to be remembered more than I wanted to put her in her place.

For the third day in a row, I was eating smoked, barbecue chicken and spinach salad from the salad bar in Sonny's Real Pit Bar-B-Q, Lake City franchise. Because of a stand of slash pine, I couldn't see the looming presence of the Hub.

Positioned at one of the rustic, overlacquered tables, I was trying to watch the entrance and the parking lot at the same time. The parking lot because I wanted to know if somebody paid inordinate interest to Christine, sitting out there next to a copy of a 1936 Cord 810, the one with the big wheel wells, wide white-walls, split windshield, and grille-grooves behind the front wheel wells, too. Watching the entrance and parking lot of Sonny's also to see if Baldy Hodgkins and/or any of his cronies I'd recognize were going to come in for lunch.

Over a spoonful of macaroni salad topped with bean sprouts and raisins, I was reading Saturday's edition of the Tallahassee *Republican*. Thank the Lord that this century's hi-tech hasn't done away with the daily newspaper. Something about reading at your own leisure, holding the printed page in your own grubbies, and smelling printer's ink. Although the modern era has changed the newspaper business radically. Since most people watch the news, etc., there aren't that many computer locations to get a paper—though you can have an outlet in your home or office through your own computer system; but public dispensers are few because they have to be large enough to contain that new skinny recycled fiber paper. The newspaper station is about as big as the normal house. The contractor who owns the distributorship pays a royalty fee for each paper he prints. Most have satellite link access to a couple hundred daily papers, from local to foreign. You go up and check their menu, punch in your selection, and stick in your card or money, and in the bowels of the machine, a laser printer whips out your paper. You pay, also, a deposit, on that superthin fiber paper it's printed on, and get your deposit back by feeding the paper, after you've read it, into any newspaper station's recycle slot. Pretty neat system. Not to mention that you can order, say, the news from AMFED TODAY, sports from THE SPORTING NEWS DAILY SECTION, comics from a syndicate, local fashion from the ATLANTA JOURNAL, classifieds from the MIAMI HERALD, and so on. If you want, the laser printer will simulate printer's ink for that realistic feeling of reading a newspaper. And while it ain't as light and easy to carry as a throwaway disk that you can run on any terminal, the wafer thin "paper" is very light and easy to carry. For that matter you can fold it up, like an old road map, and put it in your pocket, depending on how much of the newspaper you've bought. Decades of newspaper reading had me doing sports, local news, national news if I felt like it (Republic of Dixie and AmFed wide) and then the entertainment and the comics, in that order. Always the comics last, if for no other reason than to wash out the taste of the news.

The personals ad read: "Sandy, meeting agreed. But I need some assurances."

The assurances line wasn't in the script, but was to be expected. It showed how important she thought it was to meet with me. Which gave me my second or third slight misgiving about the whole damn mess. The only reason she would agree to the meeting was that she thought she could convince me to cooperate. While it was possible she might try to buy me off, I didn't think so. So she had something in reserve I didn't know about. Or some compelling reason for me to desert Silas Swallow and company. Not that I knew what the Hub wanted *me* for in the first place.

Not to mention the fact that I had no intention of ever replying to Amber Lee-Smith. The above was simply to determine if she had something to tell me. The meeting would be on my terms with me being able to control the situation.

One of the things about Sonny's which made it so popular, was that it used real people. I don't mean some poor guy assigned to clean up spills or anything like that. I mean waitresses, a guy at the cash register (which was pleasing since it was more natural to pay a person cash than use your universal credit card of which I had one or two but didn't want to use), and bus boys. A drawback to this nonmechanical type restaurant is that after a while you become obvious just sitting there. Stakeouts are easier in machine operated places. Machines don't give you the evil eye for taking up valuable customer space. Especially in a fashionable place such as this.

Nothing for three days. I was getting fat and tired of barbecue. I stalled today, too. The waitress, dressed in a jumpsuit with vertical red and white stripes reminiscent of a peppermint stick, came over and pointedly put the check right in front of my plate.

Scowling at her scowl, I said, "Thank you, ma'am."

"Yeah."

On the other hand, machines are incapable of sarcasm last I heard . . .

In the parking lot a black 1958 Edsel convertible pulled in. I recognized the two passengers. And in a moment, in walked Baldy Hodgkins and a tall, thin black woman—Janine?

I'd filled my face with a coffee cup and looked out the window. They went to another section, away from me and the front door traffic, and seated themselves.

No way they could recognize me. I was wearing a blue jumpsuit, like many other Hub workers and the town was full of 'em, and a baseball cap whose brim shadowed my face well.

Just to spite the waitress, I had a refill at the salad bar, mostly carrot salad and fresh mushrooms.

Then I paid up and casually wandered out into the parking lot.

Unfortunately, Christine wasn't parked next to their Edsel, but I'd make do.

However, they did park next to this old Shelby Cobra replica, so I went to admire the Cobra, not an uncommon occurrence. Standing on the curb between the Edsel and the Cobra I identified the location of the Edsel's battery connector. Close enough to the side to reach.

So I sat down on the curb and pulled off my boot as if to remove a stone, meanwhile leaning aside so that most of my upper torso was behind the front of the Edsel. I doubted if anyone was watching, but I must keep up appearances.

My left held the boot up into the sunlight for inspection while my right hand snaked the snap-lock cover aside from the battery connector compartment. With one hand I shook my boot, and with the other, I slid this little gizmo I'd made up over the male ends of the battery recharge connector.

The gizmo is something illegal which all oldtime mechanics have used at one time or the other: it drains and stores all the battery juice; then you can stick it on your own car's connector and charge your own battery. Kind of like a hi-tech siphon hose.

It was all done in a second. I pulled my boot back on and took a few more seconds to admire the Cobra and went and got into Christine and drove out.

Naturally, I'd figured the routes from Sonny's to the Hub and how long they would take. And adjusted my gizmo for same. I kind of hated to do it to his car: a '58 Edsel Pacer convertible. It had what we used to call the "Continental Kit," which means mounted spare tire carrier on the rear and electric windows and seats. It also was, in the old days, 400 cubes with push-button shift in the hub of the steering wheel.

Down the street where I could still see Sonny's, I parked in a Publix supermarket parking lot, near the exit.

In forty-five minutes, the black Edsel rolled out of Sonny's and drove right past Publix, where I pulled out behind them. Just like I'd figured, they took a limited access throughway to the Hub. And in about two minutes after that their vehicle cruised to a halt. My little gizmo had drained their battery right on time.

Me and Christine were about a half mile back, and I pulled up in front of them. I got out as Baldy did. I hoped he wasn't within mind-shout distance of the Hub.

I was in a blond wig with my cheeks sucked in. Should be good enough, especially with my blue Hub uniform on.

"Hey, can I help?" I asked in a friendly tone. "Not often these things break down."

Baldy's face was scrunched up. "I don't understand it either." There was a hint of anger in his tone.

"I heard some batteries could short out," I said. "Let me look." I checked the front battery charge connector compartment and palmed my gizmo. "Nothing there." I walked around the rear and checked that battery connector compartment. "Nothing here, either. Didn't the computer warn you?"

"Yes, but the discharge must have been swift, for the computer monitored the battery level and we thought we had plenty of time to get back to the Hub."

I looked up and down the throughway. "I could take you, don't look like any help nearby. Roadwatch will have your car out of here before the afternoon is over and you can call them."

It was that easy. Baldy in front with me, Janine in back. Rank Hath Its Privileges obviously, because Janine's stick-like legs didn't really fit too well back there especially when I had the front seat as far back as it would go.

"You can go to the Executives' Parking Area," Baldy told me. I had the speed up, higher than the limit.

"This certainly is a realistic copy," Janine said from the back. "It vibrates like the real thing should." Her voice was high and reedy—matched her legs perfectly.

I took the cloverleaf before the Hub.

"Where are you going?" Baldy demanded.

"This ain't the way to the Executive Parking Area?" I asked innocently.

"Not at all," he said.

So I blasted him with a hand stun gun I had under the seat. I switched hands and nailed Janine before Baldy slumped.

From there I drove to a deserted lake where no one would see us for a moment. I covered them with blankets and just waited until sundown. After dark, I got onto 10 west for about ten minutes to the exit where I had the eighteen wheeler parked. In the middle of a truck park with hundreds of other trucks. An effective hiding place, located there because of the intersection and proximity of the major arteries, 10 and 75.

I carried them into the rear of the truck and tied them up well and waited for them to recover. I'd question 'em before I visited with Amber Lee-Smith.

Janine regained consciousness first. The process took a few minutes. Preliminary body movement, head shaking, noncomprehending looking around, awareness shown in her eyes. Then hostility in those same eyes when directed at me, immediately replaced by some fashion of concern for Hodgkins when her gaze lit on him.

He was in the body twitching phase now. Janine said nothing, surprisingly, telling me she at least had some intelligence.

In the front of the truck was what I needed so I went and retrieved the bottle I'd previously bought at Publix: the hottest, spiciest jalapeño peppers available, just sitting right there aging in their own liquid. I returned to the tied-up pair wishing for brighter lighting in the cavernous enclosure. Early February, it was cool outside, but sun and closed confines made it warm and stuffy within the truck.

Four hostile eyes now.

Roughly, I jerked them upright and leaned them against the side wall so we would be on eye level as I sat down in front of them.

"What do you want?" Hodgkins demanded.

"Harry—" said Janine's reedy voice.

"Not too imaginative an opening line," I told Baldy. I pulled off my wig and let them stare at me. I don't think they recognized me right then, what with the short hair and my healthier and fuller look.

The two glanced at each other in a strange fashion, eyes almost talking to one another and I realized they were communicating with their minds.

I waved the stunner at them, shook my head, and gave Baldy a short burst in the knees. It would tingle him there for a while. "Uh uh," I cautioned. "No mind-talk. I don't want nobody at the Hub to overhear, like old Rodney. Though we aren't anywhere near." Anything to discourage 'em. Don't take no chances.

"You!" said Janine, as they both recognized me at the same time, probably more mind-link.

Hodgkins was looking me over almost professionally. "Just how *old* are you?" Even he couldn't believe the difference since he'd last seen me. Of course I'd been down and out then. Now I looked a hell of a lot younger.

"Old enough to be dead but not as old as I want to be," I told him. "Which brings us to the reason of your presence."

They exchanged glances.

"Let me tell you where we stand," I said. "You kidnapped and tortured me and Manny Temple. Manny's father is dead because of you. Since then, there has been a massive manhunt for both of us. You've split up families and ruined lives. Most of all, you done pissed me off." I stared impassively at them for a bit, wanting it to sink in. "Perhaps you can guess my frame of mind and general temper in putting up with you."

"Wyndham, I must go to the bathroom," Janine said.

"So that's the way it's gonna be, huh?"

The hard glint in her eyes told me that she'd drawn the battle lines. Hodgkins was looking back and forth between the two of us.

"Pee your pants, woman," I said.

She did, the puddle extending around her, running along a crack in the truck's floor toward Baldy. She was telling me she'd not cooperate.

To test a theory, I took out my battery juice stealing gizmo, adjusted it for a minor discharge, grabbed Janine's right ankle, and snapped the clips out and gave her a jolt.

She screamed and snapped her head back in a mean whiplash. Hodgkins was lunging at me, shouting obscenities.

Janine recovered and glared at me and I knew how it was. The two were lovers at least. Janine was the strong one, but Hodgkins was the one in charge. Their professional and personal relationships must have been a mishmash of overlapping lines. They were caught in a web of their own. Damn webs everywhere. I had a macabre vision of people growing webs between each other and entangling themselves with other webs, stumbling about, until everybody in the world was too caught up in webs to move and the entire Earth stopped functioning because of this and a giant web expanded from the Earth into space as if from a viewpoint scalding off in space at light speed with webs beginning to string from the stars and . . . damn, it was scary. I shook my head to clear the vision. Bristles had paraded up my spine and the back of my neck like a herd of buffalo across the plains. A warning? What did they call it, precognition? Something was wrong ahead of me.

Baldy and Janine were looking at me strangely. I shook my head again.

"I want to know the whys and howcomes," I said roughly.

No response.

"If you ain't gonna talk, tell me."

No response.

I lunged at Baldy, grabbing him and dragging him to the center of the truck's floor. I sat on his chest and he heaved to get me off. I crooked my leg around his head, immobilizing it.

Pulling an eye dropper out of my pocket, I stretched and got the jar of jalapeños. I unscrewed the top and sucked up a dropper full of the juice and sat the jar down away from us.

Hodgkins eyes told me he didn't understand. Well, he would. Janine was craning her neck as my body partially blocked her vision. I jammed the eye dropper into Hodgkins' mouth and squirted. His eyes bulged and his mouth spat involuntarily and he began gagging.

"Pansy ass," I said, climbing off him and picking up the jar of hot peppers. When he regained his breath and was done gagging, I said, "That was a lesson just so you'll know what the effect of jalapeño juice is."

My judgment was that he was the weak one and would talk first.

I walked over to Janine, lashed out my foot sideways into her shoulder and kicked her over. Quickly, I knelt so that my knee pinned her neck to the floor, my boot toe high enough to allow her to breathe, but not much else.

Baldy was struggling to sit up. When he'd done so, I let him watch me fill the eye dropper again. "Her eyes, Baldy. A couple drops. Unendurable pain. If I put in more than a few drops, pain and blindness. Tell me now if you're going to talk."

He sputtered, fright and a badly frowzy mouth refusing to let him talk. I waited patiently.

Janine's eyes had expanded by at least half and she was staring at me like the first Japanese who ever saw Godzilla.

I remembered José Temple and held the dropper two feet above Janine's face and squirted the whole thing at her. She jerked her head aside, costing her a partially crushed windpipe. The yellow liquid had splattered the side of her cheek, down her jawbone to just underneath her ear. I refilled the eye dropper and aimed again. This time her jerking head could not compensate enough and a small splash high on her cheekbone must have gotten a minute amount in her left eye. Her mouth opened grotesquely wide and a primordial noise tore itself from her vocal chords. It was not even a coherent scream. I refilled the eye dropper as the noise dropped a few decibels and evolved into the scream, her mouth still obscenely distended. I fired the entire load of jalapeño juice down her throat, and it must have seared the tissue of her throat and vocal chords like acid.

Not happy with myself, I rose and watched without pity as she thrashed on the floor. I shouldn't be involved with revenge, I should be after my goal: information, something which I could use to unravel the webs binding me and Manny.

Hodgkins' eyes were glued to his Janine. I could tell he was trying to help her mentally because he recoiled from what he received—or found there in her mind. I didn't really know what they did nor how they did it. And I didn't care, either.

In about five minutes, five very unpretty minutes, Janine lay there in her own wetness, panting heavily, tongue protruding out the side of her mouth, eyes pouring gallons of tears, and gasping sobbing noises.

I stood over Hodgkins and lifted his chin with the toe of my boot until he looked directly up at me. I stuck my fingers in the jar and plucked out a nice juicy jalapeño and bit half of it off and chewed lustily. I dropped the other half on his head where it bounced and dribbled seeds down the side of his head and the back of his shoulder.

"Maybe we understand each other now?" I said. I nodded toward Janine. "A good dose in her other eye and, tied up like that, she will go completely mad. Her brain will burn out right there in front of us. Then you are next."

His eyes went blanker. His mouth slacker. He drooled. Fear exuded from him like stink from a polecat. No doubt he would cooperate now. Janine had been stronger than he and now she was reduced to a vegetable state full of pain—some pain which I think he shared with his mind.

In case I needed to either implicate Amber Lee-Smith in illegal activities or use some of what I was fixing to learn from Baldy, I intended to record his answers to my questions. So I pulled out my mini-recorder and turned it on.

"Hodgkins, start talking. Who do you work for?"

He stammered. "I work for the republic at the Hub."

"What's the name of your direct supervisor?"

He glanced at the still trembling form of Janine as if

for comfort or confirmation. She wasn't much help to him. I let him work it out. He slumped back. "Amber Lee-Smith."

"Now you're cookin'. Why did you kidnap me and Manuel Temple?"

"Because he was a mindhopper."

"Was Amber Lee-Smith aware of the kidnappings?"

"She directed them." Baldy closed his eyes and faced the ceiling of the truck. Not much of the cooler night air got in here and it was stifling with no moving air, and smelled of jalapeños, sweat, fear, and urine.

"Why did she want me?" A key question.

"She never said." Baldy coughed a little. "I suspected that she wanted to see if you were a receiver or sender, too. If you were a mindhopper."

"Are you aware, Hodgkins, that Amber Lee-Smith is my great-granddaughter?" Or close enough guess.

His eyes popped open and he turned his head to look at me. "No," he whispered. "But it might explain a few things."

"Yeah." Could I get enough out of this question and answer session to use the tape for bargaining? Probably not anything that would be legally admissible in a court. Something about duress and all. "So, what's your speculation now? On why she insisted I be part of your experimentation?"

"She's . . . she's paranoid about her position. She fears espers. Oh, she doesn't say anything, but I—we— can sort of decipher how people feel about us without reading their minds—"

"*Can* you read minds?"

"No. But we do know if there is esper activity nearby."

"Continue."

"It's a combination of body language and other signals. You don't have to be empathetic to sense when people are frightened of your ability. Espers learn the signs early in life. Perhaps she wanted to know if you had any esper ability, since you were so close to the boy and could mentally converse with him, and if so, if your ability was genetic."

"Makes sense." If Amber Lee-Smith were some kind of esper-capable, she'd want to know it and develop it, thus being able to protect herself, for one thing, from possible control by espers—or to know what her esper section was doing, have access to their secret mental communications so they would present no danger to her and her position as the Administrator. In any case, enhance her power.

"Simply put," I said, "she'd want to know if she were vulnerable to esper power or influence."

Baldy let his head fall back to the floor and nodded, grating his head on the boards.

"What did you learn about the extent of Manuel Temple's mindhopping ability?"

"Physiologically, we learned of his inordinate myelination. Our instruments recorded some kind of mental transmission/reception which none of us could monitor with our own minds."

"More, Baldy."

He shrugged. "The Administrator required us to experiment with you and the boy first, to determine your involvement. We did not get into our own program to quantify and qualify his abilities. Whatever, it is far stronger than our ability. It is as if his esper ability is an evolutionary step ahead of even us, and as if he were a special case at that. Though there was some evidence he was communicating with someone or someones other than yourself."

"Why is he doing this, why is he *able* to do this?" I demanded.

His eyes popped open and locked on mine. "Epstein's brain growth stages . . ."

"Yeah, I know all about the five stages."

Hodgkins' face scrunched up and his right upper lip lifted in a "You gotta be shittin' me" look.

"I might not talk erudite," I said, "but it don't mean I'm ignorant. Answer my damn question."

"Epstein found that the brain growth stages provide children functional increases in intelligence."

"And?" He obviously didn't want to answer, so I looked around for the jalapeños and made as if to reach for them.

"We speculate that, in addition to the normal increase in intelligence, that the boy's brain growth spurts, for some reason, were not normal, and functionally increased an esper ability—such as Janine and I possess—also. We did not have him long enough to complete many of the physical tests we wanted to, but it could be that his excessive myelination has provided new channels within his brain, increased the efficiency of certain organs or signals or impulses or many other things. Perhaps this myelination precludes the natural bleed-off of mental energy, or the electrical signals necessary for the brain to operate." He talked nonsense for a few moments longer.

Changing the subject, I said, "How many people are assigned to your project?"

"A dozen pure espers, many others running computer simulations and interfacing with the engineers."

"Tell me the express purpose of your project."

"Argghh," Hodgkins groaned. But he'd already told me too much to hold back anything now. "Weapons. Faster-than-light drive."

"What is the progress of those projects?" I eased a cramped leg.

"The FTL business, I don't know. Not very far, probably, as far as my group is concerned. We haven't been able to translate biology to physics. We hoped you and the boy would provide us with the breakthrough we needed."

"The weapons?" I remembered Rodney the hunchback trying to mentally slam me in Manny's cell during our breakout of the Hub. "How's Rodney doing?" I asked, taking a guess.

His eyes were closed again. "Can I have a drink?

You seem to know all our secrets anyway. So why ask?"

"Tell me." I wafted the jar of jalapeños under his nose and he cringed.

"Rodney and his section have developed the ability to deliver small mental strokes which can be as strong as migraine headaches in people who are real espers, or somewhat less in those who are not esper but are what we've termed 'receptive.' At his best, Rodney can slam you, for instance, with his most damaging blow, and your own mental strength would determine the effect on you—probably, with a strong will like yours, Rodney would accomplish a mere brush at your mental faculties."

Old Amber Lee-Smith, great-granddaughter of mine, was going great guns to consolidate her power and possibly usurp control from the governmental charter she was operating under.

I wasn't done with him on these items yet, but I changed the subject while I was thinking of it. "Tell me your bubblevator and access codes around the Hub."

He didn't want to but I knelt on his chest and held the open jar of jalapeños under his nose and waved them over his face. He spoke and I was repeating them to make sure I got them right and he was grunting from my weight when suddenly I took a stunning blow to the back of my head.

During the last part, when I was sitting on Hodgkins' chest and we were grunting and yelling at each other, Janine must have worked her way to her bound feet by leaning against the wall of the truck to maintain her balance while rising. One hop and she was airborne. Her bound feet lashed out with a karate double kick and smashed into the back of my head.

Which knocked me over and jerked my arm causing the entire jar of jalapeños and liquid to cascade all over Hodgkins' face. And open eyes. And into his nose where it attacked the soft membranes of his sinuses.

Later, I guessed he was brain dead in the first few seconds.

His scream was higher pitched than anything I'd ever heard, ululating and echoing in the closed confines of the truck. And echoing in my own ears.

I was stunned, too groggy even to berate my own carelessness at ignoring the strong one, Janine. I swear, too, even groggy, I felt Hodgkins' *mental* shriek, the one which must have felled Janine like a blow from an ax handle.

Hodgkins continued to scream and his eyes actually rolled back into his head and then squeezed tightly shut, which must have applied some of the acidlike juice to the sensitive cells behind his eyes. If anything, his scream became louder and, I think, at that moment, his esper brain told his heart to stop beating.

His screeching scream died in midscream. His tongue shot out so far that I could see the white straining area at the base of the damn thing. His head hit the floor hard and he released gas. There wasn't any doubt in my military mind that he was dead.

Janine was thrashing around on the floor of the truck like a head with her chicken cut off. Her body movements slowed as I rose shakily to my knees.

I looked about for the stunner with some idea of washing it over her head to stun her brain and thus discontinue the obvious sympathetic pain she felt from Hodgkins.

But she just stopped breathing and was dead, too, almost immediately.

Sympathetic, empathetic death?

Well, I'd heard of stranger things.

Numbed, I stared at what I'd wrought.

Then I remembered the lives they'd disrupted. And I remembered the murderous hatred I'd developed for them when they were torturing Manny in the Hub and I had to listen to his pleas and I remembered the complete frustration I'd had at not being able to help Manny and the vows I'd made then and the kicks at a cell door which wouldn't open no matter how hard I tried and I remembered Manny's face when I'd first seen him there in his room and my determination to make *them* pay and I remembered the anger and I remembered . . .

I stood there staring at the two bodies, regretting that I didn't have two live people as leverage when I dealt with Amber Lee-Smith.

19: Amber Lee-Smith

Unfortunately, I needed Baldy and Janine alive more than I needed them dead. My plans had included them as trade bait with the Administrator.

To hell with that. Bluff it. Go ahead. I was tired of this game.

Which attitude came from the fact that I'd just figured the whole thing out. Silas Swallow was indeed a man of action, resource, and trickery.

Everything fell into place. And my kidnapping the two espers and their unfortunate deaths would precipitate a lot of activity. Doubtless I'd just put all the wheels in motion.

So it was doubly imperative I continue the bluff, elsewise my estranged great-granddaughter would figure it out just as I had.

Zell had been correct. The orbiting space ship was a blind, a fake.

What Zell had said about shapes of vehicles mostly dictated by the motivating force or the medium through which they travel was the key.

FTL, immediate translation, to elsewhere required no specific vehicular shape. Just a space- or vacuum-proof vehicle able to maintain life-support. But something big enough to carry everything necessary for space exploration, setting up a colony, and to support the few thousand people involved while so doing. And the roomier, the better.

The *Nimitz* possessed all of the above. Plus, as the current site of the PROJECT, almost everybody was already on board. As were growing edible plants, sheepaloe, etc. And it possessed a bubble. And a couple of nuclear reactors for power. Good ole CVN 68.

Which left me with two tasks: flimflam Amber, and haul ass for the *Nimitz*.

The two espers became fish bait in a deep lake, weighed down with enough cement block to build an outhouse with.

That morning I drove to Ocala, not very many miles from Silas Comfort Swallow's farm. At a flower shop. Paying for a moderately expensive selection. They showed me the small room their customers used to record their accompanying messages. I fooled around in there for a few minutes, popped the disk out of the recorder, stuck it in my pocket, and produced the disk recording I'd made of my interrogation of Baldy and Janine. I popped that in the machine and managed to erase Baldy's death scream.

To the end of the recording, I added: "Maria, play this for Silas. I'm making my play. You're advised. Do what you think you got to."

Bossman could figger it out. He knew that if I had Hodgkins, the situation was going critical. That I was making some kind of play to even up the odds and to be prepared for the consequences. That something had happened to change the equation; a jump or two and Silas would guess the two espers had croaked.

Back in the shop, the nice lady gave me a fancy, tiny envelope to put my disk in.

I addressed it: MARIA TEMPLE. WYMM? LOVE, WHANGON EMPTY

The flower-lady attached the envelope with the disk in it to the stem of one of the many gardenias and I watched a young fellow drive a battery-powered van off to Bossman's place. They'd have it within the hour. Of course, the flower-lady had called ahead to determine if the recipient of the flowers was in fact home.

Since I owed Silas at least twenty-four hours to prepare, and I foresaw a total lack of sleep and food in my immediate future, I found a restaurant and ate a giant pizza for the carbohydrates, and got some prime rib to top that off. Then I found an obscure motel far enough from Lake City to be out of the search pattern, which must be in progress, for Hodgkins. I forced myself to sleep sixteen hours and had a nice breakfast at McDonald's, fried chicken and yogurt, and was at the Hub by 0700, as we used to say when on a mission.

Like any chief of state, the Administrator's tentative daily schedule was published. So I knew Amber Lee-Smith would be in her office that morning. Not to mention her having to be on top of the search for her two lost lieutenants.

I waited for the big 0730 influx of workers and wandered in with them. Up stairs, escalators, through giant corridors, in and out of great halls. Finally, I arrived at the junction of the bubblevator where it took off up the outside of one of the great towers. To the Administrator's office for those who didn't have a chopper access or one of the more secure, direct accesses elsewhere inside this maze.

Waiting, I eventually got the bubblevator to myself. I punched in Hodgkins' personal code, which would authorize access to that floor, and punched in the destination code I'd observed from the goons when they took me to the Administrator's office.

On the way up, and too late, I realized I'd left two loose ends: Winsome and Zell. Zell wanted to go with us. Would Silas Swallow allow it? Shit, would Winsome allow it? Beat the hell out of me. The only thing I could do was ask them. So be it. After my meeting with Amber, if I lived to walk out of the Hub, I'd go straight to Daytona, and from there make my way to the *Nimitz* off Tampa Bay.

Soon I was walking down the Halls of Power, trying

to act inconspicuous among well dressed people juggling those instant coffee mugs. Times and technology can change processes, but not products. People still drink coffee.

My Hub-blue jumpsuit was not too out of place. Occasionally, I'd nod and smile at some minor official.

Of course, I wasn't armed. Doubtless the bubblevator had some sort of scanner installed, and anything which was either metal or nonmetal and resembled a weapon would have caused an SS alert and I'd have been trapped in the bubblevator. I also suspected there was a similar scanner where you step off the bubblevator into a small foyer on the Administrator's floor. Besides, here in the lion's den again, short of a nuclear bomb, no weapon would possibly do me any good.

Down at the end of the corridor sat the double doors of the Administrator's personal offices.

Just like I thought, SS were on me when I walked in. You just don't walk into a chief of state's office without reason. I guessed the cameras picked me up when my destination became obvious. Two sections of the wall, one on either side of me, slid aside and two armed SS guys stepped out of their respective left and right side hideaways.

Their weapons were trained on me and they weren't stunners. A laser and a projectile weapon.

"Hi, fellas," I said brightly.

"Your purpose?" the one on the left demanded.

I looked down and imagined I saw the spot on the floor where they'd dragged me down when I'd tried to escape with Manny and didn't know who the hell I was. I had to restrain the anger which welled up within me.

I stared him down. "I come to see my great-granddaughter, Amber. Here are my bona fides." I opened my palm and handed him the coded ID cards of Baldy and his lover.

The two guards didn't know what to do. They didn't

want to let me go, but they didn't want to anger the
Administrator if I were in fact telling the truth.

"You, sir, are not on our list," said Left.

Right took me into his anteroom revealed by the
sliding wall, and began to scan me with a handheld
machine. It would pick up anything inorganic. I guess
it could discriminate between real fillings and plastique explosives. Though I wasn't sure about that.
Nobody gets cavities any more.

Left left and went into the Administrator's office. It
would take a few minutes for them to go through the
necessary secretaries and aides. I stood and stared at
Right.

In a few moments, an Oriental aide came and got
me. He said not a word. As I followed him, I'd have
bet my last sip of Jack Blue that the communications
room here was burning up and that the senior SS guys
were reporting and/or staying on the line for immediate orders.

The aide ushered me through the main, outer office,
where they'd tried their experiment on me and Manny,
and through another office where I thought we hesitated too long—meaning another scanner.

Had these people forgot you can kill with your
hands, your feet, your head?

I know next to nothing about trains. That should be
understood from the start.

Amber Lee-Smith's office seemed as big as a parking garage, but I doubt it was much larger than half an
acre. Most of which room was occupied by fully functional model trains. Two or three of which were end-
lessly chugging along the outer perimeter of her office.

One display had a tiny engine drawing flat cars full
of tiny soldiers around what looked like a genuine
replica of the Charge of the Light Brigade. Well, I
hadn't remembered any trains involved, not that I was
there, of course, so there must have been some sort of
literary license taken.

Bubble-encased shelves held antique model trains

and attendant cars, model zoo and farm animals, all kinds of things which at one time or another had contributed to the lore and ranks of model trainery.

Standing in front of a console which must control all of this was Amber Lee-Smith. She wore what looked like bloomers, but were really loose pants with lots of folds in them. Blue. And a baggy white blouse. With a wide navy blue swath of cloth around her waist reminiscent of a swashbuckler. I guess it was the fashion these days.

"So you are my great-granddaughter?"

"Does that get you a medal?" Her voice was flat. It sounded strange coming from her Oriental features. And her face was wider than it seemed it ought to be.

So that's how it would be, huh? "Kidnapped anybody lately?"

"What do you want with me, old man?"

"What did you want with me?" I countered. "I understand about the boy."

"It is not my intention to fill in the blanks for you," she said, voice still rather lifeless. "We did not initially want you; however, your murder spree caught us by surprise and by the time we'd evaluated what to do with you, the boy was observed communicating with you."

"And by then you knew my history and that you were my descendant and hoped that genetics did their thing and you were a latent esper or something."

She nodded curtly. "I had hoped . . . well, this era has its pitfalls. It is of no more concern to me, now, for within these walls," she gestured widely, inclusive, I guessed, of the Administrator's floor here in the Hub, "I have several esper personnel dedicated to monitoring for possible tampering with me and the other high officials here. It is of no importance, because we have yet to encounter an esper of the strength and will necessary to involve herself or himself in our business."

"But you are vulnerable."

She shrugged. "I would have had it otherwise. These things are not the purpose of your presence." She tapped her booted foot upon the parquet floor.

"How is my ex-wife?" Nancy.

"Dead."

Well, I'd more or less guessed that much. Not many of my contemporaries were still around. None that I could think of. I probably had more dead ex-wives, now that I thought about it, than the law would allow. "What happened?"

"I do not intend to brief you on my family tree. But I will brag upon her and my family. She finally settled in Singapore and had daughters and granddaughters and great-granddaughters. She founded a matriarchal dynasty. She selected husbands for her offspring and their offspring. Her dynasty became important in Singapore. Hence, when Singapore began its training to bid for charter government contracts, I was there and already trained and able to take the assignment."

"And *my* daughter?" Nancy, Jr. Which should have told me something at the time.

"Yes, my grandmother," said Amber. "She controls the consortium her mother, Nancy, Senior, founded. And does not wish to see you."

"It figgers. Nobody loves me now that I don't have mindhopping ability."

"Nor are you present to discuss these items."

"A trade."

Interest peaked in her eyes. "Hodgkins and his lover. For what? For whom?"

"An end to kidnapping and harassment."

"Silas Swallow can fight his own battles."

She wasn't going to give an inch. "It occurs to me," I said, "that you will need your trusted lieutenants in order to pursue your own program."

She turned and punched a small button on a side console. Somewhere in the bowels of the room a small "toot" sounded. "Insignificant. I want the system."

"You will never get Manuel Temple again."

"I did not say I wanted the boy, old man. I said I wanted the system."

"System?" I said involuntarily aloud. My voice must have been pitched differently, for the aide stepped out of the background as if to protect Amber.

She waved him back. "It's okay, Chang."

Her laugh was a short, harsh bark. Now there was life in her eyes and voice. She pointed to a screen in the middle of the main console. "Right there I can call up every piece of equipment, all supplies and building materials which have been delivered to Swallow's orbiting ship under so-called construction. Not to mention I can review almost everything *on order* for the project."

She'd figgered much as I had.

"Stop lying to me, Wyndham. You know full well that nothing of substance has been delivered to the orbiting building site recently. It is all a blind."

Just like Zell had speculated to me. Just exactly what in the *fuck* was going on? It occurred to me to wonder: Was Silas double-crossing me? Others? What? Had I figured it out right myself?

She smiled a deadly smile, sorta like the one the puff adder must have smiled before it bit Cleopatra and croaked her. Or was it a pit viper?

"We monitor Swallow's wherabouts. Last night he and a small party helicoptered to the *Nimitz*, his PROJECT, in Tampa Bay. Not much later, the *Nimitz* sailed with the tide, supposedly to test engines and so on. But we are certain that she was heading for the twelve mile limit."

Uh, oh, I thought. Events done stampeded right over my head. "So you can't touch him." My voice was calm, but I felt like one of those trains had grown to life size and ran over me. Too late! Silas made his move and now I was stranded. Maybe I could chopper after them?

She shrugged her shrug again. "When you appeared outside my office, I ordered the SS to take enough choppers and men and capture the *Nimitz*. They are to bring the ship back and we will take it apart and obtain the system." Which meant she had wanted to see me before last night; she might even have been interested in making a deal. Or she might have been going to buy me off, bribe me or something. But she had been willing to talk. Now . . . nothing. The Nimitz sailing and Swallow's apparent run for it changed Amber's mind. Silas was probably sailing for the safety of the twelve mile international boundary. And probably had a good idea of how to translate Manny's processes into biophysics. Funny thing was, I'd brought it all down upon myself, upon us—kidnapping Hodgkins and sending the recording to Silas Swallow had started all the pieces in motion.

Goddamn. It was all my own fault. Events had superseded both me *and* Amber.

Amber flipped two switches and a train went across a bridge which exploded. The bridge crumbled and the train splashed into a miniature lake.

Manny and Maria were on the *Nimitz*. And would be hostage again. The realization hit me like the train crashing off that bridge again.

A red light pulsed on the console. The aide, Chang, sidled over to it, leaned down, flipped a switch and whispered. His face turned ashen; he stood and spoke to Amber in rapid Chinese or Singapore dialect thereof—which I couldn't follow at all.

Amber's face, for the first time, came alive. "God-*damn* it! It's impossible!" She snapped an order and the aide turned up the volume control.

From the timbre of the voice, I could tell it was a transferred radio call.

"Ah, roger, will repeat, Mz. Smith. I say again the *Nimitz* has disappeared. We were heading for it on the track that ATC gave us and they reported it was no longer there."

"Radar failure!" she shouted at the speaker receptacle.

"Double checked, Mz. Administrator. Confirmed. I

am overflying the area right now. Visibility limitless. My other choppers fanning out for search."

"Comm center," Amber told her aide.

He switched some switches.

"Go ahead Administrator," said a calm male voice.

"Mate the *Nimitz* tracking program," Amber said, "with the current film off the Gulf satellite and confirm."

"Working," said the voice. "Running . . . got it. Madam Administrator, I don't understand—"

"Tell me what you see!" demanded Amber.

"The carrier was there one second and gone the next."

Amber jerked her hand down. The aide cut the connection.

"So it is true," she said.

My mind was reeling. I didn't know what to feel. Deserted? Abandoned? Double-crossed? Used? Fucked? Conned? Had?

Manny gone. Maria . . .

Amber saw my face and barked her laugh again. "They had it, the secret, and you didn't know it, Wyndham. They used you to fool me and distract me." Her whole body appeared shrunken. Her voice was a harsh whisper. "Do you know what their success means? It negates the human equation on this planet right this minute. And we three are the only ones who realize it. Governments will lose authority, power, depending on what happens with this new thing Swallow has. But I'm not finished! We can't be out of it yet."

She strode out angrily. She paced back and forth between two tables where little oil cars went under towers which in turn squirted black liquid into their tanks while ore cars received sparkling pebbles. I must give Amber credit: she wasn't simply bemoaning her own loss of advantage. She recognized that this one single act would have an almost immediate domino impact upon the world. Amber was philosopher enough to remark on that singular occurrence in human history. And it had just happened. History.

"We have all been duped. Just as you used that woman and child in Daytona, Swallow used you." Amber paused and I could see my late, ex-wife's determination shining through the anger showing in every move Amber made. The resemblance was eerie. Hell, it scared me.

I was thinking fast and furious. I needed a ticket out of here. I must have been easy to read, since Chang watched me like an owl after a field mouse and read my intentions. The Administrator would make a fine hostage. Chang stepped between us.

Amber glanced up, flipped up a red flag on a tiny train post, and said, "Don't kill him, Chang. Wyndham is no longer important to me but I need Hodgkins and his assistant back here. I need them badly. No one else has the ability to trace down what might have happened to the *Nimitz*. Maybe he can use his group to watch for the boy's mind or the psychic vibrations or some goddamn thing that will give us a clue."

Now she was reminding me of me.

She looked at me. "We have both been used. I will trade you your life for your two prisoners."

"I have to go get them, and be alone and not followed nor electronically monitored."

"I expected no less and I am certain that you will insure same. I assume they will die within an hour or two should you not take some preplanned action?"

"Right," I said. I made my voice as hard as my face. "Having tasted your hospitality before, I know I can hold out against torture or chemicals for the hour necessary. I have to call in by 0900 and every hour thereafter. And appear somewhere personally and be observed. Any deviation and the two of 'em die. Not to mention that I must be the one to release them, otherwise any one of many physical and mechanical actions must be done in sequence or they are dead."

"Do not cross me." Her voice was commanding, but

no longer flat. I could see her mind working furiously behind her eyes. *Chang!*" she shouted.

Her hand flipped a century-old Lionel locomotive twelve feet in the air. As the locomotive came down a foot or so from the peak of its trajectory, Chang leapt. His right leg shot out and his foot smashed the locomotive, creasing it, and bending it nearly double. He landed right in front of me with fingers extended and lodged against my neck, partially cutting off my windpipe. He froze in that position.

"You could never have touched me," Amber said.

Gingerly, I reached up as if to remove Chang's fingers from my throat. Instead, I touched his throat with my own pointy finger. He wasn't worried, but his eyes showed he didn't understand.

I swiveled my head to face Amber. "And that could have been poison under my fingernail. Instant death. Can we stop posturing now?"

Surprise on her face and an incipient smile appeared. She gestured and Chang dropped his hand and stood aside.

"Grandmother said, from stories *her* mother told, not to underestimate you. And I thought they were simply stories to scare us children. Go, great-grandfather. Give me my people back. See him out, Chang."

Too nice, too fast. I'd get out free. But something else . . .

20: Winsome

Chang got me to the public area at the foot of the bubblevator. As I stepped out, I smiled widely at him and said, "Have a nice day." His face didn't change or anything.

But I was worried. It was difficult to think with emotions bouncing confusedly around in my head. Something did not fit. My mind worked the problem. Amber had given in too easily. She'd let me go and I was the only link to the PROJECT she had left—and the only leverage against Silas Swallow. Even though the *Nimitz*, passengers, and crew were ostensibly gone, and the events in her office had occurred too naturally to be faked—the *Nimitz had* disappeared.

Which pointed out the importance of Baldy and Janine. Amber wasn't going to be very happy when I didn't provide the two espers. Now she really needed them to continue her own projects and to direct an esper search for any kind of activity which might point to Silas Swallow and his suddenly missing aircraft carrier.

I was nude in the parking lot when I realized part of the answer.

Which is to say I didn't trust Amber. I stood alongside Christine and stripped to the buff. There had been too many opportunities for them to slip a minia-ture tracking device into my clothing. I didn't fear exposure, to make a pun, for Amber wouldn't let the SS detain me. While my hair was still short, I removed the wig and poured a gallon of water on my head and ran a brush through it. The same with down my back where they could have dropped a bug down the back of my clothing to adhere to my skin.

I left the clothing I'd worn into the Hub right there where it had fallen and the water puddled around it. I reached into Christine and pulled on skivvies and trousers and shirt I had ready for this very purpose.

Since they hadn't known I was coming, I wasn't worried about Christine being compromised. They didn't know about her. And I doubted if I was under observation right now—

—which was wrong for, as I ran a towel over my head and dropped it on the clothes and began to pull my shirt over my head, I saw this woman, maybe sixty, gray hair and a wide smile, sitting in the open seat of a Model-T watching me. Where were my fabled powers of observation? Damn, I was losing it.

She was one car over. I kind of smiled at her.

"I've seen stranger things," she said, voice throaty, "but not lately." She eyed me while I finished pulling the shirt down my torso. "Nice series of scars," she said, almost sounding as if she admired them. "Where'd you get them?"

"Thailand, Burma, Jordan, Panama, Costa Rica, and Lake City." I hopped up on Christine's trunk to pull on some socks and boots.

"You've been around," she said. She looked at Christine with a practiced eye. "Two originals, by dog it. Would I seem too forward were I to offer my name, address, code, and number?"

I eyed her, enjoyed the moment and boost she'd given me. I shook my head regretfully. "I've just proposed to a lady. Otherwise . . ."

"I don't care if you're lefthanded, mister."

"Madam, you tempt me, but I must be on my way."

"Well, it was worth a try," she said and smiled goodbye.

"And I'm honored. Were my circumstances different . . ."

I ducked into Christine and was off, feeling good until again the realization hit me.

Amber had no real assurance that I would keep my word and return Hodgkins and Janine. All Amber had to do after getting the two espers back was to capture me again. But I'd eluded her minions for years now so she couldn't count on that.

I blasted out the thoroughfare and knew the answer in front of Publix, right down the street from Sonny's.

Amber'd said something about me using that woman and child in Daytona. They'd questioned Winsome and Zell and knew just about everything, like how long me and Manny had stayed with Zell and Winsome. A little extrapolation and Amber knew that Winsome and Zell were important to me. It fit. Those two were the only possible hold Amber could find over me. Whether or not I still cared enough for the two didn't matter. Amber would take them anyway. Whereupon Winsome and Zell would pay for the espers' deaths.

I screamed into a four-wheel slide burning forty dollars worth of rubber off Christine and double-clutched, downshifted, and ran a plastic bodied Maserati and two Volkswagon Beetles onto the sidewalk. At the public telly, I punched in Winsome's number in Daytona. It buzzed the required five times, me praying and sweating simultaneously. The number had to be monitored, but I was calling anyway.

The picture clicked and defuzzed and there was Winsome. Before I could say anything, her voice said: "Since it's Speedweek and school's out and sales are on, Zell and I are out shopping. We will be back by two this afternoon. Leave your message when the screen indicates."

The screen so indicated it was ready to record and I wanted to shout at it, "Winsome grab Zell and run don't even stop for your purse or the bathroom just run please for God's sake run like hell!" But I didn't. SS would be monitoring and would therefore move in earlier. Maybe they'd simply wait for Winsome and Zell to return, not bothering to search Daytona and its stores for them. Adding to this confusion would be Speedweek, which culminates in the Daytona 500. But lots of tourists. That is, Daytona would be difficult to stomp around in and find a woman and child.

Two o'clock, she'd said. "Back by two." Check. Now nine. A three to four hour drive at speed limits. I could make it in time. But "Back by two" could mean noon or one or eleven. Damn.

I burned more rubber out of Lake City. A replica of a green 1942 Chrysler Town and Country Station Wagon driven by a teenager tried to keep up with me. Hah. Nice car, though. It had that wood veneer and chrome strips on the front and rear fender wells. Very wide white walls.

What used to be state road 100 leads from Lake City almost to Daytona where other roads took over. And of everybody in the entire universe, *I* knew all the roads in ex-Florida. Hadn't I been driving around them almost nonstop for what seemed forever?

On uncongested straightaways I peaked out at one thirty. I didn't know what that was in metrics and didn't care.

At Starke, about thirty-five miles from Lake City, I stopped outside the giant bubble which covered the penitentiary there. Damn bubbles were everywhere doing everything.

I punched in Winsome's Daytona number again, got the same recording, and was winding second gear out past the redline before I realized I'd just blown past a '91 Lamborghini and a cop.

Who took immediate umbrage at my noncompliance with Department of Highway Safety speed regulations.

I couldn't decide whether to stop or not. He'd be radioing ahead for somebody to nail me by turning off my motor when I next crossed a laser scanner—which there couldn't be too many of on 100 here. I kept going. The closer to Daytona, the more traffic and I had to keep slowing down, all the while cursing in frustration and worry.

At Palatka, they had a roadblock set up with their little imitation plastic cop cars. Shoulda used highway equipment like bulldozers and Cats and stuff. What they had was no match for Christine.

In the cinema, they show the old days, Robert Mitchum in a computer-enhanced *Thunder Road* blasting through roadblocks with the pedal to the metal; i.e., full throttle.

That ain't the way to do it. The faster you hit a roadblock, the more the impact is, and the more damage your vehicle sustains. Of course, you got to counterbalance this with the fact that the cops are standing there popping off at you with weapons all the time. So there is a happy medium. What you do is slew up there, kind of zigzagging to avoid hostile fire, as we used to say in the battles, which also serves to decrease your speed. I guessed a thirty mph impact with a couple of plastic cop cars wouldn't do too much damage to Christine.

I was right.

Though I did feel the tingle of a stun gun. Too bad they don't let cops play with real guns anymore. They might have had me.

To throw them off, I turned north on 17 as if heading for Jacksonville. I found a couple of back roads which returned me to 100 in East Palatka. Pretty country. Lots of lakes and green stuff. Even for February.

Because of the traffic and the fact I didn't want to attract any more attention, I slowed down. Several more Christines, all heading for Daytona. Good.

Of course, all this time I wondered. While my eyes and head were roving front and back and side to side like a fighter pilot in a dogfight, trying to eyeball for more cops, and shifting and gunning Christine and doing all that hard driving stuff, I wondered.

The *Nimitz*. Gone.

Somehow they translated Manny's esper process to engineering diagrams and into electronic and mechanical actuality. It figgered.

An aircraft carrier makes a perfect space exploration and colonization vehicle if it could be maneuvered. Which obviously it might could be.

And gone.

With Manny.

And Maria.

Silas must have been right cagey about the whole thing. He'd distracted Amber and her cronies and the rest of the world, including me, for a long time with that "it's being built in orbit" spaceship business.

Now I was cruising into Bunnell, which is the outskirts of Daytona. When I got near 95, the traffic was horrible. Which made me think I should have hired or hijacked a chopper. Well, too late to think.

When I got near the neighborhood, I forced myself to admit I had no plan of action. First time in a long time. Well, improvisation. I'd just have to park nearby, inconspicuously, and await the arrival of Winsome and Zell. Zip in, scarf them up, and burn out of there. No doubt the SS were waiting, too. It would be a race.

Except. It didn't work out that way.

A shade past noon. Cold wind off the Atlantic.

In the neighborhood, I neared the block where Winsome and Zell lived.

Two turns and a minute away.

When I couldn't help but notice two choppers hovering ahead and off to the left.

No! I wanted to shout.

They'd come home early. I should have driven faster and harder.

I gunned the engine and Christine responded as she had all day: with guts.

Me and Christine came sliding around the last corner. People, neighbors, were out on their lawns and sidewalks and porches watching. Dozens of them.

One chopper had landed and was sitting on the winter-dead carpet grass I'd mowed so often until I'd managed to con Zell into doing it himself. The other chopper hovering overhead.

Four SS pulling Winsome into the chopper by her wrists. One behind, holding Zell for his turn. Winsome struggling. She knowing damn well that this occasion would not be a Sunday school picnic. She was smart enough to know that if they took her a second time, it was for real, and this time something was bad wrong. Plus she knew all about Manny and where Manny was; she didn't know the *Nimitz* was gone. She'd think the SS could force her to tell on Manny, give away his secret and his hideout. She'd be signing his death warrant. That's what she would have to have thought. It was the only logical conclusion. She must have been scared to death for her son, Zell. She was kicking and screaming, her mouth moving grotesquely, the only sound being the overwhelming wind-chop of the giant blades.

Christine's engine protested as I jammed her down into second, the compression was such that it blew a hole into the already rusty manifold pipe and I could now hear her throaty roar over the chopper noise. I goosed the accelerator, jumped the curb, and sliced through carpet grass directly for the chopper.

I cut between the one SS holding Zell and aimed for those pushing Winsome inside the chopper, trying to avoid hitting Winsome during this process.

Christine's front end smashed one against the side of the chopper and the chopper's wheel well sliced into the area of his kidney.

Christine's door slammed open on another SS as I leapt out, and I finished him off with the butt of my Uzi.

The two SS remaining let Winsome go and went for their sidearms. My Uzi spoke selectively and they jerked back into the body of the chopper. The pilot twisted in his seat and I gave him a burst which exploded his head and starred the safety windscreen plastic.

Winsome's screams were audible even over the passage of the chopper's blades.

Number 5 SS was holding a pistol to Zell's head. I could tell he was interested in self-preservation, not in completing his mission.

I scrambled to get around Christine and circle him, but he was a street-smart fellow, for he kept Zell between me and him. I sat my Uzi on Christine's trunk lid and half raised my hands to show him my intentions. I walked toward him, forcing myself not to look up to see where the second chopper was and what it was doing.

Winsome climbed to her feet and circled Christine's hood, stepping over the body of the first deceased SS guy. Then we were advancing on Number 5 and Zell, each of us from an oblique angle. 5 kept jerking from side to side, showing Zell to both Winsome and me, backing all the while. Soon, he was against the house, jamming himself and Zell into the white stucco. He transferred the muzzle of the pistol from Zell's neck to his right ear. 5 had a look of fear about his face, a mustache strangely out of place on the young man. Maybe his inexperience would help us.

Winsome glanced behind her and I could tell from her face that the other chopper was doing something that I wouldn't like. Landing and disgorging troops, for instance.

Figgering an answer, I darted back to Christine and lunged inside, dug out my stunner, and turned back to the house. I'd noticed the other chopper was landing. And a third chopper had appeared overhead. The odds were lengthening.

I brought my stunner to bear, but Winsome was in the way now, advancing on 5 with her hands held out.

"Don't!" I shouted.

5 waved his gun at her and she grabbed his hand and I heard the unmistakable crack of a shot and

Winsome collapsed, still holding his hand with the pistol in it. Zell bit 5's wrist and I lunged for them.

I jerked his arm away from the melee, and the gun went off again, projectile pronging against the wall of the house. I held his arm aside and killed him with stiffened fingers to the throat. Chang would have been proud of me.

I didn't have time to even look at Winsome and Zell. I raced back to Christine and my Uzi.

The second chopper had landed in the street and blue clad figures were piling out. I switched to automatic fire and opened up on them. They went down, folding and falling and bleeding, gouts of flesh and blood flying. I traversed the chopper, seeking the pilot, and the airframe shook and tilted and a giant rotor blade cut a great divot out of the cement of the street and broke and metal flew like shrapnel.

People nearby were scrambling for their homes, looks of disbelief at this war in their front yards and on their street. Chopper number two died with its contingent right there in the street where Manny and Zell had played soccer.

I snapped that clip out and replaced it with one from my pocket.

The last chopper was dropping toward us. I ran to Winsome and Zell. Zell's face was hospital white and he had Winsome's head in his hands.

I knelt beside her. She saw me but had eyes only for Zell. Her right hand stroked his jawline and his tears fell freely on her face.

Blood was pumping into the carpet grass like water into a sponge. Her abdomen looked like the belly of a gaffed fish. I'd seen too many similar wounds to have any hope.

A wave of regret and sorrow washed over me.

Things had gone to hell in a hurry.

21: The Daytona 500

I had no answers. Winsome dying. Zell crying. Me. . . ?

Instead of putting Winsome in Christine and trying to make a break for it, I decided to hold off the third chopper. They'd nail us from above in this open neighborhood anyway. Again, we were fortunate they hadn't sent gunships.

The wounded chopper in the street was losing turbine blades and whining decibels higher than I thought I could endure. The streets and walks and lawns were empty now.

The first chopper behind us on the lawn kept chopping away at the air, its dead pilot slumped forward against his instruments.

Dead grass seared as a heavy laser cut through it toward me. I rolled next to Christine and came up firing on automatic.

The last chopper swooped in from the back of the house and hovered. One SS leaned out firing the laser rifle and another firing an automatic projectile weapon. A series of tracks punctured Christine's right side.

I stood my ground and aimed at the hovering chopper's vulnerable point: the housing below the blades where the shaft protrudes and the engine is most accessible to damage.

Keeping my concentration, I continued to fire, and changed clips one more time. At one point, the laser seared Christine's faded paint in a ragged line across her hood. I spared a burst to keep the gunners down.

That did it. Something in the chopper's cabin exploded and the machine lurched. Which exposed the engine housing to my fire from a much better angle. Into which I promptly emptied the rest of my clip.

Something tore at supersonic speed through the engine housing and the chopper stopped beating air and simply fell straight down.

On top of the house, crushing in the roof. The chopper tilted into the house and I could imagine the outside wall farthest from us collapsing under the weight when the chopper exploded.

The fireball, while deflected, still reached for us. The wall against which Winsome lay and Zell was crouched disintegrated above them and chunks of cement block flew into the still rotating blades of the first chopper above my head. I was least exposed, yet I could feel the heat sear my face.

Oily smoke swirled and was whipped by the rotating blades.

Out of this manmade hell crawled Winsome, her left shoulder flaming, part of her cheek missing, and most of her clothing smoldering. Her hair was mostly seared off.

Underneath her she dragged Zell, protecting him from the flames with her own body.

The explosion had deafened me and thrown me to the ground. I crawled toward her, my elbow striking the pistol of the last SS man. Winsome collapsed right there in front of me. I managed to drag Zell out from under her. He seemed to be okay—but stunned from the explosion.

Winsome's obscenely distorted mouth said, "Zell." And I got the message. He was my charge on her dead body and her soul, wherever or however she would end up after death.

"He is okay," I said. I don't think the words came

out, but her eyes read my lips. Relief flashed through them and her head collapsed on her arms.

"Jesus fucking Horseshoe Christ," I said.

How was Winsome still breathing? She was dead, but her heart continued. She must have been in her own hell. Gunshot, on fire, part of her face gone.

Quickly, I checked Zell. He was still dazed. I thumbed the pressure point and in seconds he was out.

Crying tears of frustration I groped around for the SS guy's pistol.

I found it. I shot Winsome three times in the head. Maybe she was dead before I shot her, I'll never know. But she had to have been in eternal pain.

I limped to my feet and lifted Zell with me. The beating rotors above me dried sweat and tears on my face. Something had hit the blades for their beat was no longer rhythmic. I feared the damn things would decapitate me or maybe start flying apart.

Opening the passenger side door on Christine, I put Zell inside. My head began to hurt from returning hearing. I found the Uzi and got in.

Surprisingly, the engine was still running. I backed out, careful not to come near Winsome with the tires.

I drove off slowly, driving on someone else's lawn to avoid the dead chopper in the street. People were standing at their doors and windows watching me. I glanced blankly at them. I'd seen neater combat zones. Sirens sounded in the distance and Christine was making funny noises. Shrapnel or debris from the explosion, I guessed, had penetrated the engine somewhere. With the laser seared areas and the bullet holes throughout the body, I had to get rid of Christine—much as I hated to.

It was difficult forcing my mind to think, avoiding thoughts of a dead Winsome and the horror of her death and . . . *think!* Sheathe my heart in ice and think!

My mind wasn't working well, but it didn't take much to come up with the answer. We'd be on all radios, televideos, televiewers, newspapers, and even billboards within the hour.

Back ways, alleys, side streets, residential neighborhoods, housing subdivisions where there wasn't much traffic and small likelihood of police became my route. Soon I pulled into a side entrance under the bubble of the Auto Graveyard where I'd first hidden and then retrieved Christine.

Watching my opportunity, I drove into the mass of stacked and single cars, right back to section H-44 and all the other 1958 Plymouth Furies. I backed Christine in among her sisters and slumped down. With luck, nobody would even come near this location. And I had food and water in the back. Boy Scout that I was: Be prepared.

Sure. Be prepared. Boy Scout. Yeah. Think about a neighborhood turned into a battlefield and an inferno. Think about Winsome. Think about Zell.

I couldn't remember being as down as this, ever. Well, maybe when they killed our baby, me and Lulu's, in the hills of Thailand. But that was so long ago, it was kind of blurred. Though, I must admit, I was rather depressed when locked in a cell in the Hub and listening to Manny scream for help and not be able to do anything . . .

And Zell was gonna wake up and go stark raving fucking bananas.

Winsome.

All this because Manuel Temple possessed a special talent. I cursed that talent and the trouble it caused.

"Wyndy?" Zell's voice was harsh, maybe from emotion, maybe from exhaustion, maybe from smoke inhalation.

I turned toward him, putting my scorched left arm on Christine's steering wheel. "Yeah, kid."

"Where are we?" His clothes were burned in places and there were cuts and scratches and scrapes on the exposed skin of his face, arms, and legs.

"The Auto Graveyard. We're safe for now."

His lips trembled. "Is . . . is my, is. . . ?"

"Yeah, Zell. She's dead."

"Why?"

"I don't understand myself. That's just how it worked out." Should I have surrendered when the SS guy held Zell hostage? A question I'd take to my own grave.

"Why?!" he demanded, voice firmer.

I looked into his blazing eyes. "Because of Manny. Manny's mind. His extra-special esper ability. Everybody wanted him, Zell. To unlock secrets only dreamed of. To give humanity the stars. But everyone was selfish about it. Nobody wanted to share it. And this is the final result. Now they're gone."

He shook and trembled for a while, hugging his knees to his chest with locked arms, reminding me oh so much of Winsome that I ached for him.

His voice was barely a whisper. "Those sons of bitches. Goddamn them. Those sons of bitches." He looked sharply at me. "Did you kill 'em all?" I nodded. He continued. "Good. Fuck them anyway. Cocksuckers. Sonofabitches." His words had become louder and he spat the last out. At least he was reacting with fire in his eyes.

In a little while, his voice, now small and barely discernible, said, "What do you mean, 'Now they're gone.'?"

I explained it all to him. Told him of my meeting with Amber and confirmed his earlier guess about the fake ship in orbit. "So here we are, and no doubt every SS in the republic is zeroing in on us and Daytona. The *Nimitz* and all aboard have disappeared and are apparently on their way," I finished.

Then and there it occurred to me to wonder if the FTL system from Manny's esper process had really worked. Nobody knew the answer. They could just as well have simply winked out of existence, aircraft carrier and all aboard. Don't even think it.

I didn't know what to do. Escape, I supposed.

It was Friday night of Speedweek and as dusk fell, I

left Zell to nap in Christine and walked out for medicine, boy's clothing, bandages, and hot food. From my previous stint in Daytona, I knew the code for one of the side entrances on the graveyard's bubble.

Cops and SS were everywhere. Even though I'd cleaned myself up and wore a disguise with a long, black wig, I kept a low profile. Fortunately, most of their attention was on vehicular traffic. Random roadblocks. I saw three Christines stopped, one of the Christines was stopped and searched three times while I watched it go from a parking lot down a street and onto 95. Poor bastard.

Snatches of conversation at Publix Supermarket: "Whatever is going on?" "We were stopped just driving, the car just quit—" "A whole neighborhood . . ." "Explosions . . ." "All over the televideo." "His picture. I saw him before. He was a Willie Nelson impersonator." "I can't believe it. A mass murderer. Right here!"

Maybe I'd worn out my welcome in Daytona.

That night we ate hot food and I tended Zell's cuts and burns and some of my own. I think we needed a doctor. A couple of my burns promised to infect, no matter what I did. Not to mention the pain. Well, at least that gave me something I could control for a change. Me and a bottle of Jack Blue.

Exhaustion caused Zell to sleep most of the night. He whimpered frequently and cried out once, but didn't wake. I held his hand through the rough parts, drank sour mash, listened to Willie Nelson on the disk recorder, and thought dark thoughts.

The future was bleak. First thing, to escape Daytona: best bet, go to the 500 race Sunday and exit with the tens of thousands of other cars. Next step? What? Run again? Go where?

Ex-Texas. Mexico. Someplace other than here. Anywhere except maybe Singapore.

Disguise us again. Raise Zell so well Winsome would be proud of me. Miss Manny and Maria. While I was right fond of Zell, he couldn't replace Manny and Maria.

On the nineteenth hand, I wasn't right fond of myself currently.

The next day, Saturday, the Auto Graveyard was deserted, locked up tight. Guys who work in places like this would be at the Daytona International Speedway watching the preliminary races and qualifying races for Sunday's 500.

So I didn't need to hide my efforts. Not half a mile from this section H-44 was section N, N for NASCAR. Wrecks and shells and bodies of cars which had raced in the 500. Amongst which I'd hidden another car: an '86 or '87 Buick—hard to tell on specially made stock car bodies—I'd covered with easily pulled off plastic film which had made it look gray and rusty. After the plastic was off, it was mostly red and white. A big 22 on the top and both sides. MILLER on the hood, trunk lid, and left and right rear. Stickers like CHAMPION, STP, WINSTON, GOODYEAR, TIMEX, and PEAK applied tastefully in neat rows on the sides. "Bobby Allison" over the driver's window. Bobby Allison from Hueytown, Alabama, had always been one of my favorite stock car drivers. He even won the 1982 Daytona 500. He did win well over eighty races; they called him the leader of the "Alabama Gang."

A real stock car. In which I'd installed an extra and outsized gas tank. Which I topped off back at the pumps. One thing for sure the Auto Graveyard had was its own gas pumps. Additionally, I cannibalized another bucket seat from a nearby Pontiac and installed it for Zell. Stock cars only generally got a driver's seat.

Zell was quiet all day; shell-shocked. Battle-fatigued. Me, too.

It was difficult watching Zell mourn and feel my own terrible sense of loss at the same time. I ain't altogether certain that life is ever fair.

Everybody in Daytona goes to the 500 early. To get

there in time. To have tailgate parties. To savor. To socialize. To find good positions in the infield.

Many of them were driving replicas of past 500 winners and other stock car legends. We weren't the onliest number 22 Bobby Allisons. We must have seen a thousand 43, Richard Pettys. The King. Distinctive blue and red and some white lettering, the STP Pontiacs and Plymouths and others. King Richard didn't always drive the same manufacturer's auto. Number 9, Bill Elliot Fords were right popular, too. Fireball Roberts, Kyle and Lee Petty (son and father, respectively, of Richard), Junior Johnson, Ned Jarrett, Benny Parsons, Buddy Baker, Cale Yarborough. All were represented many times over in the crush of traffic headed for the speedway.

We swung into one of the parking lots. I estimated there were fifty thousand cars surrounding the racetrack. The bubble was down. You don't run a race with the bubble up. Maybe seating for two hundred thousand—seating they'd increased every year. Plus the two-and-a-half mile tri-oval track surrounded an infield. You went through a tunnel and could park there and watch from the infield. Sit on your car or a truck and watch from the inside, mostly along the front stretch, and party.

Over close to the back stretch was Lake Lloyd, a forty-four acre, man-made lake, the excavation from which came the dirt to build up the banking for the tri-oval track.

My purpose was to park somewhere which would allow us to depart swiftly if an emergency came up. Like somebody recognizing us.

But as I drove into the parking lot, I couldn't help but notice, since I was watching for it, cops scanning cars as people paid.

Uh oh.

Quickly, I swung out of the line of traffic and into another, rudely cutting into the line, not having any choice.

Damn!

We were going to be trapped. It was a line of cars heading for the tunnel which runs under the track to get you to the infield, the pits, the garage areas.

Emerging from the tunnel, we edged ahead inside the tri-oval.

Cars inched forward and I sweated in the cool February breeze. Zell sat quietly and stared straight ahead.

You had to go left or straight to the infield parking areas. Right for the pit and garage areas.

Two cops scrutinizing autos as they stopped to pay parking.

"Zell. I don't know what's going to happen. If they catch you, tell the truth. They shouldn't hurt you. If you run like hell and escape, hide and get on the televiewer to Silas Comfort Swallow in Ocala. Got that."

"You told me he ain't there."

"Yeah, but some of his people might still be. Tell 'em I sent you and Silas owes you."

"Wyndy, we missed the trip into space." Even through his misery, the regret was plain in his voice.

"Yeah, kid. I'll make it up to you somehow."

I tugged the brim of my hat down over my eyes and pulled out to the right, edging past the traffic lined up to pay parking.

Sticking my head out the window, I waved and whistled and pointed to the pit and garage checkpoint. The busy ticket taker waved me on.

When we got there it presented another problem. We had no pit pass. Since it was a highly restricted area, they weren't wasting cops or SS manning the gates.

An old Florida cracker detached himself from a folding chair and came over. He stood there looking down at me through the open window. "Sorry, buddy. No pit pass."

"We didn't have time to get one," I explained. "Didn't want to miss anything."

"Not my problem." He needed a shave worse than I needed a shave.

"Actually," I told him, "I am very wealthy and hate waiting in line to park." I showed him the corner of a two hundred dollar bill. He nodded perceptively and I shook hands with him and the bill was gone.

He jerked his head and lifted the gate and stood aside. I drove through and parked near the garage where they were making final preparations on the race cars. Not that you can final prepare battery powered cars all that much.

The race cars were also replicas. Current rules read you could run any previous NASCAR body style, but your car had to be a battery powered job within certain mechanical restrictions to maintain parity of competition. But they had their own numbers, not 43—Richard Petty, and so on.

We sat there and watched the preparations. The 500 starts at noon and we had an hour or so to go. I chafed at the fact that we were penned up within the confines of the track. One little bitty tunnel wasn't my idea of a decent escape route.

We took a small chance, got out, made our own personal pit stops, bought hot dogs, me a beer, Zell a cherry soda.

Then back to the car. Watched the crews push the cars out to the starting positions on pit road.

I moved the car to a vantage point with a few others down toward the scoring pylon where we could see the festivities. We climbed on the roof just as everybody else was doing on their own cars.

The televideo interviews were in full progress, guys sticking mikes into drivers' faces, even though they had their own radio systems with which they communicated to their pit crews and computer-aided analysts. If I recalled last year's 500, the televideo audience worldwide would be close to one billion, maybe more. Three hundred million on North America alone.

The entire place fell quiet and a voice came over the

loudspeakers: "Ladies and gentlemen, start your engines!"

Which gave me a little nostalgia twitch since they had no real engines.

Soon the pace car led off and forty pseudo-stock cars followed. Throaty roars came from well concealed loudspeakers on each car. I love authenticity.

Gawking like a Yankee tourist, I was craning my neck here and there watching for SS and/or cops and track security personnel.

Zell was even watching for the start of the race.

Then a guy with a handheld radio stopped alongside of us. I didn't have to read his lips. Something about no "pit pass."

"Zell," I said quietly and squeezed his thigh, "into the car. Casually."

We jumped down. I shrugged and grinned at the guy. "Just didn't want to miss anything." I showed him a two hundred dollar bill.

His face fell. "I already called it in."

"Guess we'll mosey on off, then," I said. We climbed in through the windows—real stock cars have no doors or windows. Just a detachable safety net where the window is supposed to be.

We wheeled out, heading for the tunnel exit where I'd decided I wanted to go to get away from the trapped feeling of the infield. But a track security patrol pulled alongside us and waved us down. I stopped, determined to bluff it out.

Not only did a track security agent get out of the vehicle, but so did a cop.

"Oh, shit." I pulled the hat down over my eyes again. "Made a wrong turn," I told them as they came up. "Just now leaving."

The cop eyed us suspiciously, scratched his balding head, and looked curious. I saw his eyes add up a boy and an older man and his radio went to his lips and I shot him with a stunner.

But he was a tough cop; he fell to the ground

shouting into his radio. The security agent looked at me in awe and I stunned him, too.

We jackrabbited, burning rubber, heading for the tunnel. There was little traffic now since the race was starting.

Several vehicles were turning sideways at the far end of the tunnel, blocking it.

I spun the wheel, burning more rubber, and gunned the Buick back toward the garage area, wracking my brain all the while for a way to escape.

"Onliest thing I can think of, Zell, is to head for the garage, ditch the car, and sneak over to the infield with the rest of the spectators. Maybe we can lose ourselves there."

His mouth pursed up. "Let's fight, Wyndy. Let's kick some ass. Kill some SS sons of bitches."

Not if I can help it, I thought. "We want to live to fight another day." But I admired his spunk. Kid reminded me of me. It saddened me that we were going to be captured and I wouldn't be able to be Zell's father. I would like to have done that thing.

Three police cruisers pulled around the large garage building, cutting us off. I slammed on the brakes, backed up, and headed back the way we'd just come. Not many different ways to go here.

When several police cars, three abreast and two behind them, came past the entry gate where the Florida cracker was watching with interest, I knew we'd about played out our hand.

One last chance. The break in the pit wall where the race cars came from the garages to pit road. A four-wheel slide put us on pit road. But pit road leads only one place: onto the race track.

Cop cars chased us through the wall.

"Screw it," I said, jammed the Hurst shift into second and accelerated away from them like they were dead armadillos on the highway.

Just then a great shout went through hundreds of thousands of throats.

The race had started. Behind us, I saw the pace car diving onto pit road. And I saw the cop cars come to a stop.

The field of cars whipped by the exit of pit road and I let the Buick slide right up there in the pack.

A quick look in the mirror told me we were safe for just a moment. And maybe longer.

Because it occurred to me that they wouldn't stop the race in front of a billion viewers and all these spectators.

I goosed the accelerator and we leapt past three cars going into the first turn. Hostile glances from drivers told me they knew I was some sort of gate crasher.

We had five hundred miles. I had maybe four hours to come up with a way out.

And there didn't look like there was a way out.

We passed a red and black Chevy, drafting several cars behind us.

"Shit hot!" shouted Zell, a wicked grin stretching his face. He pounded the dash with enthusiasm.

Hell, yes, I thought. Go out with a blaze of glory. I'd always wanted to be a stock car racer, race on the Grand National circuit. A lifelong ambition.

"Let's win this son of a bitch!"

22: Maria

What follows comes from various accounts and communications I've pieced together.

"Sell him out; it will buy us time," said Linoleum.

"Wyndham's personal value to Amber Lee-Smith has reached a negligible point." Silas Swallow's tone was conversational.

Maria looked between the two. "Are you talking about Wyndy, *Wyndy,* the one who has been risking his life for years for us, for your PROJECT?" She didn't wait for the answer. "I cannot believe it! He is not some sheepaloe to be discussed and done away with." She still clutched the tiny envelope in her left hand. No one had seen. WYMM? Love, WHANGON EMPTY.

Bossman looked over his newly acquired ancient spectacles. "You heard the recording, my dear."

"And my ears are just as good as yours, Silas."

"And your eyes, too, Maria. But you did not read between the lines."

"What do you mean?"

Bossman looked at Linoleum who made a face and nodded. "That's the way I see it also, sir."

For a moment Maria thought Lynn was agreeing with her.

"They are dead, somehow they died."

"Wyndham probably killed them," Linoleum said.

"No!"

Bossman held his hand up to calm Maria. "He didn't kill them. They were too valuable alive. Yet they are dead."

"You can't know that," Maria said.

Bossman's voice became more mild. "I know that well. If they were still alive, Wyndy would not have sent us the recording as is. That's all there is and that's all there will be. He could not acknowledge the fact in case of interception of the recording—or, for that matter," he looked around the room uncomfortably, "listening devices."

"I swept the house this morning," said Linoleum.

"Good," Silas nodded approvingly. "Now we must decide what to do. Wyndy, ever the impulsive rapscallion, is going to do something foolish."

Maria was shaking her head. "Not foolish. Everything Wyndy has done has been calculated, planned well."

"My dear. With the death of the two espers from the Hub, Wyndy has outlived his usefulness to Lee-Smith. After a couple of days it will become obvious; if not, their disappearance will force Madam Administrator to act. She cannot afford *not* to act."

By now Maria had sorted out her feelings, damped her emotions, and caught up with the two men. "Then there is only one conclusion to be drawn."

Bossman lifted his brows, then glanced at Linoleum. "Lynn?"

Lynn Oglethorpe Lium shivered, his wide shoulders trembled, and his expressive eyes bounced around like they wanted to escape from their sockets. "If Maria means the whole thing is over, I agree. Miz Administrator is going to strike and strike hard. She won't simply settle for the boy this time, either. She'll want everything we've got. And she'd have to be a fool to buy that orbiting fake any longer."

"That is the way I see it, too." Silas sighed. "It wouldn't be too much for Lee-Smith to conclude we have Manuel, not Wyndham." He sighed again. "Well,

I wasn't exactly ready, but . . ." He grinned. "After all this time, the prospect of action, of actually *doing it* becomes quite attractive to me."

"We're going to go." Maria was divided. At least she would be permanently reunited with her son on the *Nimitz*. On the other hand, the process had not been operationally tested on this great a scale. It was possible that the aircraft carrier would explode or disappear into some dimension she'd rather not think about. "And what about Wyndy?"

Lynn's laugh was harsh, then self-conscious. "Wyndy is most tough, Maria. He's gotten along without us through some mighty rough times. He can take care of himself."

Silas spoke gently. "Maria. Wyndy is the most capable, self-sufficient man I have ever known. Wyndy can take care of Wyndy."

"We promised him!"

"And I live up to my promises." Swallow's words became hard. "However, upon the *Nimitz* are a few thousand people whose lifetime efforts are culminating. I cannot endanger the PROJECT." He stood and put his hand on her shoulder. "Of anybody I've ever known, Wyndy would understand. *He* would expect me to sacrifice him for the well-being of the PROJECT. For your safety. For Manuel's. When he sent us the recording to tip us off, he acknowledged that I should do what's best for all concerned. He knew that, Maria, else he would not have communicated thusly with us."

Maria did not want to admit that Silas was correct. She made an affirmative sound in her throat and looked around Bossman's office. The flowers were gorgeous. The sweet fragrance of gardenias had permeated the entire room.

"Get things moving, Lynn," Swallow said.

Linoleum nodded and went out the far door.

Silas said, "You have most of your records stored on the *Nimitz*, correct?"

"Yes, Silas."

"Run that program to dump everything which remains to the ship. Instigate the 'destroy' program so that if anyone other than one of us tries for access . . . well, you know the routine."

"Yes, Silas."

"What is wrong, Maria? You are going to join your son. You are going to be a part of the most ambitious endeavor any human has ever undertaken. You are going to escape from this all-the-time secretiveness, the suspicion, the danger. Yet you do not show it."

"Neither did Lynn," she said to stall.

"He seldom shows anything. It's more than just Wyndy, isn't it? What was the note on the envelope in the flowers?"

She squeezed her left hand tighter and did not answer.

"May I see it?"

She handed it to him.

He unfolded the tiny bit of envelope. "He wants you to marry him, is that it?"

Maria nodded wearily. She wished she could cry, but too many recent years of hardship precluded tears that easily.

"What is your answer?" Silas' voice was a whisper.

"Does it matter?" Her chin went up. "I can't contact him. He will be left behind. What difference does it make?" Oddly, she kept thinking of Manuel and what Manuel thought of Wyndy.

"It matters to me," Silas said. "You have been sitting on my own proposal for over a year. I . . . expected this . . . final move, the end of our efforts and our escape on the *Nimitz* to be the starting point of our new life. We'd start over together." He sat down in his leather chair heavily.

"But you suspected otherwise," Maria said.

"After all these years? Maria, I know you as well as I know myself."

Maria reigned in her emotions. "Silas—you have been so good to me, to Manuel. When we arrive

where it is we are going, I will give you my answer."
She set her jaw in determination.

"The rules state everybody must be married."

Maria couldn't help but laugh. "Silas, you shovel
that stuff better here than they do in the barn. You
are the Bossman."

He grinned slyly. "Well, I had to try it." His face
sobered. "Between us, I do feel terrible about Wyndy.
I thought before that he expected to be left behind,
and that might still be true. On the contrary, why
would he send that note with its contents and obvious
future references?"

"Maybe he figured it out and is heading for the
Nimitz right now?" Hope leaped in her voice.

"It's the only conclusion." Bossman nodded to himself. "Unless something comes up or he is unable to
join us. Well, we will be on lookout for him."

"Shall we get to work, Silas?"

"It will be my pleasure, my dear. It is something I
have been looking forward to for a long, long, time."

Maria glanced at her watch. "I have the finances set
up. A few instructions and they all revert to the Swallow Foundation."

Silas pushed his chair back. "Just make sure they
understand that we'll sort of 'appear' somewhere in
the next day or two and perhaps tap the funds for our
final supplies." They had not been able to stock the
Nimitz for long-term, as that activity would have tipped
off the authorities. Whereas in fact, he had been stockpiling supplies. Food, water, oxygen, tools, implements,
machines, and the million and one other things you
need for a few thousand people to sail the stars and
explore same and maybe begin colonizing some planet.

The remainder of that day and far into the night
they worked; messages went out and were received.
The captain of the *Nimitz* was given his instructions.
The genetic engineers and a few others at the Ocala
farm were notified and made ready for final departure. VTOL aircraft and choppers ferried a few peo-

ple, some special strains of sheepaloe, and the remaining items still at the farm which had not yet been transferred to the ship.

At midnight, Crane Plash took Silas and Maria in the last load to the *Nimitz*. As they flew, Maria sank back into one of the VIP seats, weariness overcoming her interest in the flight.

Yet she worried. And not just about me reaching the ship before it cast off. She worried about the success of the process the engineers had garnered from Manuel. Unless pushed, Silas had agreed not to try it. His initial plan was to escape past the twelve mile recognized international boundary where they'd ostensibly be safe and test the process and equipment more at their leisure. But, to her, events were coming too fast, and some kind of atmospheric pressure seemed to be driving these events. Though she hoped, she didn't really believe that Amber Lee-Smith would give them the time they needed. If nothing else, Lee-Smith could chase them and claim "hot pursuit."

Then Silas would have to give the order to turn on the Manny Machine. The nickname the scientists and engineers had given the device was "the starhopper" from Manuel's mindhopping. Though it wasn't a single device, but a series of interconnecting electronics and power grids.

And it hadn't turned out to be what she'd feared: a biolink, where somehow they connected Manuel with the ship and its power plants.

Manuel had tried to explain it to her on one of her and Silas' frequent trips to the ship.

"Look, Mom. It's like making a wrong turn on purpose."

"Do you really understand all this stuff yourself, Manuel?"

"Generally. The links and relationships. Not the math and specific physics."

Maria was relieved and her face showed it.

Manny saw her look and said, "Zell would understand."

To divert his attention, Maria said, "Go ahead, tell me more."

"It's like your brain. It takes very little energy for certain actions. Almost a perpetual motion machine. We place electronic 'gates' around the thing to be translated—the *Nimitz*. These gates are more like electronic poles. We've nicknamed 'em 'tent poles.' They weave an electronically controlled web around the item to be translated."

Webs!

Maria was looking askance at her son.

"Lemme keep going, Mom. Okay. These gates and webs work through another dimension and simply put you where you're targeted. We're translated through that other dimension, they say right away, the word—?"

"Instantaneous?"

"Yep. Not only that, but the action generates its own power which must be stored or discharged and dissapatated . . ."

"Dissipated," she corrected and thought his speech pattern reminded her of Wyndy.

"Sure, Mom." Like he was tolerating her interruptions. He continued. "So sometimes we can emerge into real space with a bang, which comes from the energy discharge. Or maybe all the air we push aside when we appear. We can appear slowly and discharge the energy or store it and not make a bang when we appear. That's the way we want to do it in case we accidentally emerge into something solid like a star or an asteroid or an ice cream cone." He giggled. Then his face turned serious again. "They learned something else, Mom. They can use all that energy to move us through the air, for example, slowly. Just keep the web powered a little, not to max necessary to translate us. We can fly!"

Maria decided she didn't understand and, what's

more, didn't need to understand, didn't want to understand.

Manny read her look. "You still don't understand?"

Humoring him, she said, "Not exactly."

"Jeez, Mom. With our nav systems we know where we're going. Just think of that as a picture in a book full of pages of pictures. When the tent poles and the web get going, it's like they grab the edges of the picture on that page of the book and we *translate* ourselves into that picture." Manny looked superior. "We've got two A4W nuclear power plants on board which give us enough initial power for the pulse to go through the tent poles and the web." He paused. "These power plants can drive the *Nimitz* at full power for thirteen years without stopping before refueling. We can be gone forty or fifty years using their energy for shipboard needs, and pulses for the starhopper. But whenever we translate, we can store the resultant energy. See?"

Manny was like Zell. He remembered the words and definitions he'd encountered in spelling bees. Not to mention the fact that hanging around scientists and engineers will change your vocabulary, if not your language. I didn't know whether he was suffering in that respect from my absence or not. More 'n likely, exposure to different things was good for him.

"So we can travel faster than light," Maria said.

Manny nodded vigorously. "Though the actual fact of doing that thing takes some time. I don't understand all I know about relativity and quantum mechanics yet."

Maria was staring at him like he was a zoo animal. Like mothers do sometimes.

Manny didn't notice. "We can even go *slower than light!*" Then he saw her face and its features saying she was overwhelmed with all this explanation. "Zell would know what I'm talking about." Then his face fell.

Maria had to take him in her arms and do another

mother thing. "From mindhopper to starhopper, you are something, Manuel Temple."

Silas had entered the spacious cabin allocated to Maria and Manny at that moment. "Starhopper? From a mindhopper? I like the sound of it. It rather rolls off your tongue like it was there all the time and you didn't know it." So the device became officially "The Manuel Temple Starhopper." Or simply the "starhopper."

Crane Plash descended to the off-angle flight deck of the *Nimitz* in Tampa Bay, breaking Maria's reverie. The ship was floating in the industrial mooring area. Access only by boat, plane, or chopper. The flight decks and the superstructure were brightly lighted. Eight football fields, she remembered the comparison. She guessed the superstructure to be nine or ten levels high, and estimated the same number of levels below decks. Men and machines were frantically active, moving equipment and supplies from the flight deck to the giant elevator for transport below. These would be stored throughout the ship, but mainly on the hangar deck below with the choppers, and VTOL and scout aircraft.

She followed Silas out of the chopper. Their luggage went elsewhere, and they took a personnel elevator to the bridge.

Manny was there and flew into his mother's arms. "Mom!"

She didn't say anything, but held him for a moment. Her eyes surveyed the elegant appointments of the bridge. Somehow, Silas fit well into this alien environment. She could see him pause as if to feel, to suck in the vibrancy of the ship.

Finally, he shook himself and strode forward to shake hands with the captain. "Skipper."

Captain Charles Nelson took Silas' hand. "Welcome aboard, sir." Nelson was a deep-voiced, slender man with auburn hair clipped in the old tradition of a crew cut. I would have been calling him "Lord" or "Admiral" or "Half" in a New York minute. His left arm was partially paralyzed from an accident, and he only moved his left hand occasionally. He was fiercely loyal to Silas. "Your orders?"

"Sail at your earliest convenience, Captain Nelson."

"Aye, sir." He looked at a subordinate officer, nodded slightly, and said, "Right away. We've already released our moorings. All is in readiness. We're holding position here by engine power."

The background rumble increased as the carrier began slowly to move forward.

"It is imperative that we reach the twelve mile limit as soon as possible," Silas said. He would have dispatched the carrier earlier since his chopper could have joined it at sea, but he was afraid to tip his hand to Amber.

"Aye, sir. Our movement and speed here in the bay are restricted and controlled by the harbormaster's computers." He looked apologetic. "It was that or accept too many tugs and a live pilot or two."

"You acted correctly." Silas looked worried. He turned to Maria. "It's three o'clock; nothing is going to happen. Why don't you try to get some sleep?"

"I will wait for Wyndy here." Maria's jaw was firm with determination.

Silas swore an infrequent oath.

"Mom, Mom," Manny tugged at her jeans. "Is Wyndy coming?"

Maria was confused for a moment. "I hope so."

Silas said, "Maybe not, son. He's still leading a wild goose chase."

"But we've *got* to wait for him!"

Silas placed his hand on Manny's shoulder. "*We've got* other responsibilities, Manuel. If Wyndy can, he will get here. He can rent a chopper or hijack one. Every pilot knows how to obtain our frequency from the harbormaster, so he'll let us know he's coming."

By dawn, they were out of the bay and under the Skyway which reaches from Bradenton to St. Petersburg, spanning the mouth of the bay. No longer did giant supports rise from the bay to hold the bridge aloft; one of the first applications of bubble technology allowed a span without intermediate support.

Once free and into shipping lanes, Captain Nelson was able to increase his speed.

While Silas went below to coordinate and organize and plan with the supervisors of the different divisions, Maria and Manny stayed on the bridge. Maria drank coffee and listened to the radio for word from me. Manny plastered himself against the great windows, against the electronic displays, and finally fell asleep in the Admiral's chair (reserved for Silas).

Slightly after eight in the morning, a soft, pulsing, electronic alarm jerked everyone on the bridge to alertness.

"Radar, report," snapped Captain Nelson.

"Ah, roger, Captain," came a voice over the intercom. "Bogies. Choppers. A herd of 'em. Swarming this way."

Nelson punched a button. "Mr. Swallow to the bridge. Emergency."

Shortly, Silas tumbled from the elevator and rushed to join Nelson at the windows. "Status?"

"Choppers," Nelson said. "More than a dozen." He punched a couple of buttons and the screen at his side showed the radar picture. "Closing fast."

"Type?"

"Gunships and troop carriers." Nelson flexed his left hand.

Silas looked over at Maria. "This is it, my dear." He turned to Nelson. "Alert engineering. We have the firepower and missiles to resist, but why risk damage, death, injury."

"Aye, sir." He flipped a switch on his console. "Engineering. Prepare for engagement of starhopper."

"Roger," came the reply. "Destination."

Bossman leaned toward the speaker. "Plan one. We go for provisioning."

Plan one was to go to the Pacific island of Saipan where Silas had been stockpiling supplies for that very purpose.

Silas said, "Captain, challenge those choppers."

"Aye, sir." He flipped another switch. "Comm, give me the leader of the choppers on the universal freak."

"Roger, Captain. You're on."

Nelson spoke into the mike/speaker. "Chopper force, this is CVN 68, the *Nimitz*. Please identify yourself and state your purpose."

Static for a moment, then, "*Nimitz*, this is Republic of Dixie chopper force. By authority of the Administrator and the Charter, I direct you to shut down your engines and prepare to accept our landing on your decks."

Nelson looked uncomfortable. "I remind you, chopper leader, that we are well past the twelve mile limit. You have no authority here."

"Call it immediate pursuit, national emergency, my instructions remain the same, *Nimitz*."

Silas spoke up. "Chopper leader. This is Silas Swallow. I would like to remind you that we have lasers, missiles, and antiaircraft guns aboard. Tell Amber Lee-Smith I will not hesitate to use them."

"Understand, sir," came the leader's voice, "but I have my orders. I also have at my disposal a satellite laser should we encounter your fire."

Silas drew his finger across his neck.

Nelson flipped a switch. "That's all, Comm."

"Roger. Disconnected."

"Shall we do that thing, Captain?" Bossman said conversationally.

Nelson said, "Stop all engines."

The rumbling ceased almost immediately. But the carrier continued forward under her momentum.

"Engineering?" the captain said.

"Ready as we'll ever be, Captain. Tent poles in position. Feed her the power and tell the computer and we're gone."

"Understand," Nelson said. "Mr. Swallow?"

Silas said, "Well, I always thought there ought to be a lot of fanfare, worldwide televideo coverage, bands, hoopla, speeches and vendors selling hot dogs and beer. But it must not have been meant to be. Power on."

Nelson sidled to another console, this one with a combination-locked bubble cover. He tapped an order into the computer from that terminal. "Power up and ready. All we have to do is tell the computer to activate the program and we're gone." Silas walked over. The Captain said, "Punch this key and the process starts."

Silas looked around and reached his hand out.

Nelson nodded to his subordinate. A voice boomed out throughout the ship. "Prepare to go translight. Prepare to go translight." An occurrence all had been previously briefed on, though nobody knew exactly what to expect.

Silas' hand touched the switch.

"Wait!" shouted Maria. Manny was clinging to her leg like a leech.

Silas looked annoyed. "And why?"

"Wyndy."

"It's too late." Silas gestured at the choppers closing in on the radar. He swept his gaze to the rear. "I fancy I can see the choppers with my own eyes, Maria. We have no choice."

"Try the radio."

Silas' features turned irritated. He nodded curtly to Nelson. Nelson flipped switches, and said in a low voice, "Comm? Give me the general freak again." He turned and nodded to Silas.

Silas spoke into the mike/speaker. "Wyndy. Calling Pembroke Wyndham. If you're out there, please respond."

All stood silent for a minute. It occurred to Maria that Silas was indeed giving Wyndy every chance he could; especially, since if he didn't, he would probably end up marrying Maria. She admitted that Silas was being more than fair when it would be to his advantage to desert Wyndy.

Silas said, "Wyndy, last chance. Speak now or forever hold your peace."

Almost a quote from the marriage ceremony. As if to remind her that she was the high stakes in this game. Which, if nothing else, pumped up her ego.

Silas Swallow jerked his head angrily. His finger darted for the keyboard and punched the key which Nelson had indicated would engage the device and send them translight.

Nothing happened immediately. Maria looked around nervously.

"Bubble first, Mom," Manny said.

And sure enough, the bubble rose slowly around the vessel and closed at the top. Then it turned opaque.

Captain Nelson said, "Next in the sequence is the night lighting." Sure enough, under the opaqued bubble, the ship's lighting all came on. Instrumentation on the bridge glowed green and red.

Klaxons begin hooting.

"Power to the poles," said a voice over the ship's speakers. "Standby." Pause.

"Better sit down," Nelson said, "and strap in. The grid around the keel of the ship is designed to use the system like the other webs. However, it has a different power requirement to provide artificial gravity. But you never can tell."

Maria sat in the Admiral's swivel chair and a sailor locked it from movement. Manny crawled into her arms.

"One minute," came the announcement.

Pressure built up in her ears as giant pumps came on, pressurizing the bubble. She worked her jaws to pop her ears.

They were going to leave Wyndy. Maria tried to think about it, but circumstances prevented her from deep remorse right then.

"Forty seconds."

"We'll know soon, Manny." Silas was as excited as she'd ever seen him. "Almost anticlimatic, ain't it, son?"

Manny didn't answer.

"Thirty seconds."

Silas turned to her. "Two step translation, this. On our first trip, we don't want to take any chances. So we'll 'appear' in space, then translate to the ocean. Kind of a line of sight thing. Didn't want to chance going through solid objects and materializing too close to the surface."

"Ten, nine, eight . . ."

Manny's arms were around her neck. She felt a mental link to him, and fed him reassurance she didn't necessarily feel herself.

". . . three, two, one, activate."

There was a moment of slight disorientation, and Maria no longer felt the swells of the Gulf of Mexico gently rock the *Nimitz*. Manny's arms were almost choking her. She felt lighter than normal.

Silas and Nelson were glued to screens and instrumentation. "Engineering, report," ordered Nelson. The same disembodied voice said, "All systems working within specks, gravity web is being adjusted; other than that, all systems operational."

"Where *are* we?" demanded Silas in a thunderous, nonmild voice.

The voice said, "A few hundred miles above the Pacific Ocean. Dimming deck lights and reducing opaque for viewing."

Deck lights dimmed, and the bubble cleared.

Stars. Brilliant stars. Millions. Maria noted one portion of the bubble remained opaque—probably to combat that side's exposure to solar rays.

A slice of the Earth. Just like from the satellite pix.

Momentary disorientation. Which way was up or down? But normal pull at seat of pants reassuring.

Incredibly deep blue. She recognized dawn coming

up on the West coast of North America. So that's why they call it navy blue, she thought. White clouds layered here and there, interrupting the blue. Color and sight belittling any gemstone, mesmerizingly attractive. Blanket of dark broken by intermittent lights directly below in the central Pacific.

The bubble opaqued again.

"One minute to translight." The same voice as before. "This time to a point a mile or so above the Marianas trench."

"The deepest part of the ocean," Silas said, "right off Saipan."

Another short spell of disorientation, then a settled feeling. Bubble went from opaque to clear. And there they were. A mile up. Many miles out from barely discernible islands. Some lights showed, but atmospheric density seemed to blur Maria's vision and she momentarily regretted the loss of clarity from space.

"Take her down, Captain," Silas directed.

"Aye, sir. Engineering, continue to run program."

"Rog."

Slowly the carrier sank to the surface of the Pacific. When she settled in, pressurization pumps turned off, the power web was discontinued and the bubble retracted. After a while, the engines began to rumble and the *Nimitz* headed for Saipan. By dawn, they were holding in a position west of Saipan.

Maria was still with Silas on the bridge. He pointed to the island in front of them, green and brown with white beaches and a lagoon on the western side. "Saipan. Fourteen miles long, five wide at the widest. Highest point, Mount Tapachou, fifteen hundred and fifty-one feet high." His arm moved slightly to indicate another island, from this distance appearing to practically adjoin Saipan. "Tinian," he said. "About three miles south of Saipan. A smaller island, more seaside cliffs, maybe ten by five at the widest. The island from where the Enola Gay departed with her atomic bomb bound for Hiroshima. In a valley there is the deepest and some of the richest topsoil on Earth. One estimate is thirty-six feet. It is my intention that while we are ferrying our supplies from Saipan, we mine a ton or two of that topsoil for our plants right here on the *Nimitz.*"

Silas' enthusiasm was contagious. Soon he had a map of the Marianas on his screen and was pointing between islands and the map.

"On the far side of Tinian, Rota. South of that, Guam. Let's see, look north of Saipan. About sixty miles. There. That smudge in the clear light of dawn. That's Anatahan. Where the last Japanese were captured a few years after World War II."

Maria thought that didn't mean much to her, but would to Wyndy.

For almost two days, choppers and rotary-winged VTOLs labored to load all the supplies Silas Swallow had stockpiled on Saipan. The quick mining of topsoil from sparsely inhabited Tinian was completed first.

The work continued all the first day, the first night, and the second day. It was completed about three the following morning and the *Nimitz* sailed, heading out to sea and away from observation. Judicious electronics countermeasures had kept any word of the ship's presence from being communicated to the outside world. After all, these days and times, there aren't any American aircraft carriers. Much less sailing around the Pacific and taking on enough supplies to last years.

Maria was well rested, for a change, and was determined to resume her full-time duties as a mother. Additionally, she intended to volunteer as a computer instructor in the ship's school. It was difficult to get Manny on a decent schedule what with all the activity and the upcoming fateful launch into space, unknown space.

In fact, of the thousands on board, at four that morning, none were asleep, no matter the exhaustion from the almost breakneck effort of recent days.

Again, Maria was on the bridge with Silas; Manny

was running the elevator up and down to his pleasure and to Captain Nelson's displeasure. He would also wander into the officer's wardroom to sneak a doughnut frequently. The wardroom was crowded as there were monitoring systems the off-duty personnel could watch to observe their launch into space.

Meanwhile, the younger officers tuned into satellite broadcasts of sporting events, many obviously going to miss the Americanism of sports. Hell, I read the sports pages first every morning myself.

Maria sat next to Silas sipping coffee, waiting for the engines to die and the translating process to begin.

The elevator doors opened and Manny wandered out desultorily. Maria thought he was simply exhausted from being so far off schedule for a young boy.

Manny walked outside the bridge onto one of the wings and stood in the night winds alone. His striking pose stirred an emotion within Maria. While there were other children on board, Manny had not yet made friends completely with them. He was still an oddity: "The mindhopper." But Maria didn't think that was his problem. He stood there for a while and then she joined him.

"Hi."

"Hi, Mom."

Maria could tell he was depressed. Well, so was she. But she was a mother and mothers gotta take care of children.

"Manuel, we have not talked much. An event of singular remark is about to take place—"

"Aw, Mom. I know all that. It's . . ."

"What is it, Manny?" she said gently. Which startled him as she seldom called him Manny.

"Lots of things."

"Like what?"

"Oh, I miss my friends, and Wyndy and Zell already. Zell really likes this technical scientific stuff."

Maria felt a pang of her own. "I feel like I'm deserting Wyndy, Manuel. I suppose it's normal. It's not nice, but it's normal. We don't have a choice."

"Yes, we do, Mom. We can go looking for him."

"I wish we could. But Silas is right. It's too dangerous. We don't know where he is. And we don't want to jeopardize all this." She waved her hand inclusively over the entire ship.

Manny spit over the railing like any kid would and didn't appear to notice his mother's disapproving look. Stars winked above and Maria wondered where the *Nimitz* would finally end up.

"Mom?" Manny brought her back to the present. "I talked to my friends. The other mindhoppers. While I was standing here a few minutes ago. We all tried together real hard to find Wyndy. I thought I could find him myself. But none of us is near enough to him."

"Wyndy is not a mindhopper, Manuel."

"Yeah. That's why I can't find him even with help. Isn't there anything we can do?''"

"No," said Silas.

Maria was startled as she hadn't heard him come up on them. A warm Pacific breeze blew her hair back and she imagined silvery flying fish leaping in the waves around the *Nimitz'* bow so far in front of and below her.

Silas said, "I would if I could, Manuel."

"Shit," said Manny.

"Manuel Temple!" Maria burst out.

"Well," said Silas mildly, "the boy speaks his mind."

"Mr. Swallow?" said an intercom nestled alongside Manny's arm.

"Yes, Captain?"

"I recommend you come in ASAP, sir. The men in the wardroom have picked up a major news story about us."

The three went inside the bridge. At the back, Captain Nelson was adjusting a large screen televideo.

The *Nimitz* appeared on the screen. The voice-over

announcer was talking. ". . . network has learned the connection to the disappearance of the aircraft carrier *Nimitz*, its entire crew and scientific community, and the elusive billionaire-in-charge, Silas Comfort Swallow, two days ago." The announcer paused. "According to intercepted police communication, the driver of the unregistered car number 22 is wanted in connection with financier Swallow and his people."

The shot segued from a still of the ship to an overhead chopper shot of the Daytona 500 Speedway and surroundings. Nestled in a sea of parked cars and buses, the Speedway was a riot of color from the stands and infield. Race cars buzzed around the track.

"An hour into the race," the network sports anchor continued, "and number 22 is actually *leading* the race. While we suspected something out of the ordinary, we were just now able to confirm it." A camera followed number 22 as it sped around the two-and-a-half-mile track. Upper left, an insert popped into view. Two photographs appeared. "It is believed that these two people are in car number 22. The one on the left has several aliases, but it is believed his real name is Pembroke Wyndham. The other is a young boy, age as yet not released, named Zell Creek. Wyndham is known to have been in the direct employ of Silas Comfort Swallow."

Manny was jumping up and down shouting wordlessly, bouncing psychic surges off everybody on the bridge.

The picture cut to an after-the-fact chopper tape of Winsome's wrecked and burning house, and the three dead choppers right there in a residential subdivision. ". . . some kind of fierce battle with police and security forces from the Hub. Many dead. Wyndham and the Creek boy are the only ones to survive this localized holocaust. Neighbors describe it variously as '. . . hell, an urban combat zone . . .' and '. . . a real war, right here in Daytona.' "

The picture flashed back to Daytona and the announcer. "We go now to our man in the pits for an update. What have you got for us, Chris?"

Cut to a young guy with windblown short, sandy hair who had to hold a microphone because of the noise from the track and the crowds. "Eyewitnesses say the car outran police and had nowhere else to go other than onto the track. It is suspected they are driving an internal combustion engine car. It is possible that their car can run the entire race without refueling. However, at those speeds, it's unknown whether the tires can last without being changed."

Maria was chewing on the knuckles of her left hand.

"Have your contacts with track security indicated what action they are going to take?" asked the announcer.

"No," replied Chris, "but speculation has it they will simply wait out the race. To stop *the* Daytona 500 would ruin this culmination of Speedweek and the race promoters will not order it. I've also heard that the local police and the authorities in the Hub do not wish the adverse publicity of this local problem on a worldwide telecast. More than a billion viewers . . ."

"They're getting it anyway," said Captain Nelson.

"Well, dip me in spit," said Silas. "Wyndy finally made his play and look where it ended him up."

"It's Wyndy, it's Wyndy. I knew he was in trouble!" shouted Manny.

Maria didn't know what to think. Wyndy cornered. Would she and Manny be disappointed again?

"Look at that," Silas said.

Cameras on top of the pressbox at the Speedway panned the immediate area and there were many SS and police choppers simply hovering or already landed on the nearby airstrip.

"He'll never escape from all that," Silas said.

"We can rescue him," Manny urged.

Silas stood, shoulders stooped, in front of the televideo watching. He turned to Maria. "Is that your wish, too, my dear?"

Suddenly, there it was. Her decision. Silas knew what he'd asked of her. It was time for her to choose between Silas and Wyndy. "If," she said hesitantly, "I ask you to help Wyndy, would you do so?"

"Yes." Silas' voice was clear and unequivocal.

"If I accept *your* marriage proposal, would you still rescue Wyndy?"

"And endanger the *Nimitz*?" Silas paused. "If you requested it, so be it."

"Damn it, Silas. I resent you putting me in this position. I resent having to make a choice between you and Wyndy for marriage. Damn you, damn you all. *You* should attempt to save Wyndy and Zell because of loyalty. Wyndy single-handedly outguessed and outran the SS and the Hub, and bought you the time to complete your PROJECT and go to space. He was tortured along with my son at the Hub. He saved Manuel from the Hub, else you'd still be talking to scientists and engineers and simply dreaming about going to space. Wyndy has been the fulcrum upon whom this whole operation has pivoted. Wyndy has been the linchpin. You owe him. You don't owe me, I don't owe you. His contribution has been as valuable or more so than anyone's and I *damn* well expect you to respond to that, and not to put pressure on me to decide whom I will marry. I'm not one of your pawns. Manuel and I are legitimate parts of this enterprise and will remain such." She had been talking closer and closer to his face and he had backed up at the vehemence in her words. Now he was backed against the screen of the giant televideo and a two-foot number 22 Buick raced around the track and disappeared behind his head.

Maria glared around. Captain Nelson had diplomatically faded back to his command station.

Silas Comfort Swallow, billionaire, started to say something, but Maria cut him off. She hardly noticed Manny standing there apart from her, staring at her with amazement.

"Silas, it is time for you to make a decision. Either stand up to your commitments as I've just outlined them to you, or let me and my son off this ship right now." She took a deep breath and stepped back from him.

Silas relaxed only a little. "But we still need the boy."

"Too damn bad," Maria said. "Your decision?"

Silas hesitated only a second longer. "We'll get Wyndy—if we can. You saw those choppers around the Speedway?"

Maria felt relieved. "Silas, I am not finished with you. You have played with me lately, toyed with me and my future life like some obscene god. You are not God. Just because you are in charge of this operation does not mean you are in charge of lives. You have assumed I will marry you. I will admit I love you to some extent, some which I cannot define, but it is not the marrying kind of love. I have been loyal to you and helped you for years, and I appreciate you standing by me and my family during our troubles. But you do not have the *right* to control our lives. Do you understand?"

"Yes, Maria," he said meekly.

"One damn last thing," she said, wagging her finger at Bossman. "Next time you court a woman who has a child, you would best serve your own cause should you not refer to her offspring as 'the boy' or 'the girl.' Sounds like 'the dog.' Kids are special to their parents and not some general reference noun. Wyndy addresses people as people, even though it may be a little rough at times."

Silas was nodding his head like a balloon in the wind. "Okay, okay. Let's go get him."

Maria dropped her finger. She turned. "Captain Nelson?" Her voice was commanding.

He looked up from his console. "Yes, ma'am?"

"If we extract Pembroke Wyndham from his predicament, will you perform the marriage ceremony for us?"

Manny sat down on the deck heavily and started crying.

Nelson glanced uneasily at Silas Swallow. "It is a part of my authorized duties, ma'am."

Silas' whole body shook and he sighed. "I will be best man."

And Maria relaxed. Maybe a new Maria. She sat on the floor and took Manny in her arms. She glanced up at Silas. "Thank you, Silas. Would you be so kind as to see to the rescue of my future husband?"

Silas hurried over to Captain Nelson. "The race is almost two hours old now, Captain. That gives us less than two hours."

Nelson shrugged. "Our problem is how. Daytona is on the coast. Simply set down in the Atlantic? Or hover over the Atlantic and send a chopper or aircraft for him?"

"Nah," said Silas, excitement at planning to beat Amber Lee-Smith one final time helping to assuage the disappointment he felt at losing Maria. "You saw all those SS choppers? There is no way our choppers or aircraft could get through that gauntlet. But, I have an idea . . ."

Maria was surprised at her own feelings. Relief. Shock at her own assertiveness. Happiness because Manuel was happy. Anticipation at seeing Wyndy again. A warm, fuzzy glow when thinking of marriage to him. She didn't want to think of . . . Winsome Creek. Those explosions in their neighborhood—a small holocaust. Only the two of them escaped. Winsome was dead. On the screen Maria saw a still photo of Winsome, a startlingly attractive woman, then alongside that photo came another, a photo taken immediately after the firefight. Maria recoiled at the sight. What kind of woman had Winsome been?

Her son Zell would need a family. And would have one.

And Wyndy? What kind of odds were in his favor? Few. He was in terrible danger. Now that she thought about it, his chances of escape were slim. And that saddened her. But he had survived plenty up until now. Would Silas be able to save Wyndy?

Silas was saying, ". . . the only way we can avoid a satellite laser threat."

It occurred to Maria that only Pembroke Wyndham could have personally fought off three chopper loads of SS and police, escaped with Zell, and wound up in front of more than a billion people leading one of the top three sporting events in the world.

23: The Checkered Flag

The current drivers of The National Association of Stock Car Auto Racing, NASCAR, had decided among themselves to eliminate number 22. Obviously, they'd tuned their car communications onto a common frequency and took umbrage at our nonunion entry.

A 1994 replica of the reborn Hudson sucked up on our rear bumper. A '58 Chevy Impala slowed up and moved in front of us. I was thankful that our Buick had a roll bar.

Most of the cars in the race had a top end of maybe one hundred and fifty miles an hour and, for safety, had a bubble encasing the driver's seat which was activated upon collision, much the same as the old airbag system, only it could be finer-tuned to higher or lower impact tolerances. So their drivers were perfectly safe.

Our number 22 Buick had only one advantage: speed. Top end maybe one eighty—but I was sticking with the safety of traffic. I didn't want to be out there by myself. Who knew what Amber Lee-Smith might try. A chopper with a magnet, a skyhook, or a laser?

The Impala driver was good. He drifted up the oval banking of turn number 1 and showed me a little daylight. I knew full well what he was doing. As soon as I surged ahead, he'd cut back down, forcing us into a spin. We'd hit the wall and prang into the infield.

I goosed the Buick gently, tapped the brakes and waited my opportunity. The Impala saw us seem to jump forward, so he cut down to where we should have been, ready to clip our front end.

But we weren't there. As he went down, I cut right, up the banking—a dangerous maneuver in the corners—and whipped by him.

As we powered ahead down the back stretch, in the mirror I saw the Impala lose it and spin into the infield, spraying grass and dirt into the air.

We blasted at the full one eighty, me slowing only for the turns at the end of the backstretch. I kept the RPMs at about the redline of 7500. The street Buick of that year would turn three, maybe four, thousand RPM.

Ahead were several slower cars we'd been lapping with regularity for the last three hours. These cars all had four hundred numbers on them, signifying rookies. Perhaps the rookies wouldn't give us as much trouble as the veterans, so I lodged us in a group led by number 419. We settled in close to the bumper of number 444.

Zell was keeping track of the number of laps we'd run and matching that with the scoreboard and the scoring pylon. Two and a half miles per lap, five hundred miles goes by quickly. Each time we passed the start/finish line, Zell would sing out the lap number. Like "Thirty. One seventy to go."

In my mind was a fear of tire wear. Regular NASCAR racers were running tires which wouldn't wear; and because of the lack of maintenance and in an effort for safety, there were no longer rules which called for mandatory pit stops. So the race nowadays was run straight through without the old requirement of at least four pit stops. But the tires I'd put on the Buick, while modern and guaranteed et fucking cetera, weren't designed for high speed racing. The tires on the battery powered cars around me were. If a tire blew at over 150 MPH, it might not be fatal if I could keep the machine under control, but it would result in our immediate capture.

Not to mention that on the two-and-a-half-mile course, we'd gone 160 of the 200 laps. Forty more laps, a hundred miles, and then we were going to be nailed right there on international televideo.

The wind howled through the open windows—though the aerodynamics shot most of it past the windows without scooping in and slowing us down.

Zell looked exhausted. He was still counting laps. Three hours of going round and round, even at these speeds, was losing its appeal. And the loss of his mother tore at him. Well, it would tear at him a lot longer.

He saw me glance at him and shouted and pointed to his wrist. And I'd thought he wasn't paying attention. "One hour," I yelled, holding up one finger.

He nodded in reply and lifted his shoulders and eyebrows in a question.

I shrugged. How the hell did I know how we would escape? If I had a plan with even a small chance of success, I'd have tried it by now. A deadly and final web was enclosing us, and I could feel the sticky strands tighten around us.

The veterans were closing back in on us now and I spurted ahead of them, weaving through the pack of rookies. The backstretch came up in front of us and I slowed to maintain about a four-car-length distance between us and our nearest pursuer.

Right then a chopper flew over us and slghtly ahead of us, disregarding the safety of the great crowd within the Speedway. Had to be illegal, but maybe they had permission as the telecasting network. Cameras hung from its belly and poked out of most of its openings. At least they weren't weapons.

Suddenly, I shouted at Zell and pointed at the chopper. Doubtless they captured that for their viewers, thinking that I'd flung a defiant finger at them. While it hadn't been my intention, I couldn't remember *which* finger I'd used.

"A plan!" my voice hollered.

Zell was all eyes and ears.

Reaching down between the seats, I patted the Uzi where I'd clamped it. I faced Zell. "We get a chance," I yelled, "we hijack a chopper." I swept my arm toward the infield. "Look for a chopper on the ground. Maybe one for televideo or emergency medical evacuation of an injured driver or spectator." I had too many things to watch while driving to do the extensive looking necessary myself.

Zell nodded elaborately to show that he understood. "Number one seventy. Thirty to go."

Two more laps of judicious driving, and I was fighting off attempts by an '85 Olds to run us off the track. The Olds, number 384, was a tenacious bastard and I was toying with him because he was the only one near us and I could stay ahead of him with some effort.

Zell touched my arm and pointed as we came down the front stretch past pit road. Zell's pointy finger indicated a building off a hundred yards or so from the garage area with a large red cross on the side. The next lap by, I eyeballed the area carefully and sure enough there was a chopper sitting there.

Where was the pilot? Sure as hell I couldn't fly the damn thing. Was the chopper jockey in the machine? Or in the infirmary? I schemed. We'd have to insure the pilot was near or onboard the chopper.

Twenty laps to go.

The 384 car snuck up on us again and I let him get closer. As we came around the final turn, I slowed and let the Olds make his play. He tried a gentle clip on the rear bumper and I seemed to lose control and shot right for the opening to pit road, faking so they wouldn't guess what I was doing. We gunned down pit road and I slowed slightly to check out the chopper. Damn. I still couldn't tell if there was a pilot on board or not.

But no longer were any cop cars on pit road. I saw

several near the opening in the fence of pit road. Maybe we could outrun 'em; I was out of ideas.

And out of time. Fourteen laps to go. Thirty-five miles. At more than 150 mph that ain't very long.

"Hang on, Zell! I'm gonna try to wreck somebody and head for the chopper."

His eyes opened wider and he seemed to gulp. Then he sat up straighter and grinned evilly, reminding me of me, and shouted, "Give them hell!"

Sure, kid. Of course, it had to happen on the thirteenth from the end lap. While I ain't superstitious, I still don't walk under ladders. But if this didn't work, I had to have time to figure another angle.

Coming into the first turn, I found a pack of four cars, one of which was a nice looking '63 Ford. Too bad, but I couldn't be choosy. I weaved through them, dodged under the '63 Ford, and slipped up right into his left side, trading some of my sheet metal and paint for his plastic.

Under his helmet I could only see a portion of his lower face which showed immediate shock and his bubble snapped up around him and he lost control and slammed hard into the outer wall. I floored the accelerator, pedal to the metal as we used to say, and shot ahead of the pack. The Ford bounced off the wall at the top of the turn and slid backward into the pack he'd been running with. I fancied I could see bubbles popping up like popcorn. For a few moments there was a real mess.

But I was blasting at the one eighty peg down the back stretch. Rounding out of those corners, I shot down pit road, braked, downshifted, and did a four-wheel slide toward the pit wall opening. All the while praying that the terrible accident would cause the chopper pilot to man his machine.

Most likely it was the number thirteen. Some smart SS or cop had blocked the opening. I swung the wheel, jammed the accelerator down again, straightened, and powered down pit road. I stood on the brakes opposite the wall where the chopper was located and watched as a dozen SS guys ran to intercept our probable escape path toward the chopper. I was still gonna try it, but Zell was having trouble releasing all the connections of his harness.

Damn.

Cops and SS were piling over the wall and I slammed the shift lever into first and raced on down pit road feeling just a tingle from a stun gun.

I looked over at Zell and made a face. "It was worth a try."

He gave me a reassuring grin. He still had faith. Well, I was running out of that commodity.

Back up to speed coming out of pit road, I discovered I'd caused myself another problem: with wicked crashes, they slow the race under a "yellow flag." The pace car went out and all the racing cars bunched up behind it running maybe eighty or ninety, going slowly through the wreck area, and waiting for a restart. With maybe eleven laps to go, I doubted any of the participants would take a shot at us and our Buick.

To insure our immediate safety, I didn't join the pack behind the pace car; I stayed ten or twelve car lengths ahead of it.

Ten laps to go—they count laps under the yellow.

No ideas.

Because of the reduced speed, more quiet. "Well, Zell, we dona't have much time. Onliest thing I can come up with: right at the end of the race, I'll stop outside the stands and we climb the protective fence and merge with the spectators. Okay?"

"Sure."

But I'd let him go and drive off again, maybe allowing him time to escape. "Race fans are sort of a strong union, they might not want to help out the SS after what we done here today," I added.

Nine laps and the web around us was about closed.

We went through the wreck area one more time and it was cleaned up. After we passed the start/finish line ahead of the pack, I glanced in the mirror. Some guy was hanging over the line waving a green flag and the pace car dived onto pit road and the pack of perhaps thirty-five cars accelerated toward us. Their loudspeakers must have had their decibel level electronically tied into their accelerators.

"Let's win this sonofabitch!" Zell shouted.

Eight laps left as we led the pack past the grandstands and the start/finish line one more time.

A glance showed more SS and cops lining pit road. Choppers hovering about the edges of the Speedway, just far enough away not to disturb the crowd. I needed a shot of optimism, but right then I couldn't even spell "hope."

Zell was shaking my arm which was being shook by the racing oval at one forty out of a corner.

"Manny!"

I jerked my head at him. "What?"

"Manny is trying to contact you."

"Mindhopping?"

Zell nodded vigorously.

One fifty on the back stretch, all the cars behind me ignoring custom and mechanical limits trying for finishing positions.

I tried to blank my mind, felt a slight brush, out of practice, recalled how we used to do it, relaxed and let Manny do all the work.

"Wyndy?"

"Yeah, it's me, Manny. Where the hell are you?"

"Here, Wyndy."

"Where the hell is here?"

"On the *Nimitz*."

"Great, kid. Where the hell is the *Nimitz*?"

"Mom says yes."

"Yes, what?" I suspected, but I'd rather he say it. And now that I thought about it, it occurred to me that the Manuel Temple FTL process must have worked for I was talking to him. Hot damn.

"She'll marry you." Manny's mind-voice was some-how smug, not an easy thing to do.

"Well, Manny, let me tell you that makes me hap-pier than a pig in shit, oops, don't tell her I said that, but it don't really matter. Six laps, son. That's all we got. Fifteen miles at one fifty. You figger it out."

"Not a whole hell of a lot of minutes—"

"You didn't learn to talk like that from me," I pointed out. And cursed myself for wasting time.

"Six minutes," he responded.

"Not no more, kid. We only got five laps to go." Goddamn. "Where *are* you?"

"Airborne and coming down, but Silas says we got to be careful, too many people down there, dangerous."

"Fuck that danger, Manny, we're short on time."

"Roger that, Wyndy. There are satellite lasers and armed choppers all about. Silas is counting on the danger to all those people down there to keep 'em from shooting at us."

"Makes sense, kid. But four laps now—"

I turned to Zell. "Manny says they're coming for us."

"Goddamn!"

Jeez, I was gonna have a double problem—that is if we got out of this mess. I explained about the *Nimitz* coming down.

"Where?" Zell demanded.

"Beats me. Lake Lloyd out there is too small. But the area around the lake plus the lake itself might fit her. I flat don't know."

Right then damned if it didn't rain, and in that rain was seaweed and even a couple of strange looking fish.

"What the hell?" I said.

A jellyfish with its long tentacles was draped across the hood until the wind stream splattered it against the windshield and then up and over the roof.

"Stuff caught when the bubble closed. They must have been at sea when it happened," Zell shouted.

"That kind of stuff would eventually be used in recycling, maybe even necessary. Iodine and all and—"

"No time for a goddamn lecture. In the back. Unharness. Get the satchel with the ammo clips for the Uzi. You carry that. And see can you find that last bottle of Jack Daniels Blue Label in the duffel."

Zell unharnessed himself, easier this time, and climbed into the back, squirming between the roll bar and fuel lines and transmission fluid coolers and so on.

"Two laps, Manny, no more time." I spoke aloud, but he received me.

"They're doing all they can, Wyndy."

Down the back stretch, driving ever so carefully on account of Zell loose in the back. One and a half laps to go.

A great shadow flat-ass overwhelmed the entire stadium. I looked around. The spectators were not watching the race. Hundreds of thousands of necks craned up.

The *Nimitz'* great gray hull loomed over the entire Daytona International Speedway. Impressive. One hell of a show. You could *smell* ocean as it dripped from her bulk.

Into the far turn and coming out onto the front stretch, I checked the mirror. The other race cars weren't paying much attention to the sudden darkening of the sky. One lap to go and they were fighting for position, for the thing they'd been working toward all day. This was their life and livelihood. A couple of rookies darted down pit road, unsure of what the hell was going on, merging with a herd of cop and SS vehicles.

Behind us at the start/finish, the guy hung down from his platform waving a white flag. Last lap. It was gonna be close.

Zell looked up. "We're the leader! We're gonna win!"

Into the first turn and the ship was coming down slower, hull settling in from about the height of the top of the stands, great screws or propellers or whatever they called 'em hanging there obscenely. Other sensors and probes dotting the hull.

"Manny?"

"Yes, Wyndy?"

I slowed for the final turn off the back stretch. "We're out of laps. The race is thirty seconds from being over. Tell Silas to hurry the hell up."

"Rog."

"Don't know how to work it, Manny. But we'll stop on the back stretch this time around. We're in a red-on-white number 22."

"We know. We've been watching you on the tele-video."

"It figgers."

The *Nimitz* seemed to fill the entire stadium like a cork in a bottle. It came to a stop maybe fifty feet above the center of Lake Lloyd and the empty area around it and simply hovered there. Neat. The ship seemed to stretch upward like an alien skyscraper, well above the top levels of the Speedway.

How were they gonna get us?

To gain time, I floored it across the start/finish and blasted by the guy waving a checkered flag doing one eighty-five. He must have gotten confused and thought we were the legit winner. At one time, that would have been the culmination of my entire life: to win the Daytona 500.

"We won, goddamnit, we won!" Zell shouted and banged the back of his seat.

Suddenly, I knew. "We're gonna make it, Zell!"

He had slid back into the front and was as enthusiastic as I was. "Fucking A."

Shit. He was gonna need some retraining.

We whipped out of turns one and two and emerged on the backstretch. I got on the brakes and downshifted, fumbling with the buckles of my harness.

We did a four-wheel slide down the banking and scraped onto the apron at the lip of the track.

"Out!"

But Zell was already crawling out his window with the satchel around his neck. He'd left the bottle of Jack Blue on the seat. I grabbed it and the Uzi and climbed out myself.

As we were doing this, the pack of cars that had been behind us blasted past on the lap after when the real winner was supposed to take his or her victory lap. Coming into turn one behind them I saw a herd of security vehicles.

"It's time, Manny."

"Standby—go up on the track, if you can."

"Gone," I said, still aloud while mind-talking.

I kicked the number 22 Buick fondly and raced around the hood. I urged Zell up the high-banked track. We had a minute or so before the posse arrived. Some cops and SS were running across the infield trying to capture us. I don't know why, because the *Nimitz*' presence showed them that they couldn't really use us anymore—except as possible hostages. On the other hand, I suspected their command and control was rather broken down. Under these circumstances, they couldn't be thinking about anything except their initial mission.

We ran up the track and lo and goddamn behold a chopper had detached itself from the *Nimitz*' deck and was descending for us.

I pointed. "When he gets down, jump in the open door and never mind anything else."

Zell nodded emotionally.

Cop cars were coming out of the turn and accelerating down the back stretch for us.

Twenty seconds, I estimated. They'd have to stop—or would they? They could drive past us like injuns at a wagon train and shoot us where we stood.

Not if we were against the wall and spectators were behind us. I hustled Zell against the protective wall and the first wave of cop cars beat the chopper to us.

I hosed 'em down with my Uzi, shooting down the

incline toward the infield. A couple of tires went and those cars swerved out of control. I ducked and felt the sting of stunners washing over us. "Down!"

But it was too late. Zell fell, unable to contol his muscles. But he was still aware. I caught a glimpse of a panicked crowd behind me. Many were down, recipients of the stun force themselves. A great amount of screaming came from that section of the spectators.

Two SS cars came more slowly, stunners out and firing. I sent 'em an Uzi message. "That's from me to Amber," I shouted.

I tried to climb to my feet, but my bad leg wasn't working too well. Using the butt of the Uzi as a crutch, I did it.

And then a withering laser fire came from the chopper and ran off the cops and SS. No way they were gonna face real fire with stunners.

The chopper hovered right in front of us. Through the open door I could see Silas Swallow crouched with a mounted laser traversing right and left out the opposite door.

Crane Plash was fighting the controls and signaling frantically at me.

Somehow I scooped Zell up without dropping my last bottle of booze and limped to the chopper. I threw Zell in and tumbled in myself, wind from the blades tearing at my clothes and hair. There went my last wig.

As I scrambled over the threshold, the chopper lifted and my belly was pressed into the floor.

Crane Plash spun a couple of revolutions and the Speedway gyrated in front of my eyes while I dragged my legs and feet into the chopper.

We rose swiftly and were soon above the top level of the stands and coming in over the deck of the *Nimitz.*

We landed on the flight deck near the superstructure and I felt another surge like a fast bubblevator as the ship itself lifted.

All about us were choppers buzzing and darting angrily like a swarm of disturbed wasps.

Then our own protective bubble went up around the *Nimitz* and I stepped out of the chopper.

Crane Plash was grinning like a stuffed racoon.

Bossman jumped down with a complaining Zell in his arms.

My bad leg gave a little but I strode out, bottle of Jack Daniels Blue Label in my left hand, and the Uzi in my right.

Right in front of me, Maria and Manny were running to me.

Manny ran mimicking my own running limp, the little devil.

Maria's smiling eyes acknowledged the picture I must have made with the booze and Uzi, and her eyes held no disapproval.

Damn, I felt good. Life was looking up. Then came a moment of disorientation and I almost stumbled and then Maria and Manny were there grabbing me.

Epilogue: Why me, Lord?

I was sitting on the very tip end of the flight deck. This part of the bubble had been cleared. I felt like I was alone in space; but acrophobia doesn't bother me unless that's the one about water.

They were still learning how to opaque and clear the proper segments of the bubble to prevent the solar rays from frying our eyeballs.

The slice I was seeing showed your basic requisite stars and night in a big pie slice. The other part of the pizza, that wasn't covered by opaque bubble, was wonderful. I'm not real good at using "wonderful." But it was. Maybe on accounta it was so different. Below is a giant blue and green and brown world just waiting for the first humans to go down and lay some claim. We were hanging up here like a spotlight in the Astrodome, still checking scientist stuff. Soil content, biologic, air, inimical lifeforms, seeable and microscopic and a lot of other junk I never hadda learn for my GED.

I was sipping a "Wyndy" on ice; being as how I was the onliest one with a still on the *Nimitz*, the name of the liquor took on the characteristics of its generator. Me. Half the crew and scientists and stuff were in hock to me up to their collective—

"Judge" Wyndy, they called me. What had happened was that somebody needed to be Solomon, and among all those military naval types and scientists and engineers and farmers and rich boys, nobody could fill the bill. They had a nice system, but it didn't allow for any deviation. And deviation was the rule, not the exception, what with all them weirdoes aboard the *Nimitz*.

My main job, besides makin' booze, was to decide problems which the system didn't take care of.

You can't mix scientists and engineers and families and civilians and military and stick them in the strict military environment of a naval warship and expect everything to click, take a likkin' and keep on tickin'. Civilians didn't recognize military and the *Nimitz* crew didn't like landlubbers a goddamn bit. At first the disputes were handled through the system: department heads would confer and confer and etc. Then the old military "chain of command" got involved and Captain Half Nelson would end up figgering everything out between what was fast becoming warring parties.

That paled right quickly with everybody. So Silas Swallow became the final arbiter. Hell, it was his show. Of course, he quickly tired of same and wasn't consistent enough to establish rules to live by. Finally, it fell to me. A couple of tough, killer decisions, and I was king of the ship. Hell, I never was afraid of making decisions.

For instance. The planet below. I'd had to use all my "Solomon's Wisdom." Names. I, of course, was the resident expert in names. One hell of a debate what to name our first attempt at colonization of someplace nonEarth.

I was tempted to name it "Solomon's Wisdom" and, doubtless, that would have satisfied all the factions.

Personally, I was inclined to name it Maria, just for pure personal gain. (I might be old, but I ain't dumb. Anybody passes up an opportunity to grease their own wheels first needs to check their wheel bearings.)

In my infinite wisdom, I'd selected the name "Winsome" arbitrarily. "If not for Winsome, none of this would have happened."

Everybody had their own "If not for this—" story. However, Winsome was the onliest one who'd died in the "If not for—" story.

The planet below was named Winsome, and Maria— after a lot of my explanation—had endorsed the idea. Zell walked around so proud, like he had enough worms in his guts to explode. He became a cult hero with all the kids. Everyone had seen the video replays of the holocaust at his house and the Daytona 500.

Hell, I even fancied Winsome up there somewhere chewing my ass—never mind that sheepaloewash.

But Winsome it stood. Why?

Because I used her sacrifice as a reason to change the course of humanity.

From the Daytona International Speedway, we'd popped out someplace near the damn moon. Can you believe it? The moon!

Silas and Captain Nelson and the scientists were deciding on a target planetary system to shoot for.

Captain Nelson, under much pressure, married me and my new bride, Maria Temple. I had two kids immediately without no sex. Manny and Zell. Who each had their own opinions of what we should do.

After a day (I say that irreverently, since I ain't certain anymore what a "day" is) of me and Maria trying to provide Manny and Zell with a baby sister or brother as the case may be, I entered the sweepstakes for the next destination.

After explaining it to my family, I had Manny and Zell and Maria on my side and the issue was decided. It just took Silas a while to realize the correctness of our position.

First, we went back to Earth and, after Manny had coordinated our appearances with his "friends," we stopped and picked up twenty-eight children and their families.

We didn't want the various powers-that-be to hitch these friends of Manny's up and burn out their brains like Baldy had attempted.

Next, we went to Beijeng—or Peking, as I always said. And sold the nonexclusive rights to the Starhopper for a billion dollars and a percentage of the profits. We sold the rights again and again. The thing gathered momentum and most large countries couldn't afford *not* to buy in.

Silas had wanted to *give* the secret away. But I prevailed.

"Don't you ever," I said, "*give* away anything you can sell."

Silas had seen the profit in that and agreed.

We sold the secret to everybody but the Republic of Dixie and anybody connected with Singapore.

If the Earth ever has a star-reaching empire, we will own ten percent of it. And there are a shitpot full of billion dollar deposits all over Earth with our name on 'em.

Manny's mind alerted me to his presence and soon he plopped down next to me. "Wow. What a view."

"Not as good as in the classroom, kid. Whyn't you *hop* your mind and butt both down to school."

"I don't wanna."

"Your mom's working and I'm in charge of you again. Why don't you want to?"

"I don't feel like it."

"No shit, Shirley." Don't tell Maria I said that.

If you don't tell her I skipped school, he thought back at me.

"But she's teaching," I pointed out.

"Not any of *my* courses."

"She ain't a dummy, Manny. She knows and cares, son. Me, too. What's the problem?"

"I'ontno."

"Twenty-eight prima donnas instead of one?"

"I'ontno."

"Now you know how the rest of us mere mortals feel."

Manny shot me a dirty look. "*Mortals? Us* mortals?

Nobody but maybe me and Mom notice. Goddamn, Wyndy. You're ageing backward!"

"Watch your mouth, boy. Way I figger, you and me, we're hitched together. The older you get, the *better* I get, see? So lay off. Maybe ole Zell will grow up and become a scientist and figger us two out."

"Uh oh."

"Uh oh, what?"

Manny had that faraway look on his face. "I gotta go." He scrambled to his feet and ran off down the deck. I guess it's nice to have twenty-eight accomplices who can warn you long distance if you've been discovered AWOL or whatever it is you do when you skip school.

I sit here and wonder.

What our, me and Maria's, kid is gonna be like. Should I attend his birth like with Manny? Suppose me and Maria's kid inherits the mindhopper business? I'd no doubt that genetic trait was Maria's. Further, suppose that kid also inherits my reluctance to age. Too many consequences for me to think about. But no doubt I'd be around to find out. I could tell by the way my body was feeling.

Why me, Lord? The more action, the more pressure, the more problems: the younger I seem to become. I don't mean I turn into some wailing infant.

What I mean is the more adversity or the more challenge, the less the years I already possess affect me. I always aged less than anybody else. Hell, I outlived more wives than most people got decendants.

Came the Manny Crisis and I grew seemingly younger. I won't let the scientists or doctors touch me. If you don't want to know the answer, don't ask the question. It *has* occurred to me—and to Maria—that something special in my old old bean up there matches well that something special in Manny's brain—else we'd never have had that super bond we have and never been able to empathize and comm together.

Hell, I can't even spell myelination. And it pisses

me off somebody took Einstein's brain and studied the damn thing.

But I do know that the more involved I became, the more active and participative I became. Sounds rather bureaucrative, I know. But, by God, I feel better. I'm physically more able to perform as my body dictates.

Hell. It was as if somebody had designed me to work backward. That is, the older I become, the more capable. The way it *should* work.

Jesus Figurative Christ. Suppose I live to be a thousand?

DAW

THEY WERE THE ULTIMATE ENEMIES, GENERALS OF STAR EMPIRES FOREVER OPPOSED— AND WORLDS WOULD FALL BEFORE THEIR PRIVATE WAR...

IN CONQUEST BORN
C.S. FRIEDMAN

Braxi and Azea, two super-races fighting an endless campaign over a long forgotten cause. The Braxaná—created to become the ultimate warriors. The Azeans, raised to master the powers of the mind, using telepathy to penetrate where mere weapons cannot. Now the final phase of their war is approaching, when whole worlds will be set ablaze by the force of ancient hatred. Now Zatar and Anzha, the master generals, who have made this battle a personal vendetta, will use every power of body and mind to claim the vengeance of total conquest.

☐ **IN CONQUEST BORN**   (UE2198—$3.95)

DAW

A GALAXY OF SCIENCE FICTION STARS

- [ ] **TERRY A. ADAMS, Sentience**   UE2108—$3.50
- [ ] **MARION ZIMMER BRADLEY, Hunters of the Red Moon**
     UE1968—$2.95
- [ ] **JOHN BRUNNER, More Things in Heaven** UE2187—$2.95
- [ ] **C.J. CHERRYH, Exile's Gate**   UE2254—$3.95
- [ ] **JO CLAYTON, Skeen's Search**   UE2241—$3.50
- [ ] **SUZETTE HADEN ELGIN, The Judas Rose**
     UE2186—$3.50
- [ ] **CYNTHIA FELICE, Double Nocturne**   UE2211—$3.50
- [ ] **C.S. FRIEDMAN, In Conquest Born**   UE2198—$3.95
- [ ] **ZACH HUGHES, Sundrinker**   UE2213—$3.50
- [ ] **CHARLES INGRID, Solar Kill**   UE2209—$3.50
- [ ] **JAMES B. JOHNSON, Trekmaster**   UE2221—$3.50
- [ ] **TANITH LEE, Days of Grass**   UE2094—$3.50
- [ ] **BOB SHAW, Fire Pattern**   UE2164—$2.95
- [ ] **JOHN STEAKLEY, Armor**   UE1979—$3.95
- [ ] **SCOTT WHEELER, Matters of Form**   UE2225—$2.95
- [ ] **DONALD A. WOLLHEIM (Ed.), The 1987 Annual World's Best SF**   UE2203—$3.95

Write for free DAW catalog of hundreds of other titles!
(Prices slightly higher in Canada.)

NEW AMERICAN LIBRARY
P.O. Box 999, Bergenfield, New Jersey 07621

Please send me the DAW BOOKS I have checked above. I am enclosing $_____
(check or money order—no currency or C.O.D.'s). Please include the list price plus
$1.00 per order to cover handling costs. Prices and numbers are subject to change
without notice.

Name _____

Address _____

City _____ State _____ Zip _____
Please allow 4-6 weeks for delivery.